ONE TRUE THING

Terrence moved deliberately and slowly toward her. When he stood just a few inches from her, he reached out and stroked her hair. "Well, Miss Head Chef, I have a few questions about what's available on the menu tonight."

"I'm listening."

He leaned forward and kissed her ears. "Is this on the menu?"

"Yes."

Her raspy voice only turned him on more. Tracing a line of butterfly kisses from her ear to her lips, he asked in between kisses, "Is this on the menu as well?"

Closing her eyes, Jasmine relaxed into his soft voice and softer kisses. "Yeah."

Pulling her to him, he caressed her back. "What about this? Is this available tonight?"

Placing her arms around his waist, she pressed closer. "It's available."

When he moved his hand down to her butt, her sharp intake of breath caused him to stop.

Jasmine glanced up into his eyes. "That's on the menu tonight too."

"I think I'll just take one of everything."

"That's a lot of stuff," she teased. "Are you sure your appetite can handle it all?"

Terrence nodded slowly. "Oh, without a doubt. When it comes to what you're serving, I'm a bottomless pit."

Jasmine laughed. "You know, my daddy used to have a saying. 'Don't let your mouth write a check your body can't cash' "

"Trust me, sweetheart. You can take my words to the bank."

Doreen Rainey

One True Thing

ARABESQUE

BET BOOKS

BET Publications, LLC
http://www.bet.com
http://www.arabesquebooks.com

ARABESQUE BOOKS are published by

BET Publications, LLC
c/o BET BOOKS
One BET Plaza
1900 W Place NE
Washington, DC 20018-1211

All Kensington Titles, Imprints, and Distributed Lines are available at special quantity discounts for bulk purchases for sales promotions, premiums, fund-raising, and educational or institutional use. Special book excerpts or customized printings can also be created to fit specific needs. For details, write or phone the office of the Kensington special sales manager: Kensington Publishing Corp., 850 Third Avenue, New York, NY 10022, attn: Special Sales Department, Phone: 1-800-221-2647.

First Printing: July 2004
10 9 8 7 6 5 4 3 2 1

Printed in the United States of America

This book is dedicated to Kiki Davis, my California connection and my friend for life.

One

Jasmine Larson wrote a few final notes in the file before closing it with a satisfied smile. It had been a tough journey for little Angela Taylor, but after surviving the death of a drug-addicted mother, an absent father, three foster homes, and too many court appearances to count, her adoption finally came through. The judge had signed the papers just a few short hours ago and Jasmine couldn't have felt happier. At nine years old, Angela could now claim a family full of love to call her own.

Placing the file back in the cabinet, Jasmine paused a moment to savor the victory. In a profession filled with suffering and pain, she relished the times when one of her cases ended with a child safe and loved. Walking back to her desk, she picked up another file and flipped it open. As she scanned the report, her smile faltered. *Jason Thomas. Six years old. Fractured arm. Bruised ribs. Immediately removed from the home and placed in a foster home—again.* Jasmine reached for her Palm Pilot and entered a home visitation appointment for Jason on Tuesday.

Interrupted by a knock at the door, Jasmine put the digital device in her purse and set the file aside. "Come in."

Monica Richards stepped into the small space and shut the door. Her hands, slightly shaking, matched her distressed expression.

A sinking feeling settled in the pit of Jasmine's stomach and a flicker of apprehension coursed through her. It was apparent—this would not be good news. "What is it?" she asked, pushing back in her chair and standing. She made a point never to take bad news sitting down. Sitting was the posture of defeat, while standing always helped her maintain her strength. And in this job, she had plenty of conversations in the upright position.

"The judge ruled on Candice Worley," Monica said, obviously displeased with the decision.

"And?" Jasmine asked anxiously. They'd been waiting for this decision for the last three days.

Exhaling deeply, Monica tried to control her emotions. "She's going back to her mother."

There was no mistaking the anger mixed with disbelief in Monica's voice. Walking around her desk with her arms open, Jasmine hoped to comfort her new associate. Hugging her closely, Jasmine suspected that Monica would find no solace in the gesture. It was next to impossible to console a social worker when a judge ruled against your recommendation—especially when it was the very first time. "I'm so sorry, Monica. You did everything you were supposed to do. Unfortunately, judges don't always agree with us."

Shaking her head, Monica sought understanding, desperately trying to make sense of what had happened today. "But she's only five and this is the second time she's being returned to her mother. What has to happen before the judge comes to his senses? Another accident? More bruises? A concussion? Death?"

Jasmine remained silent, letting Monica release all of her frustration. She knew at times like this, there was little anyone could say to make the other person feel better. In the five years that she'd been with the Alameda County Health and Human Services, she had asked those same questions at least a hundred times. No one had yet to give her the answer.

Discreetly wiping the tears that slid from the corners of her eyes, Monica stepped back and stared at her mentor with questioning eyes. "How do you do it, Jasmine?"

"Do what?" Jasmine asked, even though she could probably predict what Monica was asking.

She threw her hands in the air, her frustration growing. "Deal with the defeat . . . the failure. How can you watch a child go back to a home you know isn't safe? Do you ever feel like you work in vain?"

Jasmine motioned for Monica to take a seat. Jasmine leaned forward, resting her elbows on the desk. It wasn't that long ago that she was the one in tears, wondering how the world could be so unfair. "Monica, I know exactly how you feel right now. But it's not failure. You did the best you could. I've watched judges make unbelievable decisions more times than I care to count. But you can't let it get you down."

"How? How can you not let it get you down?" Monica said, her eyes searching Jasmine's for answers.

Jasmine didn't have to think twice about her answer. "By celebrating the victories and staying on top of the cases where you experience a setback. Make sure you never miss one of Candice's follow-up appointments. If the judge is right, you'll watch Candice grow up in a safe, solid family environment. If the judge is wrong, you'll be there to snatch her out at the first sign of trouble."

Reaching for the ever-present box of tissues on the desk, Monica wiped her cheek and stood. At twenty four years old, the youthful exuberance that had been a staple of her personality since she'd started was missing today. Monica's microbraids were pulled into a neat ponytail and her dark green pantsuit fit her five-foot-five-inch frame to a tee, projecting confidence and composure, but the light in her eyes had dimmed a little.

With a sincere smile, Monica headed for the door. "Thanks, Jasmine. That really helps." Monica paused and gazed upward, trying to collect her final thoughts.

"What is it, Monica?"

"You know," she started thoughtfully, "when I got my master's degree, I thought I was going to save the world. Nothing like a judge ruling against you to slap you back to reality."

Jasmine laughed, remembering she had had those same sentiments when she graduated with an advanced degree in social work. Reaching for Monica's hand, she gave it a reassuring squeeze and looked her colleague directly in the eye. "I still believe we can save the world. Don't ever lose that feeling."

After saying good night, Jasmine shut the door behind Monica and leaned her head against it, exhaling deeply. That wasn't the first time she'd given that pep talk to a new social worker. It was the same speech she had received from her supervisor, now manager, Marjorie Davis, five years ago when she lost her first case. It didn't make her feel any better then—and it didn't do anything for her now.

The shrill ring of her cell phone interrupted her

thoughts. She checked the number on the display and glanced guiltily at the dress hanging in the corner of her office. "Hey, Dawn."

"I was just checking to see where you were. I know crossing the Bay Bridge can be a bear during rush hour on a Friday afternoon. Just be thankful you don't have to cross the Golden Gate."

Jasmine hesitated and her silence told Dawn all she needed to know. Accusingly, she asked the question she had already figured out the answer to. "You haven't left yet, have you?"

"I got tied up," Jasmine answered, realizing that she should have left the office almost an hour before.

"Well, untie yourself and get over here," Dawn said, helping a waiter arrange crackers on a silver serving tray. She refused to buy into Jasmine's excuse.

Hearing the soft sounds of jazz in the background, Jasmine figured guests had already begun to arrive and she contemplated passing on the evening altogether. "I'm not in the mood for a party."

Popping a crab ball into her mouth, Dawn rolled her eyes, not the least bit surprised. "You're never in the mood for a party."

Twisting the telephone cord around her finger, Jasmine searched her mind for another excuse. Spending an evening smiling and nodding with people she had very little in common with didn't excite her after the day that she had had. "I don't even know the guy you're having this gathering for."

"No one knows Terrence," Dawn reminded her. "That's the purpose of the party . . . to welcome him to San Francisco and introduce him to people."

Taking a seat behind her desk, Jasmine glanced at

the numerous files stacked in front of her. "It's almost six. It would be close to eight by the time I arrived. I'm sure I won't be missed."

"You'll be missed by me," Dawn countered. It had been months since she and her best friend had had more than a quick phone conversation. She'd counted on tonight to give them some time to catch up.

Jasmine closed her eyes and thought about it. After such an emotional day, was she really up for a party?

After a long silence on the other end, Dawn handed the serving tray to a waiter and waited for Jasmine to respond. Still nothing. She wondered if the long commute was the only reason Jasmine didn't want to come. Becoming concerned, she switched the phone to the other ear. "Talk to me, Jasmine. What's really going on with you?"

The corners of Jasmine's lips curved into a slight smile. No one knew her better than Dawn, so she wasn't surprised that she picked up on her somber mood. "I was just talking to a new social worker. She had a case that didn't work out like she'd hoped. Needless to say, she was extremely disappointed."

Hearing the frustration in her voice, Dawn felt her heart going out to her friend. It was always a challenge for Jasmine to balance her emotions when it came to the children she worked hard for on a daily basis. But that was all the more reason to make sure she had a life outside of work. She knew emotional burnout could quickly become a problem when you didn't learn to take some time for yourself, friends, and family. "You need to take some time to enjoy, to relax, to have some fun."

"I don't know," Jasmine started. She'd heard many

times before from coworkers and friends that she needed to make time for life outside of her career. "I haven't changed clothes yet and it's going to take me at least forty-five minutes to get there. And that's if traffic works in my favor."

"I can send a car for you," Dawn offered. "That way you won't have to drive and fight the traffic. You could start relaxing on the way over."

Glancing at the file on her desk, she realized Dawn was right. She couldn't work twenty-four hours a day. And it was Friday night. Reaching for her dress, she said, "A car isn't necessary. I'll change and be out of here in less than thirty minutes."

"Good," Dawn answered, "because I have someone I've been dying to introduce you to."

"Oh no, Dawn," Jasmine said, agitated that she'd waited until she agreed to come before letting her in on that little tidbit of information. "Not tonight. I'm not interested, nor am I in the mood for one of your crazy hookups."

"But I've told Jonathan what a great person you are," Dawn said, as if that made everything okay.

"I couldn't care less what you've told this Jonathan person."

"He's thirty-three, a chiropractor who owns a wonderful home just outside the city."

"It doesn't matter what he does or where he lives," Jasmine said, amazed that she was ignoring her objections. "I don't need you to find me a man."

"Of course you do," Dawn teased. "You haven't done such a good job in that category on your own."

Jasmine couldn't disagree. But that didn't mean that she wanted Dawn to make her the object of one of her matchmaking missions. "Dawn, I'm warning you. I won't come if I have to spend the entire evening avoiding you and this Jonathan person."

"Okay, okay," Dawn reluctantly agreed. "I'll lay off of the matchmaking . . . if that is what it takes to get you here."

"That's what it takes," she said adamantly.

"You have my word," Dawn said, disappointment laced in her tone. "I won't introduce you to Jonathan."

Jasmine's shoulders relaxed and she reached for her dress. "Good. I'll see you soon."

Two

Terrence McKinley felt his facial muscles tighten as he maintained a forced but polite smile listening to the young woman compliment him on his stellar career and his move to the West Coast—once again. As a matter of fact, she'd told him at least seven times in the past fifteen minutes in her high-pitched, squeaky, annoying voice.

When Dawn initially introduced Terrence to her, he found the woman physically attractive, dressed in a light blue, beaded cocktail dress. But that was where the attraction ended. The moment she uttered her first words, any attraction he could possibly have felt toward her quickly disappeared.

Aimee Wilkes had a voice that sounded like a cross between a mouse and a cricket. High-pitched, nasally, and distinctly aggravating. Even if he could have gotten past the whining sound coming from her mouth, he definitely couldn't excuse her conversation. After practically reciting her resume, she went on to explain her not-so-successful career as an actress, hairstylist, and part-time belly dancer, only to follow that up with details of her fascination with anything related to reincarnation.

He'd tried unsuccessfully on several occasions to extract himself from the conversation, but couldn't get a word in. It had been an excruciating twenty minutes since Dawn made the quick introduction before conveniently disappearing to speak with other guests, and he wasn't sure how much longer he could keep it up.

When Terrence's good friend Eric suggested that he and his wife, Dawn, throw a "welcome to San Francisco" party in his honor, Terrence didn't think it was a good idea. He liked to keep to himself and the idea of being the guest of honor at a big party didn't appeal to him at all. Only after Dawn promised to keep it small and simple did he reluctantly agree. Judging from the more than one hundred guests, the various introductions to single women, and the fact that Aimee Wilkes was now performing the lines from her latest audition for a soap commercial, this night was turning out to be something very different from small or simple.

Having just moved from New York to accept a position at Eric's law firm, he'd hoped to spend his first month getting familiar with the city he would now call home. But with a busy workload, and Dawn's never-ending matchmaking, he hadn't been able to find much downtime. Even though he and Eric had been great friends at Howard Law School, he had only been in Dawn's presence a handful of times, as she met Eric after he moved to California. In the middle of a large trial when they got married, he had been unable to attend their wedding. Looking back, he knew he should have found a way to be there. At least he would have met all of Dawn's single friends at one time. Now, he was forced to endure Dawn's meddling into his personal life by introducing him to her friends one by one.

Initially, he didn't mind Dawn trying to set him up every now and then. But somewhere along the way, it had turned into her full-time job. Things weren't too bad when he had lived on the opposite side of the country. He could conveniently lose the phone numbers and e-mail addresses Dawn passed on to him. But from the moment his plane touched down at San Francisco International Airport, Dawn had been quite relentless in her pursuit of finding him the perfect mate.

First, Dawn steered him toward Michelle, a woman who sat next to her in yoga class. Dawn claimed she was smart, successful, and loved to cook. When Terrence passed on her, Dawn quickly moved on to Renee. A former marketing coordinator at Dawn's firm, and recently divorced, Renee had been described by Dawn as a "free spirit." Terrence had visions of colorful clothes and lots of jewelry—not exactly his type.

Declining the invitation to have dinner with her, Terrence pleaded with Eric to get his wife to leave him alone. But Eric was no match for Dawn. Having fallen completely in love with Eric four years ago and marrying him two years later, she wanted everyone around her to be blissfully in love too. But Terrence wasn't interested in falling in love just yet. He'd tried his hand at love and it practically laughed and spit in his face. The job offer wasn't the only reason he decided leave his Manhattan apartment for a loft in San Francisco.

"Terrence, there you are."

His stiff posture relaxed and his look of relief was evident as Terrence turned his attention away from Aimee to Eric.

"I have someone who's been waiting to meet you."

Focusing his attention on Aimee, Eric smiled sweetly. "You'll have to excuse us."

As soon as he was safely out of earshot, Terrence hissed through gritted teeth, "Took you long enough."

"Sorry, man," Eric said, making a quick scan of the room to make sure Dawn didn't see his successful rescue mission. "It seems like every time I rescue you from one of my wife's hookups, she has you locked down with another."

"Just how many single women are here?" Terrence asked, hoping he'd just been saved from the last one.

"Trust me, man. You don't want to know," Eric said, patting him sympathetically on the shoulder.

Terrence heard the laughter in Eric's voice, but couldn't bring himself to join in. He had a strange feeling this was going to be a long night.

Jasmine handed her keys to the valet and headed up the walkway. The drive from Richmond into the city had taken longer than she planned, and if she hadn't promised Dawn that she would come, she would have turned around and headed back home. At least it was a clear May evening. The weather was perfect.

Before she could knock, the door swung open and a waiter immediately took her wrap as she stepped into the entryway. The home of Eric and Dawn Westfield was perfect for entertaining. Located in the exclusive neighborhood of Pacific Heights, their house and its surroundings mirrored their success as corporate attorneys for two different law firms. With high ceilings and large, formal rooms, it could easily accommodate a hundred people.

The party was in full swing when Jasmine made her

way into the great room where most of the guests gathered. Waiters passed with trays full of tasty crab balls, spinach pastry puffs, and glasses of wine and champagne. The background sounds from a three-piece jazz ensemble drifted from the far corner where they played. It appeared that many lawyers from Eric's firm, as well as clients and potential clients, came out to welcome the new addition to the firm. Jasmine, who had no idea which man he could be, couldn't have cared less about anyone other than the host and hostess. Dawn had convinced her that it wasn't just about the party, it was the idea of spending a little quality time with her best friend.

Growing up with Dawn in Richmond, California, about fifteen miles northeast of San Francisco, Jasmine couldn't remember a time in her life that she didn't share with her. Puberty, the senior prom, freshman roommates at the University of California at Berkeley, and graduation. Dawn was there when Jasmine walked across the stage to pick up her master's in social work and Jasmine applauded the loudest when Dawn graduated from law school.

Once Dawn accepted an associate's position at Benson & Clark, a midsized firm in the city, and Jasmine began working, the time they had to spend together greatly diminished. Shopping, taking in a play, or meeting for dinner became more difficult as they began building their careers. When Dawn met Eric four years ago, it limited their time even more. She and Jasmine often needed to schedule time together weeks in advance. Now, at thirty years of age, they made a commitment not to neglect their friendship and agreed to get together at least once a month. But as often happens in busy lives, it had been almost two months since they'd been able to carve out time for each other. And while Jasmine was looking forward to the two of them spending time with each other, she wasn't pleased that she had to go through this party to get it.

"You finally made it."

Jasmine turned to the voice and spread her arms for a hug. The deep purple chiffon cocktail dress with matching strappy stilettos contrasted sharply with the conservative suits and pumps Dawn usually wore to work and to court. With her long black hair resting below her shoulder blades, her café-au-lait complexion, narrow eyes, and high cheekbones, Dawn's exotic features often made others mistake her for an actress or a model instead of a corporate attorney.

Dressed in a black halter dress that gathered at the waist and fell midthigh, Jasmine, with her chin-length brown hair styled in a blunt bob cut, probably wouldn't pass for a supermodel, but would definitely turn heads. At five feet six with a thin frame, she, along with Dawn, always garnered attention from the opposite sex whenever they ventured out together.

"How did you find me?" Jasmine asked. "There has to be a hundred people in here."

"Actually, I think there's more than that," she answered with a teasing sparkle in her brown eyes. "But you'll be glad to know that out of all the people here, I've managed to find the one person you should definitely meet."

Recognizing that scheming glint in her eyes, Jasmine moaned loudly. "Oh no, Dawn. You promised—no more matchmaking."

Dawn shook her head, ready to defend her statement. "I promised I wouldn't introduce you to Jonathan. Derrick is an entirely different story. He's thirty-nine, owns two car dealerships, and can get you a great deal on a Ford."

"I should have known," Jasmine mumbled under her breath.

"And did I mention he's quite handsome?" Dawn asked, completely ignoring Jasmine's agitated expression.

Jasmine shook her head in disbelief. "What would make you think I would be interested in a man ten years older than me?"

"But Derrick—" Dawn started.

"How many times do I have to tell you?" Jasmine said pleadingly. "I am not interested in Jonathan, Derrick, Lawrence, Antonio, Demetrius, or Michael. I couldn't care less about a chiropractor, a car dealer, a mechanic, a professional bowler, a college professor, or any of the hotshot corporate lawyers from your or Eric's firms, whose only allegiance is to the almighty dollar."

"Hey, watch it," Dawn said lightheartedly. "I'm a hotshot corporate lawyer."

"Then I've proven my point," she said with a definitive nod.

Ignoring the sarcasm in her response, Dawn, not quite ready to give up on Derrick, tried one more time. "Aw, come on, Jas. This will be the last time—Scout's honor."

She'd heard that pleading innocent tone before and had fallen victim to it. But this time, Jasmine was determined to stand her ground. "I warned you before I came that I wasn't—"

"Oh," Dawn interrupted, waving to a gentleman making his way toward him. "Here he is now."

Jasmine watched the man approach. Dressed in a black suit, with small circular-framed glasses, and a smattering of gray hair around his temples, he reminded her of her father. Cutting her eyes at her friend, she hoped to convey the message to back off. But it was too late; Dawn purposely ignored her. After making quick introductions, Dawn excused herself under the pretense of meeting more guests, leaving Jasmine and Derrick to fend for themselves.

Terrence couldn't believe it was close to midnight. Scanning the room, he saw the crowd had swelled to the largest of the night. He'd hoped that after he'd met a few people, had a drink, a little food and polite conversation, the party would wind down and he'd be back in his own home. Wishful thinking. The jazz ensemble had been replaced an hour ago with a DJ, and judging from the latest hip-hop song blaring through the speakers and the number of people moving and grooving on the makeshift dance floor, this party was far from over.

At least he had finally managed to shake Dawn and her never-ending line of single women. But it hadn't been easy. He'd only extracted himself from Aneisha, the last woman introduced to him by Dawn, about thirty minutes ago. Unfortunately, that only left him to wonder how long it would take for Dawn to strike again.

He leaned casually against the back wall, the first time all night he'd had a moment to himself. Taking a sip of his drink, he cut his eyes from one side of the room to the other, deciding to take matters into his own hands. Quietly, he scoped out his options. As the guest of honor, he would be rude to leave, but he needed a break . . . a moment of peace.

The entrance at the front of the room led to the foyer. He spotted Dawn in the arched entryway laughing with three other women. Women he had yet to meet. To his left was a swinging door that led to a small

butler area and a short hallway to the kitchen. With the
catering staff still serving, he knew it would be the last
place he would find any peace and quiet. Directly across
from him was another opening, but he couldn't remember where it led. Deciding to take his chances, he
placed his empty glass on the tray of a passing waiter
and slowly began walking across the room.

Giving a nod here and there and a smile to this person and that, he tried to appear friendly, while maintaining enough speed in his walk that people would
think twice before stopping him. When he was just a few
feet from freedom, he heard his name being called.
Without a backward glance he took those final steps,
hoping the caller would just assume he couldn't hear
over the music and the conversations. Three seconds
later . . . he reached freedom.

Filled with relief, he continued down the hallway passing a powder room, a formal dining room, and a staircase leading to the second floor. He paused when he
came to a closed door. He knocked. Getting no answer,
he cautiously opened the door, and for the first time that
night his shoulders relaxed and a genuine smile graced
his face. He'd found the library. If there was one place
that should be able to provide some peace and quiet, this
was it. A large comfortable chair sat in the corner and
the dark wood shelves and warm-colored wallpaper gave
an inviting feel. Stepping inside, he started to shut the
door, but stopped when he heard music.

Straining his ear toward the sound, he tried to decipher what was playing. Realizing the melody was neither jazz nor hip-hop, he couldn't quite place it. The
band left hours ago and the DJ couldn't be heard in
this part of the house. The music sounded live.

Unable to squelch his curiosity, he shut the door to the library and continued down the hall. The sounds grew louder until he finally found the source. Quietly, he stood in the entryway in what he assumed to be the music room.

The white grand piano sat majestically in the center of the room. The walls and carpet, also done in shades of white, added to the grandeur of the space. Remaining in the shadows, he watched as a woman played with fiery emotion, moving her fingers swiftly and effortlessly across the eighty-eight keys. The piece, a moving composition he couldn't name, verged on classical music and jazz. It reminded him of a lost soul, searching for a place in the universe. Watching her body sway back and forth, she seemed entranced in the world she'd created with her music. Wanting to be a part of that experience, he joined her by closing his eyes and swaying back and forth, enjoying the private concert.

With a powerful crescendo and a commanding final chord, the room suddenly became engulfed in complete silence. Before he could stop himself, Terrence clapped loudly. Obviously startled by her audience, she rose from the bench abruptly, stumbling back a few steps before regaining her balance. Continuing the applause, he stepped into the room, locking eyes with hers. His heart skipped a beat at the vulnerability he noticed reflected in the brown eyes that looked at him. "That was magnificent!"

Closing the lid to the Steinway grand piano, she cut her eyes downward, looking slightly embarrassed. "I thought I was alone."

Terrence didn't stop walking until he was just a few feet from her. The woman was just as beautiful as the music she played. For a moment, he completely lost his train of thought. "I . . . I didn't mean to intrude. I just wanted to get away from the crowd for a moment. I stumbled upon this room and the beautiful sounds coming from it."

Jasmine smiled at his words. "I rarely play for an audience, but thank you for the compliment."

"You mean you're not a concert pianist?" he asked with sincere surprise.

Giving a slight laugh, she hoped he couldn't pick up on her nervousness at having him stand so close—invading her personal space. "Far from it. I'm a social worker."

"The way you play, you may have missed your calling," he said, breaking into a charming smile.

"Again, thanks for the compliment."

An uncomfortable silence ensued and Terrence took a moment to get a good look at the woman standing in front of him. Against his six-foot frame, she stood several inches shorter. Her hair, tucked behind her ears, exposed beautiful eyes and sensuous lips. He immediately wondered if she was one of the women Dawn may have wanted to set him up with. If that was the case, what was taking her so long?

"I guess I need to get back to the party," she said, breaking the quietness. Clasping her hands together, she realized her nervous gesture and quickly placed her hands at her side. "Believe it or not, I haven't even met the guest of honor yet."

"How long have you been hiding out here?"

Jasmine's back stiffened and her eyes narrowed. "Who said anything about hiding?"

Terrence noticed the defensive stance and knew he

had touched a nerve. "There's a room full of good food, great drinks, and an abundance of interesting people, and you're in the back of the house, alone."

Jasmine could have sworn the temperature rose at least ten degrees as he took another step closer, staring at her with compelling and magnetic eyes. Refusing to attribute her arousal to his muscular frame and the mocha-bronze skin that appeared so smooth, she had to force herself not to reach out to stroke his cheek. Clearing her throat, she shook the thought from her mind and took one step back. "Taking a moment to get away from a party does not equal hiding."

"It's nothing to be ashamed of," he said, putting his hands in his pockets. "The truth be known, I'm hiding out myself."

Jasmine relaxed. Had she met someone who abhorred these corporate shindigs as much as she did? "I'm not really big on parties either, especially ones like this."

Intrigued, Terrence repeated, "Like this one?"

"I love Dawn and Eric like family," Jasmine said, "but these firm events have never been for me. Most of the people here are rich lawyers talking about what they bought, what they are buying, or what they are going to buy. Definitely not my type of crowd."

"Then why are you here?"

Shrugging her shoulders, she said, "Like I said, Dawn and Eric are like family."

"There you are."

Terrence and Jasmine turned to the voice as Dawn entered like a whirlwind.

"Everyone has been looking for you," she said, locking arms with Terrence. "I can't have the guest of honor hiding out."

Smiling, he answered, "I wasn't hiding. I was actually drawn here, by the beautiful melodic sounds coming from this woman's fingers."

Looking at Jasmine, he continued, "I apologize for disappearing for so long, but this woman had me mesmerized."

Glancing from Jasmine to Terrence, Dawn took in the slight smiles of each and the closeness of their stance. At that moment, the lightbulb clicked in her brain. Who would have guessed? The one person she would have thought would never go for the newest corporate lawyer was staring at one with interested eyes.

"This *woman?*" Dawn asked Terrence.

"I say that because I have yet to find out her name," Terrence explained. "We haven't officially been introduced."

"Then, please," Dawn said, ecstatic at the prospect of her best friend and Eric's good friend. "Allow me to do the honors."

With the giddiness of a teenager, Dawn dramatically cleared her throat. "Jasmine Larson, meet Terrence McKinley."

Terrence held out his hand and watched closely at Jasmine's slight hesitation. Finally, she slid her hand inside his.

"Very nice to meet you, Jasmine."

Terrence's gaze bored into her and Jasmine's breath caught. Realizing they still held hands, Jasmine quickly extracted herself from his touch. The moment the physical contact was broken, she felt she had regained some semblance of control. "Likewise."

Dawn watched the sparks fly and could barely contain her excitement. She had spent the entire evening working on getting them hooked up with different people. But now that she had witnessed the undeniable interest they had for each other, she immediately canceled all the plans she had to introduce them to other people. This was going to be her best match yet, and she didn't even have to scheme to make it happen.

Three

Jasmine sat at the breakfast table savoring a cup of her favorite hazelnut coffee when Dawn, still in her nightclothes and robe, sauntered in humming an up-beat tune. Having been up for almost an hour, Jasmine, already showered and dressed in comfortable jeans and a pullover top, ignored Dawn, hoping they could at least get through breakfast without discussing Terrence. Even though Jasmine could inwardly admit that she was slightly intrigued, a little interested, and physically attracted to him, she wasn't sure if she wanted to date someone like him.

The fact that Dawn knew she was interested in Terrence only complicated the situation. The past had proven that once Dawn got wind of a possible love connection, she clamped down on those involved like a rottweiler gnawing on a steak bone. It was next to impossible to get her to let it go.

"Hey, girl. You want an omelet this morning?"

Jasmine turned to the voice in surprise and raised a

suspicious brow. She thought for sure the first words out of her mouth would include "Terrence" and "hook-up." Maybe Dawn had suddenly realized that she and Terrence would not make a good couple.

"I could whip up something with dark brown eyes, skin the color of smooth Hershey's chocolate, a body that could make you scream for your mama, a voice that could melt your soul, and ears that love to hear you play that piano." By the time she'd gotten all of the words out, her laughter resonated around the room.

So much for hoping that Dawn would give up her matchmaking ways. Reaching for the morning paper, Jasmine opened it up to the sale pages. "It's too early for this, Dawn."

Pointing to the clock on the stove, Dawn shook her head. "It's almost eleven o'clock."

"Not too early *in the morning*," Jasmine said sarcastically. "Just too early for you to make comments about Terrence and me. I talked to the man for less than five minutes."

Opening the refrigerator door, Dawn pulled out eggs, cheese, green peppers, and onions. "It's not the length of time you spend with someone, it's whether you get the woo-woo."

Debating as to whether she was walking into a trap, Jasmine closed the paper and set it to the side. "Okay, Dawn, I'll bite. What's the woo-woo?"

Dawn's eyes widened in surprise. "How could you ask that question?"

"Oh, I'm sorry," Jasmine said, feigning concern about the subject. "Tell me this . . . would that have been covered in my psychology class, or maybe that would have been freshman English?"

Grabbing a mixing bowl from the cabinet, Dawn began cracking the eggs. "The woo-woo is the defining factor in compatibility. It's the spark, the interest, the physical attraction, the butterflies, the intangible feeling that the person you're looking at could be the one."

Jasmine observed the far-off look in her best friend's eyes and couldn't stop her lips from curving into a slight smile. Ever since they were little girls, Dawn had bought into the fairy tale. The princess. The knight in shining armor. The white horse. Jasmine was just glad that Dawn finally met her prince charming. Meeting at a lawyers' convention for young associates four years ago, Eric had adored Dawn and vice versa. No one was surprised when they married, because they practically oozed happiness their entire courtship. The sunny morning two years ago when Jasmine stood beside her best friend as she repeated the vows that some so carelessly spoke, there was no denying that this marriage would go the distance.

Unfortunately, not every woman could be that lucky. Jasmine had witnessed too many situations where the woman thought she'd found Mr. Right, only to learn that he was the devil in disguise. The worst part was that some of these couples had children that sometimes made their way to her office.

"You and Terrence would make a fabulous couple," Dawn continued, pulling Jasmine from her thoughts of work. "Just think what a romantic story it would be of how the two of you met. Your grandchildren would absolutely love to hear about it."

It always struck Jasmine as odd that her friend could be so tough in her professional life and so soft when it came to love and relationships. "How would your high-powered executive clients react if they heard you talking that way? Aren't corporate attorneys supposed to be unfeeling and tough? No emotions? No mush?"

"Believe me, at the office, I'm all business," Dawn said sternly. After a few seconds she relaxed her expression and continued. "But when it comes to my best friend and her love life, I absolutely love being all mush."

Playfully holding her hand over her heart, Dawn continued her theatrics. "I can see it now. He reaches for your hand, and your heart skips a beat. He pulls you close, his eyes moving slowly down to your lips. His head lowers, waiting for you to object, but you open your mouth slightly, giving him silent permission to take possession of your lips."

Jasmine unconsciously closed her eyes as the scene became a vivid picture in her mind. Even though their time together the night before was extremely brief, she remembered every detail about the way he looked, including the crinkle in his eyes when he smiled and his luscious, very kissable, lips.

"Jas?"

Jasmine snapped out of her daze and glanced at her friend just as she poured the omelettes into the pan. *How long has she been calling my name?* Not wanting to admit she'd been caught daydreaming, she stood to refill her coffee mug. "Well, I don't know about the 'woo-woo' or the scenario that you've obviously gotten from reading one too many romance novels. All I know is that I've never been a good match for someone who has spent his entire professional life in a corporate job where his only loyalty is to the almighty dollar. Men who are solely concerned with their careers never appealed to me. Terrence and I are just too different."

"What do you mean by 'different'?"

"Come on, Dawn," Jasmine said, knowing full well Dawn understood exactly what she was referring to. "I'm sure he drives a car that costs more than I make in a year."

"What does that have to do with anything? If you're interested, you're interested."

"I'm not interested," Jasmine declared, hoping to sound convincing.

Dawn didn't respond right away and Jasmine realized she didn't believe her. "I spent less than five minutes with him."

Dawn stared at her with knowing eyes and Jasmine struggled to ignore her, shifting uncomfortably in her chair. "He probably doesn't even remember my name."

Jasmine watched Dawn casually lean against the counter and cross her arms at her chest. After several seconds of silence, Jasmine relaxed her shoulders and finally relented to her friend's accusatory looks. "Okay, okay, I will concede that he is fine," she said, hoping the admission would put an end to the discussion.

Dawn shifted her weight to the other foot, staring and waiting.

"All right, all right . . ." Jasmine said, realizing she had to come clean about all her thoughts about Terrence. "I'm interested. Are you satisfied now?"

Dawn's expression remained serious as she slowly uncrossed her arms and walked over to Jasmine. Stopping only when she stood directly in front of her, she slowly placed one hand on her shoulder and stared directly in her eyes with a blank look. Suddenly, she burst into laughter and started doing her version of the happy dance. "This is great. You and Terrence? What a great couple."

"Calm down, Dawn," Jasmine said, trying to squelch

Dawn's excitement. This was exactly the reaction she had been trying to avoid all morning. "In case you've forgotten, he lives and works in San Francisco. I live and work in Richmond. I spend my days helping people who are fighting for their lives. He spends his days with people who are fighting for money—even though they probably don't need it."

"That's not fair, Jasmine," said Dawn, hearing Jasmine's condescending tone.

"It might not be fair, but it's true," Jasmine said, glad that the minicelebration had come to an end. "Being physically attracted to someone doesn't make up for all the other differences."

"I don't see all these differences you keep talking about," Dawn responded.

Jasmine shrugged.

"So you won't even give him a chance?" Dawn asked, obviously annoyed that she would let this opportunity slip away.

Jasmine thought about Dawn's words carefully—but still came to the same conclusion. A relationship between the two of them wouldn't work. "Give him a chance? Correct me if I'm wrong, but unless I'm invited to the next firm event, I don't think I'll be seeing Mr. Terrence McKinley any time soon. We don't exactly move in the same professional or social circles."

"I think you should see him at least one more time before you completely write him off. Besides, you sound like he's the only one who can make the first move," Dawn said, flipping the omelettes over like a chef making Sunday brunch. "The man doesn't always have to be the one to initiate contact."

Jasmine refused to respond. She had never been the forward type when it came to men. She figured if he was interested, he'd find a way to let her know.

Dawn cut her eyes at her friend's silence. When Jasmine refused to make eye contact, the truth became crystal clear. "You can't be serious!"

Jasmine took another sip of her coffee, still not answering.

"Are you saying you've never made the first move on a guy before?"

"You make it sound as if that makes me weird or something," Jasmine said defensively.

"It does!"

"Maybe I've never had to make the first move," she answered, sticking her chin out defiantly.

Dawn didn't believe her and decided to call her on the carpet. "You're trying to tell me that every guy you've ever wanted to go out with asked you out. You've never been disappointed that someone didn't call you, and you didn't try to approach him. You've never lost out on a relationship, because every man you've ever been interested in has asked you for your phone number, asked you to lunch, or invited you to dinner?"

Jasmine heard the disbelief in Dawn's tone, but refused to acknowledge it. She didn't want to admit the truth. Many opportunities had passed her by because she wasn't willing to make the first move.

She remembered Robert Mancel, a high school math teacher she'd met while working one of her cases. In several meetings regarding the student, they'd had conversations that revealed their similar interests, and even flirted with each other. She didn't notice a ring and he never mentioned a girlfriend. She'd waited for him to ask for a number, a lunch date—anything. But he never asked, and she didn't have the nerve. She hadn't seen Robert since the child moved out of state to live with relatives.

Then she thought about Calvin Bridges. Calvin had eyes that would make the clothes melt off your body. He walked into her church one Sunday morning with his sister, Rochelle. Visiting from Texas, he was thinking of relocating to the Bay area to be closer to his family. She'd flirted, made witty conversation, and then waited. Surely he would ask where she worked, where she lived, or how he could get in contact with her again. But nothing. She hadn't seen or heard from him in almost a year.

Not willing to admit that she may have let "the one" slip away, she decided to avoid the topic altogether. Reaching for the newspaper, she opened it up forcibly and stared at the words, hoping to end the discussion once and for all. "This is a ridiculous conversation. If a man is interested, he'll let the woman know."

"I can't believe your old-fashioned thinking."

"Call it what you want, but it still holds true," said Jasmine, refusing to look up from the newspaper. "I'm not putting myself out there just so I can be embarrassed, rejected, or worse—humiliated."

"But you expect a man to put himself out there over and over again?" The indignant tone in Dawn's voice resonated around the room.

Finally looking up, Jasmine exhaled deeply in frustration. "That's their job."

"Says who?"

"Says . . . says . . ." Jasmine searched her mind for the answer to justify her point of view. "Says the universe."

Dawn howled with laughter at the ridiculous statement. "So it's okay for men to get embarrassed, rejected, or humiliated over and over and over again?"

"I don't make the rules," Jasmine reminded her.

"That's just it . . . nowadays, there are no rules."

"Spoken like someone who's happily married and not still out there looking," she said with confidence.

"How do you think I became happily married?"

Jasmine glared at her friend suspiciously. "What is that supposed to mean?"

"It means exactly what you think it means." Dawn grabbed two plates from the cabinet and placed them on the table. "I made the first move on Eric."

"I thought you said you met him at a convention?"

"That's how we met. But that's not how we started dating."

Dawn slid the omelettes onto plates and put the dirty pan in the sink. Grabbing two forks and napkins, she slipped into her seat. "It had been months since the convention, and even though we exchanged business cards, I hadn't heard from him. He seemed interested enough when we met, and there wasn't a wedding ring. Finally, I took a chance and called him up one Saturday night and asked if he'd like to go dinner. He happily accepted and the rest, as they say, is history."

"But why didn't he ask you out?" Jasmine asked.

"Does it matter?"

"Yes!" Jasmine said. It would drive her crazy if she asked a guy out and he said yes but hadn't asked her first.

"No, it doesn't," Dawn insisted. "The bottom line is, someone has to make the first move. So why not you?"

"Why not him?"

"Why not you?" she countered.

"This could go on the rest of the day," Jasmine said, picking up her fork. "This is supposed to be our day to hang out and shop. So let's drop the subject of Terrence, eat this food, and get ready to hit the mall."

Four

Terrence entered his condo wiping the sweat from his forehead. His normal three-mile jog had turned into a five-mile minimarathon. It had been years since he'd run that far and that hard, but his feet just kept moving. His morning runs typically took on a life of their own when something put his mind in overdrive—a case or a woman. Having just settled into his new job, he had no case pending that got his legal juices flowing. So that left only one thing—a woman.

Determining who that woman was would not be difficult. Jasmine Larson. The moment he'd heard the music, he'd been drawn to it. The instant he saw her face, he'd been intrigued, and the second he heard her voice, he was enthralled. It wasn't because of her looks, even though with her straight brown hair, smooth skin, and shapely figure, she could easily win a beauty pageant. It was the passion, spirit, and complete emotion he heard in her music. With her eyes closed and her body swaying slightly, her fingers glided effortlessly across the keys, drawing him into her world.

Out of all the women Dawn tried to steer his way, he wondered why she wasn't one of them. It was obvious they were good friends. Was she married? Attached? Or worse, was she another bitter black woman with expectations too high for any man and too low of herself? That had been the case with Felicia.

From the outside, Felicia Harris appeared to have it all together. Educated. Great career as a marketing manager with a large computer corporation. She owned her own brownstone where she rented out the top floor. But that was just a facade that covered up the fear and insecurities that lay just beneath the surface.

After dating for almost a year, they began to talk of getting engaged. That was when everything changed. Suddenly, he didn't recognize the person he had made a commitment to. Felicia became demanding and critical, and expected him to read her mind. Why didn't he take her to the new soul food restaurant for her birthday? Why couldn't he pass up Sunday football with the guys to spend the day with her? Why didn't he go to her friend's wedding with her?

All he wanted to know was, why didn't she tell him up front what she wanted? If she wanted to try the new restaurant, why wait until they were seated at another restaurant before saying something? If she would have preferred him to spend the afternoon with her instead of watching the Giants take on the Redskins, why didn't she tell him before he left for the game, instead of giving him the silent treatment when they saw each other later that night? And the friend's wedding? She had talked about it, and talked about it and talked about— but never asked him to go. Why didn't she just invite him instead of arguing over it later, claiming that he should have known she wanted him to go?

Eventually, Terrence got tired of being expected to use his psychic powers to make the relationship work. He couldn't convince her that the best way to stop the fighting was for her to just be honest and up front about what she wanted from him. But she responded as if he were speaking a foreign language. So they parted ways. That was almost two years ago and he hadn't had a serious girlfriend since—which suited him just fine. Dealing with women had become too hard.

Reaching in the fridge for a bottled water, he unscrewed the top, took a big swig, and leaned against the counter. He surveyed the area; boxes surrounded him at every corner. He'd been on the West Coast for almost three weeks and had yet to finish unpacking. Between settling in to his new job, meeting with clients, and catching up on some of his new cases, he'd barely had time to unpack the things he absolutely needed.

He'd never forget the look of shock on his family's face when he told them he was leaving. With his being born and bred on Long Island, and having lived the last five years in the heart of New York City, everyone thought he must be losing his mind when he announced his departure. There were hundreds of law firms in the city, his family reasoned. He could easily accept a position at one of them and not have to leave New York. They didn't understand his need for a change—not just the law firm, but from everything.

Staying in touch with Eric over the years, he never took his offers to join his firm seriously until last year. This time, Terrence was the one who initiated the conversation. A few cross-country trips for interviews, another one to find a place to live, and the final trip that moved his life from the East to the West, and the deal was done. No more winter snowstorms. No more Felicia. Even though their relationship had ended, they still shared some of the same friends, favorite restaurants, and occasionally ended up at the same parties.

The sound of the phone ringing brought him back to the present. "Hello."

"Are you ready to come home yet?"

A slight grin escaped his lips at the sound of the woman's voice on the other end. "It's only been a couple of weeks."

"So you should definitely be ready to come back."

Terrence heard the laughter in her tone, but also knew she was dead serious. The last thing Yvonne McKinley wanted was for her big brother to move to what she often referred to as "the other side of the world." Just twenty-six, she'd been married for a little over five years and had already blessed him with a niece and nephew. Thinking back to the day he told her he had accepted the job and would be gone in less than a month, he remembered that she had accused him of letting Felicia run him out of town, explaining that if he just gave it a little more time he would get over her once and for all. But Yvonne didn't understand that he needed to get away from more than just Felicia.

At thirty-one, he felt he'd come to a pivotal point in his life. On the partner track at his old firm, he needed to decide if this was where he saw himself working for the rest of his career. Ready to buy a home instead of renting, he had to decide if New York was really where he wanted to put down roots. After visiting San Francisco several times over the past years, he decided to give the city a chance. Of course, Yvonne still blamed his leaving on his breakup with Felicia.

"I'm on my way to my hair appointment, but I wanted to check in and see how the party went. Did I win the bet?"

Terrence laughed out loud when he thought of their conversation last week. Yvonne found it hysterical that Dawn continually tried to set him up with her friends. She warned him that he'd spend the entire evening ducking all the women that Dawn would want him to meet. Terrence disagreed with her, believing that Dawn would invite as many single women as she possibly could, but would let nature take its course, as opposed to making obvious introductions throughout the night. How wrong he'd been. "You win."

"I knew it!" Yvonne cheered through the phone. "So tell me, were any of them a hit or were they all a miss?"

Terrence remembered the parade of women that he'd been introduced to the night before and gave his sister a brief recap of the disastrous results. "Not one woman discreetly steered my way was right for me."

"Were you giving them a fair chance?"

Terrence heard the skepticism in her voice and tried not to take offense. "What's that supposed to mean?"

Yvonne hesitated a moment. "Maybe none of these women interests you because you haven't gotten over Felicia."

"Oh, please, Yvonne," Terrence started, annoyed that she kept bringing his ex-girlfriend into the equation. "Felicia doesn't have the power to stand in the way of me finding another girlfriend."

"Then explain to me how you can be introduced to at least ten women in three weeks and not be interested in at least one of them."

"That's an easy one to answer," Terrence said. "The first woman's divorce had just become final and she spent the entire conversation in tears, wondering how he could just abandon her after all they had shared together. The second woman spent the entire time pressing me for job leads for the catering business she was just starting."

Terrence heard his sister about to interrupt, but he wouldn't let her. "And let's not forget my all-time favorite. The belly-dancing, out-of-work actress whose voice sounded like a mouse and who spent most of the conversation explaining to me how she thought she was a princess in her previous life."

"Okay, okay," Yvonne said, finally able to cut him off. She couldn't help but laugh at his strange encounters. She couldn't believe that Dawn's friends could be so weird. "I guess it is possible that you haven't met one woman that actually piqued your interest."

Terrence's thoughts immediately went to the music room. "I wouldn't say that was a completely true statement."

"Really?" Yvonne asked. "I thought you just said that none of the women Dawn introduced you to appealed to you."

"Except . . ."

"Except who?" Yvonne said impatiently. She had a feeling he was holding out on her.

"For some reason, Dawn didn't introduce her to me."

"Who?"

Terrence could tell by her voice that she was getting irritated with his evasiveness, so he rehashed the scene starting with the moment he heard the music. When he finished, he tried to calm his racing heart. It was the same feeling he had gotten when she finished playing the song.

"Terrence?"

How long has she been calling my name? "I'm here."

Yvonne smiled when she heard him finally answer her. *This must be some woman if she can preoccupy his thoughts like that.* "Why didn't Dawn introduce her to you instead of those other women? This one sounds more your type."

"I've asked myself that same question," Terrence said thoughtfully. "Maybe she's already involved with someone."

"Aren't you going to find out?" Yvonne asked, unable to conceal her excitement at the prospect of her brother dating someone. "All you have to do is call Eric."

"No, thank you," he answered without hesitation. "I've been after him to get Dawn off my back ever since my plane landed. No way am I going to encourage her by asking about her friend. Besides, there has to be a reason why she didn't introduce us, so let's just drop it."

The slight irritation in his voice wasn't lost on Yvonne. Whether he wanted to admit it or not, he was attracted to this woman. The only thing Yvonne had to do was convince him to do something about it. Knowing her brother, that was not going to be easy.

Five

"I can't believe you paid four hundred and thirty-five dollars for a pair of shoes," Jasmine said as she set their packages on the floor just inside the living room before following Dawn to the kitchen. They'd been shopping all afternoon and it never ceased to amaze Jasmine how much money Dawn was willing to spend for material things.

Jasmine could remember asking her mother for the latest pair of jeans or the newest tennis shoes to hit the market. Her response was always the same. *"There are people starving all over the world. No need of us wasting money."* But fifteen years later, there were still people starving around the world, even though the last thing Jasmine did was waste money.

"And I can't believe you won't call Terrence," Dawn answered.

Jasmine pointed to her watch. "That's a record. You haven't mentioned his name in . . . what . . . almost ten minutes?"

"Has it been that long?" Dawn said, feigning shock. "I must be slipping."

Jasmine folded her hands in front of her face as if she were praying, pleading with her eyes. "Will you *please* give it a rest?"

"I would if you weren't interested. But you are. I'm just doing my job as your best friend to encourage you to do what you really want to do anyway."

Jasmine dropped her hands and decided to turn the tables. "If you're so gung ho about me and Terrence, why didn't you plan to introduce us?"

"What do you mean?"

"For weeks you've been talking about all the women you could set him up with. Not once did you mention me. Why?"

Dawn hesitated, not wanting to admit that she had thought the same thing Jasmine had been saying all along. "Because I didn't think he was your type."

The words were said so softly, Jasmine wasn't sure she'd heard them. "I'm sorry, Dawn. I didn't hear you. Can you repeat that?"

Dawn knew Jasmine had heard every word she said, but she repeated it—this time it was a little louder.

"Bingo!"

"You know how you are, Jas," Dawn said, trying to explain her initial reluctance to introduce Terrence. "You said it yourself, this morning. You don't like lawyers, you don't like men who don't feed the hungry or work in soup kitchens. You refuse to date men who spend their money on expensive things when there are 'children starving around the world.' The only reason you've stopped lecturing me about how much I spend on material things is that you know how much Eric and I give back."

Jasmine stood up and clapped slowly and loudly at Dawn's admission. "Thank you . . . thank you . . . thank you. You've just succeeded in confirming why I wouldn't want to go out with someone like that."

Playfully slapping her hands down, Dawn refused to give up. "He might be a successful lawyer, but he's also a pretty good guy. He wouldn't be Eric's friend if he weren't. And now that we know you want to get to know him better, all you have to do is call him."

Jasmine heard the words but couldn't agree with them. Not only had she never been the pursuer, but she definitely couldn't see herself making the moves on a guy she didn't think would be a good fit for her—no matter how fine he was.

"I know that look," Dawn said.

"What look?"

"The look that says, 'I really want to do something but I'm not going to let myself—for no good reason.' "

"Okay, okay, let's just say—hypothetically speaking—that I give this Terrence guy a call. What on earth would we possibly talk about? Our professions are worlds apart, we move in different circles, and he's probably into activities that I have no interest in."

"When did you get so pessimistic?" Dawn said, retrieving the steaks from the refrigerator she had left marinating.

"I'm not pessimistic, I'm realistic," Jasmine declared. "I see things every day at work that remind me that the real world can be a disappointing and dangerous place. I just prefer to protect myself by looking at each situation without the help of rose-colored glasses."

"So the fact that you're attracted to him and vice versa doesn't matter?"

"Attraction doesn't mean anything if ultimately you're not compatible," Jasmine said, taking a seat at the table.

"Then let's find out if the two of you are compatible. Call him."

Jasmine's patience was beginning to run thin. Six hours. That's how long they had been having this same conversation. "You sound like a broken record, Dawn. Call him. Call him. Call him."

Reaching for the cordless, Dawn handed it to her. "There's one very easy way to shut me up."

"No," she said, refusing to take the phone.

"Five-5-5-9056."

"Not gonna happen."

"I dare you," Dawn said, dropping it in her lap.

"Don't be childish, Dawn."

"I double dare you."

"Oh yeah, that's real mature," she said, ignoring the phone thrust in her face.

"The reason you don't want to call him has nothing to do with compatibility—it's because you're scared."

Jasmine twisted her lips in a sarcastic smile. "So we're moving from childish dares to reverse psychology?"

"No," Dawn started slowly. "I think I finally hit the nail on the head."

"And what nail is that?" Jasmine said, not sure she wanted to pursue Dawn's line of thought.

"I saw the way you looked at him last night. I watched your eyes light up every time we've talked about him today. You actually do think you two could get something going . . . and that scares you."

Jasmine's nervous laughter seemed a lame attempt at discrediting Dawn's reasoning. "What do I have to be scared of?"

"Brian."

That name hadn't been uttered in years, but it could still stir immediate anger in Jasmine. "What does he have to do with any of this?"

"Think about it . . . Brian broke your heart almost six years ago, and you haven't been serious about another man since."

"You know what, Dawn?" Jasmine said dramatically. "You may be on to something. It couldn't possibly be that the reason I haven't had a serious boyfriend has something to do with the fact that I've been busy getting a master's degree and building a career. No, I'm sure it has everything to do with knucklehead Brian."

Ignoring her sarcastic tone, Dawn shook her head. "You made time for Brian."

Jasmine decided to remain quiet. This conversation was grating on her nerves, and she felt herself being worn down. There was no denying the spark of interest that had ignited in her the moment she saw Terrence. But Brian Jenson had taught her a valuable lesson—two people from different worlds don't mix, no matter how many butterflies flutter around in your stomach.

Dawn realized she couldn't get her friend to budge and decided to take matters into her own hands. Retrieving the phone, she shrugged. "Fine, Jasmine. Don't call him."

Relief surged through Jasmine's entire body. Finally, they could end their discussion of Terrence McKinley. "Thank you. Now can we please move on to another topic?"

"I'll call him for you."

Before Jasmine could figure out what was happening, Dawn had already dialed the number and was awaiting an answer.

Jasmine reached for the phone, but she was a split second too late. Dawn stepped around her just as he came on the line.

"Hi. Terrence? It's Dawn."

"Hey, Dawn." Terrence tried to sound cheerful, but he couldn't help but wonder why she was calling. Every time she had spoken with him, the subject usually revolved around introducing him to somebody. And frankly, he'd had enough. If Eric couldn't get her off his back, he'd have to do it himself.

"I just wanted to call to say that I hoped you had a good time last night. Eric and I just wanted to make you feel welcome." She stepped around the table as Jasmine once again reached for the phone.

"Yes, I did. I'd planned to call you guys sometime this weekend, but I've been busy unpacking."

"Still trying to settle in?"

"You could say that."

"Then you must be ready to take a break."

Terrence paused as his attorney instincts kicked in. The words sounded innocent enough, but he smelled a setup, and if it had anything to do with one of her flaky friends she'd tried to set him up with, he would have to put an end to her matchmaking once and for all. Hesitantly, he started to answer. "I'm fine—really."

"That's too bad, because Eric and I are having dinner tonight with a friend that's great at organizing. I'm sure she could give you some tips."

Terrence cringed at the thought of having to deal with yet another one of her blind date hookups. "Listen,

Dawn, while I appreciate your trying to make me feel welcome in a new city, I'm just not interested in—"

"Jasmine Larson."

Terrence heard the name and couldn't get a response out of his mouth.

Dawn's smile grew wider as the other end of the line went silent. "Terrence?"

Finally, he found his voice. "Dawn, why are you calling me instead of her?"

"She's right here," Dawn said, giving Jasmine the thumbs-up sign.

Jasmine heard the words and felt her heart hammer against her chest. A part of her wanted to run out of the room, proving once and for all that she had no interest in talking to or seeing Terrence. But it was the other half that kept her feet firmly planted where they were. That was the half that scared her.

"But she didn't call, you did," Terrence said.

"Minor technicality," Dawn explained.

"No, Dawn," he said, catching her before she could pass the phone. "Obviously there's a reason why she didn't call me, which means this call probably has more to do with your matchmaking desires than her wanting to talk to me. So, while I appreciate you thinking of me, if Jasmine is interested in seeing me, please have her call me herself. Have a great afternoon."

Hitting the end button on the phone, Dawn set the phone on the table and remained silent.

Jasmine watched her replace the receiver and panic struck every nerve in her body. "What happened? What did he say?"

Realizing how anxious she sounded, Jasmine quickly

toned it down a notch. "I mean, how did the conversation go?"

"For someone who didn't want me to make the call, you seem mighty concerned about the conversation." Dawn turned her attention back to preparing dinner, ignoring her friend on purpose.

"Cut the crap, Dawn."

"Oh, feisty, are we?" Dawn teased, turning back to her. "I knew you liked him."

"Just tell me what he said."

"He said that if you want to talk to him, call him yourself."

Jasmine remained silent.

"I'm going to go up to shower and change before dinner. Eric's going to grill the steaks. In the meantime, if you want, you can just push redial."

Jasmine took a seat and watched Dawn leave the room. After several minutes of staring at the phone, she picked it up, placing her finger right above the redial button. She took a deep breath and made her decision.

Later that evening, Eric, Dawn, and Jasmine savored the tender steak, corn on the cob, and baked potatoes.

"I can't believe you didn't call him back," Dawn stated for the fifth time.

"I can't believe you won't give it a rest," Jasmine said, again. Truth be told, she couldn't believe she didn't call him either. But ultimately, it was for the best. Between their careers and where they lived, it just wouldn't work.

"Yeah, Dawn. Please give it a rest," Eric chimed in. "You've been driving everyone crazy with your matchmaking. Jasmine. Terrence. And especially me."

Dawn turned to her husband to plead her case. "But you didn't see them last night, Eric. It was definite attraction on both their parts." Turning her attention to Jasmine, she looked for confirmation. "Tell him."

"Leave her alone, Dawn. And please leave Terrence alone. You're in the process of ruining a very good friendship, and a very good marriage," he added pointedly.

"Okay, okay. I'll let it go."

Both Eric and Jasmine sighed in relief.

"But don't blame me if what could possibly be my best match doesn't happen."

"I'm sure we'll get over it," Eric said.

Jasmine glanced at Eric and gave him a silent thank-you.

Jasmine turned her entryway light on and walked straight down the hallway to the kitchen at the back. Sorting through her mail over the trash can, she immediately discarded the junk and set the bills to the side. After she said good night to Eric and Dawn, the unusually light traffic on this Saturday evening allowed her to make the trip from the city into Richmond in less than forty minutes.

Heading up the stairs, she thought about Dawn's assessment of her. *Afraid to get involved with another man. Fearful of taking a chance. Absolutely not true!* She'd dated plenty of men since Brian. She just hadn't been able to find someone whom she made a connection with, felt a spark of attraction to—until last night.

Jasmine paused as his face flashed in her mind. Even though she hated when Dawn tried to set her up, she had to admit that this was one hookup she wouldn't mind.

Staring at the phone, she silently recited the number she'd memorized hours ago. Contemplating for the hundredth time whether to call, she shook her head no, and instead headed to her closet to change into something more comfortable.

Twenty minutes later, she sat on her bed flipping channels. The clock on her television read 10:03 P.M. It was Saturday night and she was sitting at home—alone. Was this what her life had become? Before she could talk herself out of it, she grabbed the phone and dialed.

Terrence lay across his bed watching television. He'd spent most of the afternoon and evening unpacking and still had a ways to go. But figuring he'd done enough for one day, he found the only thing left to do would be to decide if he wanted to order pizza or Chinese.

Thinking of his earlier conversation with Dawn, he wondered if she'd relayed the message to Jasmine about contacting him. He had wanted to speak to her the moment Dawn offered to pass the phone to her. But no one knew better than he how relentless Dawn could be when she was trying to make a love connection. She insisted that he meet and talk to a woman he'd already told her he had absolutely no interest in. Could she have been doing the same with Jasmine? Trying to force them together when she really wasn't that interested? But the more he thought about it, the more he realized he wanted to see Jasmine again. Setting his concerns aside, he decided to give Dawn a call to get Jasmine's number. Just as he reached for the phone, it rang.

"Hello?"

"Hi. Terrence?"

He'd only heard her voice in one conversation, but he'd recognize it anywhere. "Jasmine?"

The half smile that escaped her lips was only a small indication of how happy she was that he knew her voice. "I hope I'm not disturbing you."

"No, not at all. I'm just taking a break from unpacking."

The phone went quiet as neither spoke.

After a few seconds, Jasmine leaned back stiffly against her headboard, getting her words together. "I wanted to call and apologize for Dawn's behavior. I know she's been playing matchmaker with you and I know how annoying that can be."

"Are you speaking from firsthand experience?" he asked, clicking off the television.

"Are you kidding?" She laughed, feeling her body begin to relax. "I must have met at least ten guys that have 'accidentally' run into us when we've been having dinner, shopping, or just hanging out."

"How does she manage to set up all her single friends and hold down a full-time job?" he asked jokingly.

"Your guess is as good as mine. I was hoping she'd heed my advice and leave me alone. But as you can tell from her phone call this morning, that was just wishful thinking on my part."

"Ah yes, the phone call," Terrence said. "She never gives up, does she?"

"Not when she thinks she's right," she answered flippantly.

"Is she?"

"Is she what?"

"Right."

"About . . .?" Jasmine wondered.

"Us."

She paused before answering. "You and me?"

"Yeah, us."

The small word hung in the air. "Listen, Terrence, I know Dawn thinks she saw an attraction between us, but she didn't initially introduce us for a reason."

Terrence sat forward with interest. He figured there had to be a reason why Jasmine hadn't been one of the many women on Dawn's list for him and he couldn't wait to find out what it was. "Which is?"

Deciding to hold nothing back, she put the truth out there. "I don't date guys like you."

Terrence paused and wondered what she meant. "Guys like me?"

She heard the confusion in his voice, and started to explain her answer. But before she could continue, he spoke.

"You mean guys from the East Coast?"

She heard the hint of humor in his voice. "No."

"You must be referring to guys who love to listen to the piano being played by a beautiful woman?"

She couldn't stop the smile. "No."

"Oh, I know. You must be talking about guys who duck out of parties to find a little peace and quiet."

Charmed by his wit, she almost thought of tossing her concerns aside. Then she thought of Brian. That pushed her to continue her explanation. "I'm talking about guys who put money above everything else."

Terrence sat back as he attempted to digest her words. "Did I miss something? Have I been placed in this category?"

"I know you were heavily recruited by Eric's firm," Jasmine continued to explain. "You probably make more money in a year than I ever will and you do it by helping people who already have so much—sometimes through extremely questionable practices."

"And you got all of this from our five-minute conversation about music?" he asked, completely dumbfounded.

"No," Jasmine said, "I got all of this from dating men just like you."

Terrence chuckled at the absurdity of her words. "I'm sorry, Jasmine. You gotta give me more than that."

"No offense to you, Terrence," Jasmine said, and she meant it. She wasn't saying that he wasn't a good man, she was just pointing out that he wouldn't be the man for her. "I'm not compatible with men whose goal in life is conquering the professional world by any means necessary. More interested in billing hours, schmoozing with clients, and impressing their boss than with what's right. To do what you do, a person has to be calculating, removed, and somewhat unemotional. Not to mention pushing personal feelings aside for the sake of the client and the almighty dollar."

Terrence listened to her monologue and started to get the picture she was trying to paint. "And you, as a social worker, are there for the little people, helping the underdog, giving a voice to those who seemingly have none."

"Exactly," Jasmine said, satisfied that he understood.

"And never the two shall meet?"

"Oh, they meet," she said confidently, "they're just usually on opposite sides."

"And I assume you've tested this theory of yours?"

Jasmine thought of Brian. "I have . . . and it was one hundred percent accurate."

"You know," Terrence said carefully, "the more I think about it, the more I see your point of view."

"Really?" Her heart sank and she hoped the disappointment she felt didn't come through in her voice. Not that she didn't believe the words she'd just spoken, that just wasn't the response she expected from him. If he was interested in getting to know her, wouldn't he challenge her thinking a little more?

"Yes, really."

"Then I guess I'll say good-bye," she said, trying to sound upbeat. "It was for the best anyway."

Hearing the disappointment in her voice, Terrence smiled. Regardless of the spiel she'd just given him about her theory of opposites, he could tell an attraction still remained. "There's just one thing."

"What?"

"As a lawyer, I deal in facts, in concrete evidence," he started. "And all I have to go on is hearsay."

"From a reliable source," she added.

"From a source I've known less than twenty-four hours," he reminded her. "Unlike you, I'm not able to tell everything about a person in one conversation. So, I can't truly assess how reliable you are."

"And your point?" she said, ignoring his dig at her assumptions about him in their short meeting.

He could hear her impatience, but he didn't mind. If she really wasn't interested in talking with him, she would already have hung up. "My point is, I suggest an experiment."

Jasmine smelled a setup, but she was in too far to back out now, and she wasn't sure she wanted to. "What kind of experiment?"

"According to your so-called theory, a relationship

between the two of us would never work because of our differing views stemming from our professional lives."

Jasmine remained silent. She could easily guess where this conversation was headed.

"How about we spend some time together? You know, put your theory to the test. See how it holds up."

There it was. A challenge. "Terrence, I can't say that I don't find you physically attractive, but you can trust me on this one, a relationship between you and me wouldn't work."

"Fine. All I'm asking you to do is prove it."

Jasmine didn't answer immediately. She'd taken enough psychology classes to know when she was being manipulated. But a small part of her didn't mind. When she had dialed his number, she tried to convince herself that she only wanted to apologize for Dawn's behavior. But if she were to be completely honest with herself, she would admit that somewhere, despite her assumptions about him, was a desire to see him again. "And how do you suggest we do that?"

"Oh, that's easy," he said nonchalantly. "By going on a date."

Jasmine wasn't completely surprised by his answer, she just didn't know if she wanted to take him up on his offer. "And what will one date prove?"

Terrence was about to answer her question, when another thought came to his mind. "You're right. It won't prove anything."

It was a good thing they were on the telephone. If they were face-to-face, he would have witnessed the disappointment settling into her expression.

"We should agree on at least three."

Her smile returned and without a shadow of a doubt

she decided she would accept his offer. Still, she didn't want to give in too quickly. "I see manipulation is not beneath you. But what can you expect from a lawyer?"

He laughed at her humor. "Is that a yes?"

"You're forgetting one thing," she explained. "I don't need to prove my theory. You do. You can go find any social worker and test your theory out."

"First of all," Terrence corrected, "this is your theory, not mine. And second of all, I don't want any old social worker. I want you."

Jasmine didn't miss the lowering of his voice and shivered as goose bumps made their way up her arms. "Again, just like a lawyer. Always expecting to get what you want."

"Will I?"

"On one condition," she said seriously.

"I'm listening."

"We don't tell Dawn. She gets too involved sometimes and it will make things easier—especially when things don't work out between you and me."

"*If* it doesn't work between us."

"Okay, Terrence, *if* it doesn't work out."

"It's a deal. How about we get together tomorrow?"

"You don't waste any time, do you?" she said, pleased that he wanted to get together so soon.

Now that he'd gotten her to agree to a few dates, he didn't want to give her the chance to change her mind. "If you don't already have plans, you can show me the sights of San Francisco."

"Be your personal tour guide?" she teased.

"If you'd do me the honor."

"Let me check my calendar, make sure I don't have any pressing engagements that require my attention," she said, still wanting to hold out a little longer.

Terrence waited patiently, knowing full well that if

she had something important, she wouldn't have to check her calendar to remind her of it.

"What do you know?" she said in fake astonishment. "I'm available."

"Then it's a date?"

Waiting a few moments, she responded with a slight feeling of anticipation, "It's a date."

Six

Jasmine checked the street sign before making a left onto the one-way street. Finding a parking space, she cut the engine of her Honda Accord and took a deep breath. A little before ten, she had agreed to meet Terrence at his place to begin their day of sightseeing. Dressed comfortably in a pair of blue jeans with a deep purple button-down short-sleeved shirt, she'd pulled her hair back in a short ponytail and opted for minimal makeup.

The Waterfront district had been revitalized over the past few years, but Jasmine had yet to come to this part of town. With its trendy restaurants, businesses, and up-scale housing, the area looked like its own little city. Walking up the short set of stairs that led to his building, she pushed the button on the security panel. Staring into the security camera, it took only a few seconds for the buzzing sound to indicate the door was open.

Finding his apartment number, Jasmine suddenly felt the butterflies in her stomach. Agreeing to this date had been a major move for her, considering she thought they had nothing in common besides physical attraction. But now that she was here, somehow, someway, she wanted this to be a love connection.

It had been almost six years since her breakup with Brian Jenson, and it had taken half that time for her to recover from a broken heart. When they had met in graduate school, his charm and good looks only complemented his desire to make a substantial difference in his community. They'd volunteered together on several nonprofit committees and had even mentored two high school students preparing for college. But something happened on the road to "giving back."

It began their final year of graduate school. She noticed that his ambitions for what he wanted to do after graduation began to change. Instead of continuing to pursue his work with nonprofits, he began to talk about how much money he could make by working with a large, Fortune 100 company. Soon, their time together became limited as he started to spend his nonstudying hours joining the right organizations, attending every business event he could, and meeting every company recruiting executive that came to their campus. And in the end, all his efforts paid off. He got the offer of a lifetime from a top management consulting firm in Chicago. It came complete with the six-figure income, the seemingly bottomless expense account, box seats for the Bulls and the Bears, and unlimited access to the city's business elite.

At least Jasmine could say that she never asked him to choose between his job in Chicago and her. He didn't give her the chance. He accepted the offer without consulting her, calling it the fulfillment of his dreams—the opportunity of a lifetime. Believing it would be best if he went to Chicago first, to set things up, he didn't push her to join him. All he said was that she could come later.

But later never came. After several unreturned phone calls, Jasmine picked up on the hint. Brian had ended it without having the decency to notify her. Her only clue that he wasn't lying dead in a dark, back alley somewhere was the Christmas card she received the year he left. *Hope things are going well. Have a great New Year.* To this day, she hadn't heard another word from him.

Two years ago, however, she came across an article in the *Wall Street Journal.* Brian had led a team of consultants working with a major pharmaceutical company to put a positive spin on the legal fallout from not telling users of one of its drugs about the severe side effects. Several deaths resulted from the company's withholding of the information. His public relations savviness helped them avoid paying a substantial settlement to patients who had unknowingly taken the drug.

The disappointment of the failed relationship paled in comparison to what she had to endure after he left. Between her trying to explain to her friends, family, and coworkers what happened and trying to make sense out of the way he had treated her, the experience had given her insight into what it must feel like to lose your mind.

If it hadn't been for her work and Dawn, she wouldn't have made it through. Helping others deal with their problems made Jasmine realize that hers weren't so bad. Now that she had recovered from Brian, she didn't forget the lesson learned. It was hard not to let money, power, and position get the best of you. Very few people she'd known had been able to do it. A part of her wanted to believe that something special could develop between her and Terrence. But she had met enough lawyers to know what their top priorities were: billable hours and fat bonuses, regardless of whether the client was right or wrong.

Reaching apartment number 653, she rang the doorbell and held her breath. She was making either the biggest mistake of her life or the best decision ever.

The door opened and his stunning good looks greeted her. At the party, Terrence had looked debonair, but she credited the three-thousand-dollar suit he wore, the gold cuff links, and the expensive tie. This morning, in a pair of tan khakis and a white button-down shirt, he was just as handsome.

"I hope you didn't have any problems getting here, especially on Sunday. Traffic should have been light."

"Are you kidding me?" she said, forcing her eyes away from his body and onto his face. "Traffic is never light in northern California."

Stepping aside, he gestured for her to come inside.

Just inside the door, she started to speak but the words lodged in her mouth. She froze. It was well known that lofts in the Waterfront area of town were pretty pricey, but the layout of Terrence's apartment was absolutely spectacular. *And it probably cost more than my entire block of houses.*

Terrence watched her facial expression, trying to gauge what could have made her have such a look of disbelief and annoyance. "You'll have to excuse the boxes," he offered. "You would think that after three weeks, I would have finished unpacking."

The boxes lining the walls weren't the reason for her reaction. It was the sheer overwhelming opulence of such a beautiful place. "Your place is . . . umm . . . nice."

Terrence watched her eyes pan the loft and it hit him what was going through her mind. After all the talk about how she felt about his profession and money, he could see the judgment in her eyes.

His sister, Yvonne, had come out with him to help decide on a place to live. She was the perfect person to choose. His baby sister by five years, she had style and flair. And while all he wanted was a nice place to lay his head, she wanted to choose something that fit his style. He had to admit, she did a great job. The loft boasted three floors with two bedrooms, a beautiful U-shaped gourmet kitchen, two fireplaces, and a breathtaking view. The garage was a bonus, as parking in the city could be scarce. With the urban feel of the neighborhood, it reminded him of his life in New York. "Can I get you something before we head out? Coffee? Juice?"

Turning her attention away from the loft and toward Terrence, Jasmine wondered what she was doing here. She'd already proven that the lifestyle she'd chosen to live didn't fit in with the rich and famous—no matter how handsome he was. But now that she was here, she had no choice but to go through with it. She would play tour guide, eat a few meals with him, and be on her way. "No, thanks, why don't we just get started?"

Following Terrence to the garage, he turned to her and started to say something just before he opened the door. Abruptly, he changed his mind. Without saying a word, he held the door open and stepped aside to allow her to walk ahead. This time he heard the judgment before he saw it. She exhaled loudly and he knew, just as she reacted to his living quarters, she reacted to the car. He opened his mouth to speak but decided against it. He had nothing to apologize for, and he refused to make his material possessions a factor in building a relationship with her.

As he pressed the button on his key ring, the locks

clicked and he held open the passenger-side door for her. Only after a slight hesitation did she get in, without saying a word.

Jasmine put on her seat belt and watched him trot around the car to the driver's side. Leaning back in the soft leather seats, she inventoried the wood trim and the custom sound system. Nothing like a custom 745IL BMW to make a statement. *Just as I thought, his car cost more than I make in a year.*

"Where to first? Fisherman's Wharf? Alcatraz? The wax museum?"

Jasmine's attention quickly turned from the car to him when she heard his questions. At first, she curved her lips into a slight smile, but it quickly turned to laughter.

Terrence didn't know what was so funny, but his body relaxed now that he'd gotten a laugh out of her. "Did I miss something?"

"You've got to be kidding me," she said, shaking her head in disbelief. "The Wharf? Alcatraz? Those places are nothing but tourists' traps."

"But when I told people I was moving out here, those were the places they suggested."

"Spoken like people who obviously never lived in San Francisco."

Jasmine watched his crestfallen face and decided to give in. "Okay, okay, we'll do the touristy stuff. Maybe another day I'll show you the real San Francisco."

Terrence started the car and backed out. He liked the fact that she already agreed to see him another day.

Four hours later, Jasmine and Terrence leaned against the rail watching the seals lie out in the sun. According to him, she'd been the perfect tour guide. They started by driving down Lombard, known as the most crooked street in the world, followed by a tour of the famous wax museum. The lifelike figures looked as if they would move at any moment. Finally, they ended with a tour of Alcatraz. Terrence even managed to convince her to have her picture taken in a striped prison uniform standing behind makeshift bars. Deciding to take a break from their adventures, they grabbed a snack in the late afternoon sun.

Taking a bite of her large pretzel, Jasmine laughed as Terrence pointed to a seal that seemed to be putting on a show for them, sliding in and out of the water without stopping. Despite the fact that she had had no expectations of having a good time, she found herself thoroughly enjoying the day.

It had been years since she'd been to this area. She didn't think she'd be able to take the crowds or the constant sales pitches from vendors and novelty shop owners. But with Terrence's genuine interest in the sites and his talkative nature, this was the best Sunday afternoon she'd had in a long time.

Watching his attempts at balancing several plastic bags full of T-shirts, key chains, and San Francisco mugs, while taking a bite of his pretzel, Jasmine offered a hand, taking half of the packages from him. "I can't believe you bought all this stuff. The vendors must have seen you coming a mile away."

Terrence appreciated the relief and handed her two of his bags. "I guess I did go a little overboard. But I'm sure my niece and nephew will get a kick out of everything I got them."

"How old are they?"

"Delaney is five and Marcus is three. My sister, Yvonne, and her husband, Troy, spoil them rotten."

Jasmine watched his expression as he talked about his

sister and her children. His love for them shone. "It's great when children have a loving environment to grow up in."

The wistfulness in her voice didn't go undetected.

"Delaney and Marcus are lucky," she said. "Every day I see children who don't have it that good."

Finishing off his pretzel, he assumed she was thinking of the children she dealt with on a daily basis. "What made you decide to become a social worker?"

Jasmine paused when he asked the question. Over the years, men that she'd dated had asked general questions about her job. Things like what she did, if things were going well, or how her day was. But none had asked why she chose to do what she did. Not even Brian. In a way, she was glad, because it was extremely personal to her.

"My first day in sixth grade I sat next to a girl named Lorraine Martin. In those days, we usually sat in alphabetical order. In the first two weeks of school, we became best friends—inseparable. At the beginning of the third week, she didn't show up. The next day, her seat remained empty, and it remained that way for the rest of the week.

"Worried and confused, I asked my teacher what happened to Lorraine. That's when she told me that she'd been moved to another home. I didn't comprehend what the teacher was saying, but other students in the class said that she'd been living with a foster family because her mother was on drugs and she wouldn't ever have a real home.

"I came home and told my mother about it. She explained that there were children who grew up in families that had problems. And when the problems got so bad that the child might not be happy, they were sometimes given to another family."

Jasmine paused and stole a glance at Terrence. The genuine interest on his face gave her a sense of comfort and a feeling of calmness. "I couldn't imagine being taken away from my parents, no matter how many problems we had. How would I survive the separation?

"My mother went on to explain that sometimes it couldn't be helped and that for the safety of the children, it was necessary for them to leave their mother and father. But the good thing, she told me, was that there were people called social workers who made sure that a child would always be safe and happy."

The passion with which she relayed this story revealed how much she valued her career, thought Terrence. "And you wanted to become one of those people, offering safety and happiness to children."

It was a statement, not a question, and Jasmine heard the understanding in his words. For the first time in her life, someone finally understood—not just what she did, but why she did it.

Terrence gave her an encouraging smile and made her an offer he hoped she couldn't refuse. "As a way of saying thank you for the marvelous job you did today, how about I cook dinner for you?"

"That depends," she said.

"On?" he asked.

"Can you cook?"

"Overall, no," he said, not sure how to answer the question without scaring her off. "But I make a pretty good spaghetti and meatballs."

"What do you know?" Jasmine said playfully. "That just happens to be one of my favorite dishes."

Forty minutes later, they had returned to the loft. Terrence entered first, tossing his keys on the small table beside the door. Balancing two bags of groceries, he held the door open for Jasmine with his elbow, kicking it shut behind her. Giving her a boyish grin, he said victoriously, "Told you I didn't need any help."

Following Jasmine into the kitchen, he put the bags on the counter. "I haven't cooked since I've been here, so it'll take a few minutes to look through these boxes to find the right pans."

"I can help with that," she offered. Leaning over one of the larger boxes, Jasmine started sifting through the items. "Just let me know what you'll need."

Terrence turned to respond to her, but choked on his words. With her leaning over and reaching deep into the box, Jasmine's butt was the first thing he saw. Small and round, it was perched in the air. The jeans she wore hugged her in all the right places.

When she didn't get a response, she stood and faced him. Her eyes caught his line of vision and she felt her cheeks grow warm. "I think I'll sit on the floor and finish going through this box."

I think that's a very good idea. Otherwise, I won't be responsible for my actions. "Cool," he said, clearing his throat. "I'll unpack the grocery bags."

For the next few minutes, they worked in silence. Suddenly, Jasmine howled with laughter. Startled, Terrence stepped over to her. "What's so funny?"

For several moments, her hearty laughter kept her from answering his question. She could only point to something inside the box. Peeking over, Terrence moaned when he realized what she had come across. Reaching down, he picked it up, unable to suppress his own smile. Somehow, the photo album must have gotten mixed up with the kitchen items when the boxes were packed. Taking a seat on the floor beside her, he leaned his back against the center island.

"I will have you know that this was the style in those days."

Jasmine finally found her voice. "How tight were these jeans you're wearing?"

Trying not to join in her laughter, he attempted to defend his fashion choices. "What are you talking about? Those were Jordache jeans. Top of the line."

Jasmine refused to let him off the hook that easily. "Then how do you explain that haircut? Exactly how many parts do you have running through your scalp?"

Terrence stared at the picture, working overtime to maintain a straight face. "I'll have you know that me and my boy, Corey, spent many Saturday mornings cutting each other's hair."

"Seems like you needed a few more Saturdays to get it right," she offered, shaking her head in astonishment.

"Oh, okay, you got jokes," Terrence teased, trying to pull the photo album out of her hands.

"Tell me this," she asked, refusing to let it go. "Is that a muscle shirt you're wearing—with no muscles?"

"You're enjoying this, aren't you?" he said, finally giving in and joining in the laughter.

"I'm just trying to reconcile in my mind the handsome man I met Friday in that custom-fit suit. Or the good-looking man sitting beside me today in khaki pants and a crisp button-down shirt with this—what were you, fifteen?—with this guy with a high-top fade dyed on the top, at least five lines in his head, and jeans so tight you couldn't possibly sit down."

As he leaned in closer to her, she stopped laughing and his voice lowered. "So are you calling me handsome and good-looking?"

Refusing to acknowledge the warming sensation that

tingled through her body, she pointed to the picture. "Not in 1985."

Terrence laughed and sat back. "I'm sure if we checked out some of your teenage photos, we could probably have a bigger laugh. I'm sure you have at least one photo with an asymmetric haircut. Or how about an outfit complete with brightly colored leg warmers? Oh, I got one. I'm sure you have at least one picture with you in a New Edition sweatshirt. Every girl I knew I had something with New Edition on it."

Hearing the teasing in his voice, she playfully nudged him in the arm. "I plead the Fifth."

"Yeah, I thought you would."

Jasmine flipped to the next page in the album and pointed to a young woman in a cap and gown. "She favors you."

The smile on his face was instant when he looked at the woman in the picture. "That's Yvonne. She's smart, beautiful, and the best sister any guy could ask for."

"Does she live in New York?"

"Yeah," he said, thinking of all the conversations they had had when she tried to convince him to stay. "She thought I was crazy for wanting to move across the country. Between her and my parents, they tried just about everything to get me to stay."

"Sounds like you guys are a close-knit family. Hard to believe you left all of them for a job."

Terrence hesitated before he spoke. He rarely talked about his relationship with Felicia, always feeling the hurt and betrayal of their breakup. When it had seemed they wouldn't be able to salvage what they had tried to build with each other, that was when he made the decision to take Eric and his firm up on their offer. Yvonne had told him not to let "that woman" run him away from his family—his home. But Terrence knew in his heart it was time for a change.

So while his family tried to persuade him to change his mind until the moment he boarded the plane, he couldn't deny that deep inside he'd made the right decision. And glancing at the woman sitting next to him only confirmed the good things that were coming into his life as a result of his leaving New York.

"Sometimes it's just time for a change," he said thoughtfully.

Hearing his tone, Jasmine looked up. A moment ago, his voice carried the sounds of levity and fun. Now it was more reflective, as if he was deep in thought. The social worker in her couldn't let it go. "Anything you want to talk about?"

Pausing, he shook his head. "Not really."

If there was one thing Jasmine had learned in her line of work, it was that you couldn't push a person to talk before he was ready. Even though she had an inkling in the pit of her stomach that there was more to his answer than just being "time for a change," she decided to let it drop. Flipping the page in the album, she pointed to an older woman. "And who is this?"

Terrence relaxed when he realized she wasn't going to pursue the topic. Standing, he reached into one of the grocery bags. "Let me get us a glass of wine and I'll tell you all about them."

For the next half hour, Terrence went through the album, introducing Jasmine to all the characters that made up his family. There was Uncle Raymond, who, at age forty-eight, decided after September 11 to leave his job of twenty-three years working in city government to become a sculptor, claiming life was too short not to follow your desires. He was preparing for his first showing at a small art gallery in Soho.

Next, there was Aunt Gracie. She was loud and boisterous and never had a problem telling it like it was. His mother's sister, Gracie often alienated family members with her brutal honesty, but by the time the next big family gathering rolled around, all had been forgiven. Finally, there was Michael and Carolyn McKinley.

Jasmine secretly smiled as she listened to him talk fondly about his parents. His father had worked as a computer operator and his mother worked for the telephone company as a supervisor in customer service. Describing their middle-class lifestyle, he detailed his childhood memories with funny stories.

His parents had wanted more for their kids than they had had; Terrence spoke of the educational vacations his parents forced him and his sister to take. The countless road trips to Washington, D.C., Philadelphia, and Williamsburg, Virginia, to visit museums, historical sites, and other places. But there was also the trip to Disney World they took when he was eleven.

Rehashing the two-day car ride, he thought his parents would smack him and Yvonne silly if they didn't stop arguing. But once they rode Space Mountain, all the crankiness and complaints about the car ride quickly dissipated.

Closing the book, Terrence placed it back in the box but didn't get up. "Look at me. Some interesting first date I've turned out to be. Have I completely bored you talking about my family?"

Taking another sip of her wine, Jasmine couldn't help but begin to think that he was punching holes all through her theory that they wouldn't be compatible. Bored?

Hardly. She'd always **heard** that listening to a man talk about his family could provide insight into his character. Hearing his words today definitely scored him points. "Not in the least. In my line of work I rarely hear about the all-American family."

Hearing the hint of sadness in her voice, he could tell her mind had gone to one of the many cases she handled. Standing, he reached his hand out to help her up. When the palm of her hand slipped into his, a faint trace of electricity forged a trail from the tips of his fingers up to his arm.

Jumping to her feet, she lost her footing and leaned into him. With his arms wrapped around her, neither moved. Just inches apart, he gazed into her face, taking in her natural beauty. With her hair windblown from their day out in the city and her lipstick gone from the snacks they'd eaten throughout the day, she looked like the most beautiful woman he'd ever met.

Raising her eyes to meet his, Jasmine felt her heart skip a beat. He was handsome, successful, and seemingly grounded in family and friendships; she could easily allow her attraction to him to grow. When she watched his gaze lower to her lips, she knew what he wanted, but saw the hesitation, as if he waited for permission.

Clearing her throat, she stepped around him, avoiding the very thing she wanted. She wasn't ready to offer a piece of herself, no matter how small. "We better get these groceries put away. Hopefully the ice cream hasn't melted."

Terrence didn't move as she began taking the items out of the bag. He released a slow breath, and several seconds passed before his breathing became normal again. He couldn't recall a time when he wanted someone's kiss so badly. Not just for the physical satisfaction, but for the emotional connection that had started between them. In the year that he and Felicia had dated, he didn't think she learned as much about his family as Jasmine had in just the last thirty minutes.

Thinking back, he remembered that Felicia rarely seemed interested in learning about his past and what made him the person he was. Her main concerns revolved around his ascent to partner, the next new restaurant opening, or the next fabulous vacation she wanted to plan. Besides their careers and love of travel, what else did they have in common?

"How about I make the salad?"

Hearing her voice brought Terrence back to the moment. "Sounds like a plan."

Forty-five minutes later, Terrence lit the candles he dug out of one his boxes and placed a bottle of wine on the table. Holding out the chair, he motioned to her.

"Candles, wine, holding out my chair. A girl could get used to this."

"That's the plan."

Scooting closer to the table, Jasmine eyed him suspiciously. "You think this is going to work, don't you?"

"What?" he asked innocently, as he took a seat across from her.

"You and me."

"Have you noticed that you always say 'you and me' and I always use the word 'us'?"

"So?"

"It's as if you want to keep us separated while I'm working to bring us together."

Jasmine thought she was the one with the psychology background. "You, me, us. Whatever term one may choose to use doesn't change the fact that one good day doesn't prove anything."

"Are you always this pessimistic?" he asked, placing salad in each of their bowls.

"I'm not pessimistic, I'm real," she reasoned.

"So you're telling me in a matter of one day, you've made a complete assessment about us and have, without a doubt, determined that any type of personal relationship between the two of us will not work?"

When he put it that way, it did sound just a tad presumptuous and slightly ridiculous. But her theory had been proven right one too many times to toss it aside so quickly. "We are from two different worlds."

"Different careers, different income brackets, and different types of cars are all circumstantial. It doesn't mean that it equals what you say it equals."

"Your priorities are different from mine," she countered.

"Cause for speculation," he said with confidence. "You haven't asked me what my priorities are."

"Am I on the witness stand?" she said, listening to all of his legal jargon.

"If you've reached a conclusion with facts that haven't been proven, then yes, you're on trial."

Putting the sauce over her spaghetti, she decided to present her side of the case. "Well, counselor, let's just say that precedents have been set that have proven my theory time and time again . . . regardless of whether the names have been changed."

"Then tell me, what was his name?"

"Excuse me?"

Even though the food was in front of him, he had yet to take a bite. This conversation was too important. "No matter what you expect me to believe about how you derived your theory, I'll stake my case on the fact that you only have one precedent. Your own."

"Now who's being presumptuous?" she countered.

"Am I wrong?"

Jasmine didn't answer right away, contemplating how much of her life she wanted to reveal on a first date. "It's getting late. We should finish our meal so I can head back across the bridge."

Her avoidance of the question only made his curiosity grow, but he hadn't been able to share Felicia and she respected that. He could only offer that same courtesy in return.

An hour later, she gathered up her purse and jacket, as she made her way to the door with Terrence following close behind. Earlier, she had avoided his kiss. This time, she wasn't sure if she'd be able to resist if he tried again.

Reaching around her, he opened the door. Turning the corners of his lips into a slight smile, he leaned in closer and whispered, "What does your theory say about kissing men you have no intention of developing a real relationship with?"

Jasmine cut her gaze from his eyes to his lips and inhaled a short breath. In just one day, he had managed to break down some of the barriers that held her heart in check. "It says one kiss never hurt anyone."

Without hesitating, his lips captured hers as he had to hold back the powerful force of a man who had finally found what he'd been searching for. Tentatively, he wrapped both his arms around her waist, caressed her, coaxing her to give him further access. Just when he thought she would refuse him, she opened her mouth and he slipped his tongue in.

A bolt of fire coursed through Jasmine's entire body and she went warm from head to toe the moment his lips touched hers. Trying to maintain a sense of composure proved fruitless against the assault. Kisses like this could make any woman throw away her theories.

Pulling back, she needed a moment to catch her breath. If she wasn't careful, the night would end with more than just one fabulous kiss.

Terrence felt her step back, but still kept his arms around her. Steadying himself from the impact, he waited several seconds to get his breathing under control. "Next Saturday, I'm invited to a reception hosted by Chandler Enterprises. They're a huge client of the firm. Won't you join me?"

And just like that, the spell was broken. This time, she stepped completely out of his embrace. "I don't think so. That's really not my scene."

"Good music, good food, and good conversation are not your scene?" he prodded.

"You're one to talk," she reminded him. "At the party Friday night, you were hiding from good music, good food, and good conversation. And that event was planned especially for you."

"That's different."

"How?"

"This is business."

"This is exactly why you and I wouldn't work," she mumbled under her breath.

"Us."

Rolling her eyes, she ignored his play on words. "I'm not one for schmoozing with people I don't like for the sake of a deal."

"It's how business gets done."

"Not interested. Enjoy your night."

"Jasmine—" he started, hoping to convince her to change her mind.

"Besides, Dawn and Eric will be there. I really don't want her in my business, pushing you and me together."

"Pushing us together, would that be so bad?" he asked, reaching for her hand.

Jasmine ignored his question. "Have a good time at your business party. I won't be able to join you."

Terrence moved on to plan B. "Then how about dinner Friday night? I'll come to your part of town."

Sliding her hand out of his, she couldn't ignore the fact that the conversation they just had about Saturday night reminded her of the very reason a relationship between them wouldn't work. "Terrence, I don't think—"

"Stop thinking," he commanded, taking her hand again. "If you don't want to go to the party, that's fine. But what reason could you possibly have for not joining me for dinner?"

"I'll let you know," she said, stepping into the hallway.

"Is that the best answer I'm going to get?"

"Yes."

"Then I'll anxiously await your call," he said sweetly, leaning in for one more kiss.

Jasmine savored his lips before she stepped back. If she wasn't careful, he would use those kisses to get her to agree to anything.

"Good night, Terrence."

"Call me when you get home?"

Jasmine chuckled. "You've got to be kidding me. I think I can handle a forty-five-minute drive."

"I didn't say you couldn't handle it. I'd actually offer to follow you, but I know you definitely wouldn't go for that, so I'll settle for a phone call."

"I don't believe this. Opening car doors, helping women to their feet, offering to follow them home. You're an old-fashioned kinda guy. And they say chivalry is dead."

"I'll take that as a compliment."

She gave him a sincere smile. "It is."

An hour and a half later, Jasmine snuggled under the covers with several files and her Palm Pilot, mapping out appointments for the upcoming workweek. Before looking at the first case, she grabbed her cordless.

"I thought I would have to send the calvary out to check on you," he joked.

"I had to get settled in."

"I had a great time today."

"Me too," she answered honestly.

"See you Friday?"

If persistence was a necessary attribute for a successful attorney, then he was definitely at the top of his profession. She decided to go against her theory one more time. "See you Friday."

Seven

Jasmine waited for Monica to pay for her lunch before they found a seat at a table by the window. Spending the morning in the office, they decided to grab a quick bite to eat before heading out for some afternoon visits.

"Can you believe he actually thought she would believe that the woman she saw coming out of his apartment was a plumber? What kind of plumber do you know who will come to fix your pipes in a miniskirt, midriff tanktop, and stiletto heels?"

Jasmine nodded at her words and took a bite of her sandwich.

"And then she got in her spaceship and headed for Mars, where she joined her family of androids."

Jasmine nodded again. After several seconds of silence, Jasmine looked into her friend's face, her words finally registering with her brain. "Androids!"

"Oh, so you were listening," Monica said teasingly. "For a while, I thought I was having lunch with myself. What's on your mind?"

Not responding immediately, Monica narrowed her eyes and caught an unfamiliar expression on her friend's face. "Oh my God."

"What . . . what is it?" Jasmine asked, alarmed at her tone.

"Your face!"

"What's wrong with my face?" she asked, running her fingers across her cheeks. "Do I have mustard or something on it?"

"No, you've got a man on it," Monica exclaimed, excited that it appeared that things were picking up on the dating scene for her friend.

"What are you talking about?"

"The slightly turned downward eyes, the ever so light coloring of the cheeks, the slight upward bend on the ends of your lips. That's the 'I got a man' expression."

Taking a sip of her iced tea, Jasmine waved her assumptions off with her hand. "That's the most ridiculous thing I've ever heard."

"You think so?" Monica challenged.

"I *know* so," she said with assurance.

"Did you meet a man?" Monica asked smartly.

"What kind of question is that?"

"It's a question that will prove or disprove how ridiculous my statement is."

"This is a stupid conversation," Jasmine said, wondering if she did, in fact, look different today.

The fact that Jasmine was dancing around answering the question was all the answer she needed. "I rest my case."

"What is it with all this lawyer talk?" Jasmine asked, throwing her hands in the air.

"Oh, that must mean he's an attorney. Do tell."

One of the first rules Jasmine followed when she had

started working was to keep her private life private. And she had managed to do that for five years. But Monica was different. They seemed to click the moment she came on board, and since Jasmine couldn't share this information with Dawn, she set her food aside, opting to share the details of her weekend with Monica.

When she ended with the good night phone call, she could see the dreamy look in Monica's eyes.

"He sounds absolutely perfect," Monica squealed with excitement.

"Nobody's perfect," Jasmine reminded her pointedly.

"He's got to be close. Successful, rich, a loft on the waterfront, and he loves his mama? Girl, what more could you be looking for?"

Monica's assessment of Terrence did make it seem as if Jasmine could be declared insane for not pursuing a relationship with him. "I don't know, Monica. We'll see."

"At least you agreed to dinner on Friday. I would have made you call him right now and accept if you hadn't already."

"Don't get too excited," Jasmine warned. "It's only our second date and I'm still not convinced we can overcome our differences."

"Second, third, twentieth, or a hundred. Who cares about the number of dates?" Monica said. "Just give him a fair chance."

Jasmine remained silent.

"And ask if he has any brothers."

Popping a chip in her mouth, Jasmine delivered the disappointing news. "Sorry, no brothers."

"Oh well, can't blame a girl for asking."

Feeling a little overwhelmed by all the Terrence talk, Jasmine decided to go back to a topic that didn't make her palms sweat and her stomach flip-flop. Work. "So back to Jeannie Downs. You said when you met with her yesterday, she was complaining about a woman—a so-called plumber—coming out of Elvin's house."

Monica put her sandwich down and wiped her hands on a napkin. "Yes, and of course, I wanted to know what she was doing at Elvin's apartment anyway. She promised me a month ago that she was finished with him."

"Did you tell her that she risks losing Joey for good if she doesn't stay away from him?" Jasmine asked, concern etched in her voice. Jeannie had been doing so well. Jasmine would hate to see her backtrack because of Elvin.

"I tried," Monica said, exhaling in frustration. "But she's insisting that he's changed. That he's not going to touch her or Joey, and that he was through dealing drugs, blah-blah-blah."

Jasmine tried to think of a way to get through to Jeannie. She'd been in and out of a relationship with Elvin for the past seven years and Jasmine had hoped she'd finally broken free six months ago. But it looked like that might not be the case. "Tell her to let him prove himself first, and then if she wants to go back, she can start seeing him again."

Monica pushed her food away. The conversation had completely stolen her appetite. As a matter of fact, she'd missed eating meals several times during the week because of conversations like this. "I've been trying. I encouraged her, letting her know that she was on the right track, reminding her that she had been clean for nine months. Because we'd been successful in finding her a job, she finally had a steady income, which would work in her favor in her efforts to get Joey back.

"When is her hearing?"

"Next month," Monica answered. "I really hope she stays away from Elvin. I want to recommend that she gets custody of Joey again. But how can I do that if I know she's back with Elvin?"

Jasmine sympathized with her. These were the type of calls that could wreak havoc on her mind. "Try to touch base with her more times than usual. Keep encouraging her like you have been. This is a crucial time for her."

"I know," Monica said. "Unfortunately, it's a crucial time for just about everyone on my caseload."

Jasmine acknowledged the frustration in her voice and offered her own words of praise. "You're doing a great job, Monica. Don't let it get you down."

"I'm trying, Jasmine. I really am."

Reaching across the table, Jasmine pushed her food back in front of her. "Eat."

Leaning forward, Monica smiled and picked up her half-eaten sandwich and took a big bite.

It was almost eight o'clock, and Jasmine was just getting home. She had yet to have dinner. Making Joshua— a nine-year-old who had just recently come into the child welfare system—her last visit of the day, she'd intended to stay only about a half hour. But that quickly grew to more than an hour. New to foster care, she'd tried to make the transition as easy as possible for him. His foster parents were caring enough, but there were two other foster children in the home, and she wanted to ensure that his new environment wasn't too overwhelming.

But as usual, she left him feeling as if she still didn't do enough. What if his mother couldn't find a job? What if he stayed in the foster care system until he was eighteen? What if his grades dropped and his rebellious behavior increased as a result of all the upheaval in his life? You couldn't control the what-ifs. Shaking those thoughts from her mind, she opened the refrigerator just as the phone rang.

"Is this a good time?"

The automatic smile at the sound of his voice caught her by surprise and she realized just how much she missed him. "Did I give you my number?"

"Caller ID," he confessed.

"Ah yes. The wonder of technology."

"Do you mind?"

"Not in the least, but I was just about to get something to eat," she said, pulling lettuce, grilled chicken, and cucumbers out of the refrigerator for a salad. "I'm just getting home from work."

"And I thought lawyers kept late hours," he said, pounding away on his computer.

"Can I call you back?"

"Sure. I'm actually still at the office," he said, glancing at his watch. "I'll be leaving in about ten minutes."

"I'll call you later."

Almost two hours later, Jasmine snuggled underneath her covers and reached for the phone. "Terrence?"

"I was wondering if you'd forgotten about me," he teased.

"I'm sure you weren't sitting by the phone," she said, even though she secretly smiled that he must have been missing her, just as she missed him.

"I was working, but the phone was never more than a few inches from me."

"Sounds like we keep the same schedule."

"I don't believe it," Terrence exclaimed triumphantly. "You actually discovered something that we have in common. You better be careful, Jasmine. We wouldn't want you thinking we actually have a chance at making this thing work."

"You're right," she joked. "So we better change the subject."

Terrence shut down his laptop and put his files away. "I told you all about my family, why don't you tell me about yours?"

Over the next hour, Jasmine shared stories of her childhood and growing up in the same house she lived in today. Her parents, both teachers, provided a nice life for their only child. Her mother, Janice, died nine years ago from a stroke, and her dad, Calvin, died one year later from a heart attack. With only a few distant relatives spread about the country, her friends had become her family.

"I was devastated when my mother died and nearly lost my mind when my father died. Both were taken from me so suddenly. It seemed like one day they were here and the next day they were gone. If it wasn't for my work and Dawn, I don't think I would have made it. Helping families work through their problems kept me going during the days, and Dawn coming out to stay with me several times during the week got me through the nights."

Jasmine paused to collect herself. She hadn't shared those feelings with anyone and desperately tried to understand why she opened up to him. Grabbing a Kleenex off the nightstand, she discreetly wiped the tears that hadn't been shed in more than seven years.

"I'm sorry about your loss," he said, with genuine concern in his voice. "They sound like they were terrific parents."

"Thanks, Terrence. And you're right. They were the best."

* * *

As the week continued, Terrence and Jasmine fell into the routine of talking to each other every night. No subject was taboo. They talked politics, religion, and race relations. They discussed the best movies, the greatest singers, and the best places to buy everything from clothes to stereos.

When Jasmine answered the phone on Thursday night, not more than three words had been spoken before Terrence realized something was bothering her. In the short period of time they'd known each other, he'd already become familiar with her moods.

"I just had some disappointing news today."

"One of your cases?"

"Yes. A six-year-old boy has been with a great foster family for four years. His mother has resurfaced seeking custody again."

"And that's a bad thing?"

"In this situation, it could be," Jasmine explained. "The mother is a drug addict who's been in and out of jail a few times. She just got out of rehab less than a month ago and has shown up ready to file papers to reclaim her son."

"I thought you would want the child placed with the biological parents whenever possible," he said, trying to recall things he'd read and learned regarding family law.

"Not when they're drug addicts," she answered, slightly agitated.

"Didn't she just get out of rehab?"

"For the second time," she added pointedly.

"Maybe this time, she's really going to beat her addiction and is ready to take care of her child," Terrence said hopefully.

"And how will we find that out—when she's high and unable to pay attention to her son? When the little boy goes another two days without eating because his mother couldn't remember to buy food?"

Terrence heard how worked up she was getting and backtracked to calm her down. "All I'm saying is that maybe she's changed."

"And all I'm saying is that I can't take that chance. Not yet. We can help her get her life back on track, then work with her to get custody of her son back."

Terrence let the subject drop, moving onto other topics. But the ease of their conversation had become strained. After several more attempts at reviving the conversation, he agreed to call it a night. "I'll see you tomorrow. Seven o'clock."

"Terrence, maybe we should—"

"Seven o'clock," he said matter-of-factly. He wouldn't let her use the conversation about her job as an excuse to cancel their dinner plans.

Leaning back on her pillows, she relaxed her shoulders and smiled at his refusal to let her break this date. And even though her frustration at her job appeared to be taking over her emotions, deep inside she didn't want to cancel either. Besides, she reasoned, Monica would kill her. "See you tomorrow."

The next morning, Terrence sat in his office reviewing files. It was not quite lunchtime, and he wanted to get through his paralegal's case cites for a brief he needed to file by the end of next week before taking a break.

"You look to be deep in thought."

Terrence glanced up at the voice and Eric stood at the door, dressed for casual Friday in tan dress pants and a button-down white shirt—without the tie.

Dressed in black jeans and a gray pullover shirt, Terrence motioned for his friend and colleague to take a seat. "But I can definitely use a break."

"I'm not staying long. I've got a meeting in a half hour. I just wanted to see what was on your schedule for tonight. We haven't had much time to hang out since you got here, and since Dawn has depositions scheduled well into the evening, I thought you might want to grab a drink after work?"

"I would love to join you, but I have other plans," Terrence said, thinking of his date with Jasmine.

"Other plans meaning 'I have more cases to review' or other plans meaning 'I met a hot babe and we're getting together tonight'?" Eric questioned.

"I'll go with 'other plans' option number two," Terrence said, casually leaning back in his chair.

"Thank God," Eric exclaimed, raising his hands in the air as if his favorite football team had just scored a touchdown.

"What's with this overwhelming excitement?" Terrence said.

"Don't you see?" Eric explained. "Now Dawn can leave you alone and get off my back about setting you up. All you have to do is give me a name. Once I relay this tidbit to Dawn, her matchmaking days will be over."

Terrence tapped his pen on his desk, the nervous gesture signaling his attempt to stall for time.

Eric watched his friend closely, as his expression indicated his uncertainty in sharing more information. Then it hit him. "I know her, don't I?"

Terrence didn't answer.

"Oh," Eric started, leaning forward with interest. "This must be a doozy because I don't ever recall a time when you didn't spill the beans on who you were spending your time with."

Terrence put some documents in a folder and set them aside, ignoring his nosy questions.

"Is it Bridgett in accounting? Rumor has it she's had the hots for you since your picture went up on the Web site under new employees." Getting nothing in response, Eric tried again. "It must be Joyce in recruiting. I over-heard her asking Melinda in benefits if your insurance coverage was single or family."

Terrence stood and walked over to the file cabinet. "I used to wonder how you put up with Dawn. Now I understand. You're both the same."

Placing his hand over his heart, Eric feigned being offended. "I resent that. I'm not trying to hook you up . . . I just want to know who you've already hooked up with."

"Then keep wondering, my friend," Terrence said, ignoring the pleading look in his friend's eyes. "My lips are sealed."

"Are you bringing her to the reception tomorrow night?"

"Nice try, Eric." Terrence thought back to her refusal to escort him. Even though he truly believed that she was starting to realize that he didn't fit the mold she'd created for all guys who were successful professionals, she still refused to join him. "No, she's not able to make it."

Heading for the door, Eric said, "No problem. I'm just happy I can pass on the news to Dawn that you're officially off the market."

Terrence's look of surprise prompted Eric's next question. "You are off the market, aren't you?"

Terrence rang the doorbell at seven o'clock sharp. Traffic out of the city was heavier than he imagined, so he was glad he left early. When the door opened, he held out a bunch of fresh flowers. "A beautiful arrangement for a beautiful woman . . . and that's not a line. You look absolutely wonderful."

Jasmine took the flowers, along with the compliment, and ushered him in. It had taken her almost an hour to decide what to wear, something she hadn't done since Brian, finally settling on a deep purple pair of ankle pants with a white silk sweater. Her hair, usually worn in a bob, was slicked back behind her ears, showing off her glittering earrings and stunning makeup. An hour earlier as she added mascara in the bathroom, she had scolded herself for taking such measures for him. But his smile and sincere words made her realize it was well worth the time and effort.

"I'll be ready in a moment. I just need to get my jacket."

Terrence stepped into the small entryway where a flight of stairs was against the far left wall. Motioning to the right, he followed her into the living room. Decorated in burgundy and beige, the room had a warm, friendly feeling. The upright piano made him remember the night he'd met her. Maybe he could convince her to play for him again.

Taking a seat on the sofa, he gazed at the various photos while waiting for Jasmine to return.

"Are those your parents?" he asked, pointing to a picture on the fireplace mantel.

Jasmine walked back into the room. "Yes, that was taken about a year before my mom passed. They had been planning that trip to Paris for years. With the Eiffel Tower in the background, I think it's one of my favorite photographs of them."

Hearing the wistfulness in her voice, he went to her, placing his arms around her waist. Without saying a word, he lowered his lips to hers. When their tongues became intertwined, he thought he would collapse from the sweetness he was experiencing. Pulling her closer, their bodies melding together, he felt all of him come alive.

Jasmine melted into his touch, finding comfort in the cocoon he created around her. She never doubted the physical attraction between them, but the kisses they shared went beyond that. In the short week that they'd gotten to know each other, she could no longer deny what he had been telling her all along. They had what it took to make this relationship work. Feeling her body react to his sensuous kisses and stirring touch, she stepped away. "We better get going. I'm starving."

The couple headed out of Richmond to Bay Street, an outdoor mall featuring upscale shops and restaurants, just ten miles west. Seated after a short wait at a popular Mexican restaurant, they ordered a round of margaritas.

"How was work today?" she asked. In all their conversations, he rarely talked about his firm or the cases he was working on. She wondered if she'd made him gunshy about discussing that topic with her.

"Uh-uh, nope. We're not going to do that tonight," he declared.

"Do what?"

"Talk about work," he said, reaching across the table to hold her hands.

The waiter delivered the drinks and left when they indicated they weren't ready to place their order yet. "Fine. What would you like to talk about?"

"In a word—*us.*"

"You mean you and me?" she corrected.

"No, I mean *us.*"

"And what is it about *us* that you would like to discuss?"

Terrence smiled at her use of the word. "Eric stopped by my office today—wanted me to join him for drinks tonight."

Though not sure why the sudden change in topic, Jasmine didn't object. The topic of "us" made her uncomfortable, as she was starting to have feelings for Terrence that she wasn't ready to completely explore. "Are you saying you'd rather be with Eric tonight?"

The humor in her voice made him smile. "Of course not. But he did want to know who I had plans with."

A moment of sheer panic crossed her face as she realized the impact of answering that question. She would never hear the end of it from Dawn.

Watching the color drain from her face, Terrence quickly put her out of her misery. "Relax. I didn't tell him it was you."

Exhaling loudly, Jasmine had never felt so relieved.

"But he did ask me something that I wanted to run by you," he said.

"Something about a case?" she asked. What could Eric possibly want to know from her?

"No."

"A question about Dawn?"

Watching closely for her reaction, he leaned forward.

"He said that he was glad to be able to tell Dawn I was off the market so that she could stop setting me up."

Taking a sip of her drink, Jasmine pretended not to understand the roundabout question he was asking.

"Jasmine?"

"Hmm?" she said, purposely scanning the restaurant, trying not to make eye contact.

"Am I?"

"Are you what?" she asked, feigning ignorance.

Terrence decided to play along and spell it out for her. "Am I off the market?"

"Do you want to be off the market?" she asked, returning his gaze.

"That depends . . ." he started.

"On?"

"On who wants to take me off."

Just then the waiter arrived to take their order, but Terrence waved him off.

"I was ready to order," she said, hoping to stall to avoid finishing the conversation.

"Uh-uh. Not until I get my answer."

Jasmine set her menu aside. "If you come off the market, doesn't that mean I'm off the market as well?"

"Without a doubt," he said emphatically.

"You want an exclusive relationship with me after knowing me only one week." The skepticism in her voice rang in his ears.

"I want an exclusive relationship so I can continue to *get* to know you," Terrence said, taking her hand and explaining his point of view. "I've played the dating game, and I've even played the serious relationship game. And that's what they all were. A master game of chess—people making moves on each other, hoping to stay one step ahead of the other person. So I've decided to approach this relationship differently. No games. Just me getting to know you and you getting to know me. To see if we can be that thing that so many people search for. That one true thing."

Coming from any other man, the speech he just gave would have sounded rehearsed and tired. The "no game" talk was considered one of the best game moves of all. But Jasmine heard his heart in his words and believed that he spoke with the conviction of the truth.

When the waiter arrived this time, it was Jasmine who shooed him away. "You're asking a lot of me. Between my work, our careers, and my theory, I'm not sure if I can give you what you're looking for."

"The only thing I'm looking for from you is a chance. I'll take it from there."

Jasmine didn't answer, but instead glanced around the restaurant for the waiter. Catching his eye, she waved him over. Picking up her menu, she scanned the selections. Without looking up, she said, "Then I guess, you, Mr. Terrence McKinley, are off the market."

Two hours later, Terrence cut the engine and hopped out of the car, trotting around to the other side to open the door for her. Walking up her sidewalk, he held her hand. When they reached her front door, the motion lights came on and illuminated both of them.

"Do we give the neighbors a show, or are you going to invite me in?"

"Neither," she answered truthfully as she unlocked the door. The evening had been perfect. Too perfect. If she wasn't careful, she'd find herself giving in to desires she wasn't sure she could emotionally handle yet.

"Not even for a cup of coffee?" he coaxed.

"Not for coffee, tea, a drink of water, to use the phone or the bathroom," she said with a slight grin.

"What's the matter?" he asked, wrapping his arms around her. "Don't you trust me?"

"It's not you I'm worried about," she answered candidly.

"Can I at least have a kiss?" he said, already lowering his lips.

The kiss was soft and sweet, and Jasmine backed off as soon as it began to turn into something more.

Before turning to leave, he decided to ask her one last time about tomorrow night. "It's not too late to change your mind. Come with me to the reception tomorrow."

"Sorry, Terrence." Jasmine already felt like she'd conceded quite a bit in the young relationship, but this was one topic she wouldn't budge on. "I have some work to catch up on anyway."

Hiding his disappointment, he nodded in understanding. "I'll call you tomorrow."

Eight

Over the next month, Jasmine and Terrence spent most of their spare time with each other. Alternating between San Francisco and suburban Richmond, they enjoyed exploring the area, trying new restaurants, and catching up on movies they'd missed in the theaters. Their routine of talking every night had become a ritual, and soon, Jasmine found it difficult to fall off to sleep if she hadn't heard his voice telling her "good night and sweet dreams."

The relationship was going so well that she had all but thrown her theory out the window. While she still didn't want to attend firm events, Terrence had shown her over the weeks that he wasn't fully focused on making money and climbing the corporate ladder. Still disappointed that she wouldn't accompany him to work-related functions, he said he understood and respected her decision. That was why he wasn't seeing her tonight. He was having dinner with Richard Montague, owner of

Nationwide Auto Parts, a company that raked in hundreds of millions of dollars a year.

When Terrence had left his New York firm, Richard agreed to let him retain him as a client. Richard reasoned that they didn't need to be in the same state for Terrence to provide him with legal counsel. And with one of his manufacturing plants located twenty miles north of San Francisco, he would be in the area at least once a month and could see Terrence, if necessary, at that time. While several of his clients agreed to move their business with Terrence, this client was without a doubt the biggest. And his new employers took notice. And why wouldn't they? Terrence had just added over a million dollars to their annual revenues.

By four o'clock on Friday, Jasmine started to pack up early. She'd spent the afternoon in family court with a seven-year-old who had been in foster care for two years while his mother served out a sentence on drug possession. Now that the mother was out, Jasmine wanted to help reunite her with her son. But with the mother's having no job and questionable living conditions, Jasmine recommended that the child stay with his foster parents. The judge concurred, giving the mother six months to find steady income and a place to live with adequate space to raise a child. Jasmine would be working with the mother beginning next week to help her find a job and secure a decent place to live.

It was situations like this that reminded Jasmine that there really were no winners or losers. Did the child really win? Ultimately, he was away from his mother. If he stayed in the foster system, he would most likely live in at least three homes before he turned eighteen. And the mother? She was caught up in a system that pun-

ished her for having a drug-dealing boyfriend. The sec-
retarial and computer skills she learned in jail meant
absolutely nothing if no one would hire her because
she had a record.

"Jasmine?"

Clicking the intercom button on her phone, she
said, "Yes?"

"Dawn Westfield is here to see you," the receptionist
said.

Jasmine wondered about the unexpected visit. She
had to think back years to remember the last time Dawn
had come to her office during a workday. She hoped
everything was okay. "Send her in."

A few moments later the door opened and Dawn
breezed in looking as if she just stepped out of a *Vogue*
fashion shoot. The gray, fitted, double-breasted suit
reeked of success and money. The matching sling backs
only added an exclamation point to the bold statement
she made when she walked into the room.

Jasmine, on the other hand, opted for a more casual
professional attire. The pleated blue dress pants with
the blue-and-white silk button-down shirt was appropri-
ate and comfortable.

"What are you doing here? Is something wrong?"
Jasmine's concern echoed in her barrage of questions.

"You tell me," Dawn said. "You're the one that's been
MIA the past month. I've called you three times to try
to get together for lunch or dinner. Each time, you've
been busy. I've called a couple times during the week to
talk and catch up, and you're always on the other line.
Now, I know I could just as easily have called or e-
mailed you my question, but there's nothing like a face-
to-face visit to make sure I get a truthful answer."

Having absolutely no idea what Dawn was talking about, Jasmine sat in her chair, perplexed. "And what questions do you have for me?"

"Who is he?" she said, leaning in as if she was about to get a juicy bit of gossip.

"Who is who?" Jasmine asked, even though she really didn't need an explanation.

"The only thing I could think of that would throw you into this 'I'm unavailable' mode would be a man. But in the times that I did manage to get you on the phone, you haven't mentioned any name."

Taking a seat in the chair opposite her desk, Dawn leaned back and got comfortable. "And I'm not leaving until you tell me."

"How did you know I would be in the office?" Jasmine asked. Her schedule was subject to change on a moment's notice.

"I called the receptionist to get your schedule. I took a chance that you'd be out of court by now. And don't even try to change the subject."

Jasmine couldn't believe that Dawn had left work to find out what was going on in her personal life. "Are you able to hang around for dinner? My treat."

"Oh, this must be good if you're paying," Dawn said, rubbing her hands together.

Twenty minutes later, they sat at the Olive Garden enjoying a glass of house wine. Jasmine had been feeling guilty about not sharing her budding relationship with her best friend and had actually decided to tell Dawn the next time they got together. Leave it to Dawn to take matters into her own hands.

After they ordered, Dawn couldn't stand it one second longer. "So spill it. What, or should I say who, has been occupying your time?"

Jasmine took a deep breath and jumped into her story. "You're right, Dawn. I met a guy."

"I knew it!" Dawn exclaimed. "Eric tried to tell me that you were probably busy with work, but I know you too well. Your excuses of being unavailable didn't jibe with his work theory."

Jasmine couldn't believe the overwhelming enthusiasm Dawn had. Had it really been that long since she'd had a boyfriend?

"I'm sorry for interrupting," Dawn said, forcing herself to calm down. "Go on."

Taking another sip of her wine, Jasmine decided to have some fun with the story. "I met this guy at a party and . . ."

"A party . . . what party? When?" Dawn jumped in. "Why wasn't I invited? In Richmond or the city?"

"Are you going to let me tell the story or not?" Jasmine asked. Dawn had the least amount of patience of anyone she knew.

"Okay, okay, sorry."

"So I met this guy at a party, and initially I thought he wasn't my type. But after having my arm twisted, I decided to go out with him. And surprisingly, we had a great time. That one date led to another, and the next thing you know I'm off the market."

Dawn heard the phrase and stared at her friend. "Did you just say you were 'off the market'?"

"Yes," she said, not offering any more information. She didn't think it would take Dawn too much longer to figure it out.

Dawn narrowed her eyes and looked to be in deep thought. "Eric just used that phrase when he was talking about . . ."

Recognition flashed in her eyes and she stared at Jasmine with excited eyes. "You said you met him at a party . . ."

Jasmine started to speak but was cut off.

"You didn't think he was your type . . ."

After a few more seconds, Dawn continued, "You had to be convinced to give him a chance."

Jasmine nodded to all her comments.

"Oh my, I don't believe it. Please, please, please tell me it's—"

Jasmine decided to finish the phrase for her. "Terrence McKinley."

"Yes!" Dawn exclaimed, practically jumping out of her chair, causing several other patrons to wonder what was going on. "My matchmaking works again."

"Oh, please, girl," Jasmine teased. "You weren't even going to introduce me to the man."

"Good thing I arranged for him to find you in the music room," Dawn said with a sly grin.

"Yeah, right," Jasmine mocked. "But I will say thank you for making me come to your party."

"Okay, girl," Dawn said with the excitement of a child at Christmas. "I want every detail. Blow by blow. Don't leave anything out."

Over lobster ravioli, Jasmine rehashed her courtship from the moment she had entered his loft to take him sightseeing to yesterday when she came back from lunch to a beautiful floral arrangement filled with exotic flowers. Everyone in her department admired them and tried to remember the last time the man in their life had sent them a similar gift.

By the time she finished her story, they had finished their meals and had moved on to dessert.

"I'm so happy for you, Jas," Dawn said. But then her smile faltered and her face looked crestfallen. "But I'm also a little hurt."

Jasmine didn't need to hear her explain why. For so many years, they had shared everything. In the sixth grade, Dawn had her back when Cathy Sikes wanted to fight her because she thought Jasmine liked the same boy she did. Jasmine was there for Dawn when she got stood up for the junior prom. She was also there a year later when that same boy, after apologizing profusely, asked her to the senior prom and she proudly told him to go to hell.

Jasmine had been there when Dawn got her acceptance letter to law school and was sitting next to her when she got the call offering her an associate's position at the law firm. Dawn had helped Jasmine make it through the first time one of the children from her caseload died from injuries sustained by an abusive father. She had also sat beside her last year at a banquet that honored Jasmine for her work in her community.

"Why didn't you tell me?"

Setting her fork aside, Jasmine inhaled deeply. Knowing how hurt she would feel if the roles were reversed, she tried to explain the best way she could. "I'm really sorry, Dawn, that I held this from you. But you have to admit, you had gone a little haywire with your matchmaking."

"But I was just—"

Jasmine held Dawn's hand. "All I'm saying is that

one minute you don't think of hooking us up, and then once you see us talking, you're all over me to call him. I just didn't think I could take that kind of pressure, especially if things didn't work out between us."

Reluctantly, Dawn agreed. "I guess I can see your point. I just wanted you to be happy."

"I was already happy," Jasmine explained. "I have a career I love and friends who love me. I never needed a man to make me happy. I know you think I did, and that's why you've tried so hard to find me one."

"I guess we women sometimes forget that a man doesn't complete us, he complements who we are."

Jasmine watched some of the hurt and anger that was evident in Dawn's eyes a few moments ago dissipate. "So now do you see why I didn't tell you?"

Nodding her head, Dawn finally understood her point of view. "I understand. But now that I do know, how would the two of you like to come over for brunch Sunday?"

"I don't know . . ."

"I promise," she said, raising her right hand. "I'll be on my best behavior."

"I'll see if Terrence is available."

"Fair enough. Speaking of available, where is he? It's Friday night. You two didn't plan to get together?"

"No, he had a dinner meeting with one of his clients. I think it was Richard something . . . Richard Montague."

Recognizing the name, Dawn nodded. "Eric was telling me about that. Your man created quite a stir with the partners when he brought that client in."

Jasmine liked the sound of those two words. *My man.* "Really?"

A twinge of guilt twisted in Jasmine's heart. While

Jasmine constantly shared what was going on at her job, Terrence rarely opened up about the goings-on at his firm. She wondered if he did it on purpose, knowing how she felt about what he did.

"Let's just say that when any lawyer brings in a client that almost guarantees a million in revenue, people stand up and take notice."

"Hmm."

"What's that for?" Dawn asked with a raised brow.

"What?"

"I know your sounds and that one means you don't approve of something."

Jasmine hesitated. She wasn't sure if she was up for having this conversation again.

"It's not that I don't approve," Jasmine said.

"It's just what then?"

"Let's just say that he has his career and I have mine, and I'm not interested in people whose sole purpose in life is to make money—at any cost."

Dawn sat back and placed her hands in her lap, searching for the right words. "That's such an unfair statement, Jasmine. A very broad generalization."

"Then answer this," she said. "You're a lawyer who represents large corporations and extremely wealthy clients. How many times have you questioned what you were doing, or disagreed with their requests, based on your personal beliefs or principles?"

"We don't represent personal beliefs and principles, we represent the law," Dawn reminded her.

"I deal with the law every day and I know that it allows some crazy things to happen that morally aren't right."

"Why are you so against what we do?" Dawn asked.

"Because in your line of work, you can't always do what you know is right. How many times have you put up with a client, gone against your better judgment on something, or tried to take a stand, but caved because of the money—the billable hours?"

"That's not a fair question," Dawn stated. "Every career is full of compromises."

"Lawyers represent companies that willingly make products they know are dangerous or harmful—and help them explain it away. The concept of giving money to someone to cover up their mistakes is ridiculous. People have been hurt and lives are lost. Corporations lobby Congress—throwing their money around, making sure laws are passed that assist them in their business objectives—but their objectives may not necessarily be good for people."

Dawn leaned forward, trying to contain her mounting anger. "I can't speak for every company out there. But I do know that the companies I represent operate within the boundaries of the law. Lawyers play a vital role in helping truth and justice prevail. I won't apologize for what I do."

A sudden chill settled in the air at her words and neither said a word.

Finally, Jasmine reached for and squeezed her hand. "I'm not asking you to apologize for what you do. You have every right to represent your clients in their best interest within the confines of the law. I respect that. I'm just asking that you respect my opinion about it."

Dawn could respect it, but she didn't have to agree and told her so. "Social workers haven't cornered the market on helping people."

"I know," Jasmine said.

After several more moments of silence, Jasmine leaned forward. "Friends?"

Jasmine asked the question just as they would when they were kids and had a disagreement. It was their way of starting over.

Dawn relaxed and smiled. "Friends."

Nine

Terrence pushed the print button and leaned back in his leather chair. Turning, he stared out the window. The view from the twenty-first floor could be breathtaking once the fog burned off. It was just too bad he was enjoying the view on a Saturday morning, but working weekends was par for the course in his profession. With the brief he prepared for one of his clients regarding a breach of contract suit just completed, he'd be home by noon.

As he stared out over the skyline, he thought about the past month of his life. The move, the new job, and Jasmine. It was that last item on the list that brought him the most joy. Yvonne had badgered him constantly for updates on his relationship with Jasmine. But the only information he would offer was that they were seeing each other. Terrence smiled at the last conversation he had had with Yvonne yesterday. It was practically driving her crazy that he was keeping the details of him and Jasmine to himself. She even threatened to fly out here and see for herself exactly what was going on.

"I thought I'd find you here."

Turning to the voice, Terrence smiled. "Eric, how's it going, my man?"

"Everything's cool."

Stepping into the office, Eric looked more ready for the basketball court than a courtroom in a dark blue Nike sweatsuit and sneakers. Before Terrence could offer, he took a seat and jumped right in to the purpose of his visit. "My wife came home stirred up last night. So excited I could barely get out of her what caused that huge grin on her face."

"Sounds like good news," Terrence said, picking up his document from the printer and scanning the contents for errors.

"Oh, believe me, it didn't just make her day, it very well may have made her life," Eric said. "And even I must admit that it makes me feel pretty good too."

"Wow!" Terrence said, intrigued. "This must be something. What is it?"

"She had dinner with Jasmine last night."

At the mention of her name, Terrence stopped fooling with the papers in his hand and a smile automatically appeared across his face. His eyes immediately softened.

Eric noticed the change in his expression, which only confirmed what his wife had shared with him. "Judging by that expression on your face, I guess it's true?"

"What's true?" he asked cautiously.

"Your 'off the market' woman is Jasmine."

"She told Dawn that?" he said, not wanting to give anything away if Jasmine hadn't truly told her.

"Yep. Over a bowl of pasta and bread."

Terrence couldn't help but feel the relief flow through his body. For weeks he'd been wondering how long she was going to hide their relationship. It seemed as if she didn't want to have to deal with other people if they didn't work out. But now that she told Dawn, that had to be a good sign. Maybe her feelings for him had grown just as his had for her. "We've been seeing each other since my party."

"And?" Eric prompted.

"And it's going great. She's warm, caring, beautiful, and smart. What's not to . . ." Terrence caught himself before the word came out.

Eric heard the hesitation in his voice and leaned forward. "Are you saying . . .?"

Terrence stood, suddenly anxious to move around. He'd only thought he was in love once in his life—with Felicia. But now that Jasmine had entered his world, he wondered if what he had felt for Felicia was real. He'd spent most of his relationship time with Felicia trying to keep her happy. With Jasmine, she brought her own happiness to the relationship, allowing him to enjoy just being with her.

"Terrence?"

Interrupting his thoughts, Terrence stared at Eric, not quite ready to share where his mind was taking him. "Let's just say that my relationship with Jasmine is going just fine."

Eric rose out of the chair and headed for the door. "I'm glad to hear that. Especially because I know Jasmine has her issues when it comes to what we do for a living."

Terrence didn't need an explanation of that comment. In all the time they'd spent together, their differences still hovered over them. At least the issue seemed to have moved to the back burner, declining in importance over the past several weeks. And Terrence intended to keep it that way.

Later that evening, Jasmine opened the oven door to check on the Cornish hens. For the past month, she and Terrence had eaten out in so many restaurants she decided to do the old-fashioned thing and cook for him.

Her mother, originally from South Carolina, had been a fabulous cook. Her southern flair had their mouths watering before the food was even ready. And while Jasmine didn't inherit all of her mother's culinary skills, she was able to retain a few things. It had been a long time since she'd spent this much time in the kitchen, but as she inhaled the aromas wafting through the air, she knew it would be worth every minute.

Setting the dining room table with her best china, Jasmine surveyed the results. Her smile faltered as she took in the scene that she'd created. The wineglasses, the candles, the dimmed lights. The tone had definitely been set for seduction.

The thought jumped into her mind, causing Jasmine's heart to flutter. Glancing down at her outfit, she took note of the tight sweater that dipped suggestively in the front. She'd even selected her Victoria's Secret lace panties with matching bra. Suddenly, she broke into a smile. Her conscious mind had just confirmed what her unconscious mind had already known. She was ready to move their relationship to the next level.

For the past month, they ended their dates with tantalizing kisses that set her soul on fire. Each time, it got harder and harder to break away. But each time, she pulled back, and he, albeit reluctantly, followed. Now, Jasmine wasn't fooled. There was every indication in his body, his eyes, and his touch that all she had to do was say the word, but he never pressured her and that made her want him even more. Tonight, she just might give in to her desires.

When she answered the door a half hour later, she stepped into his arms, welcoming him with a kiss firmly on the lips. Never the aggressor, Jasmine's greeting caught him off guard, but offered a promise of things to come.

Dressed casually in linen pants and a multicolored shirt, his handsomeness could not be denied. "Have I got a meal for you!"

Terrence's eyes perused her body from head to toe and secretly admitted that he could survive just feasting on her. "Good, because I'm definitely starving."

All through dinner, the conversations that usually came so easy weren't there. There was a charge of electricity in the air that neither wanted to acknowledge or admit to each other. Jasmine barely tasted the three cheeses she'd put in the homemade macaroni and cheese and Terrence couldn't tell you if he was eating chicken, pork, or beef.

Jasmine started to clear away the dishes. "Do you want some coffee?"

"No."

"Dessert?"

"Uh-uh."

Jasmine heard the erotic undertones in his answer and turned to face him. "Then what would you like?"

Terrence watched her sexy sway and heard the innuendo in her voice. "What I would like might not be on the menu."

Shrugging nonchalantly, Jasmine said, "Menus are always subject to change. What was unavailable yesterday might suddenly become available today."

Terrence eyed her with interest. "How would some-one know when there's been a menu change?"

"They have to ask the head chef—the person who decides what gets added and what gets taken away."

Terrence stood and moved deliberately and slowly toward her. When he stood just a few inches from her, he reached out and stroked her hair. "Well, Miss Head Chef, I have a few questions about what's available tonight."

"I'm listening."

He leaned forward and kissed her ears. "Is this on the menu?"

"Yes."

Her raspy voice only turned him on more. Tracing a line of butterfly kisses from her ear down her cheeks, finally resting on her lips, he asked in between kisses, "Is this on the menu as well?"

Closing her eyes, Jasmine relaxed at the sound of his soft voice and softer kisses. "Yeah."

Pulling her to him, he moved his hand gently up and down her back. "What about this? Is this available to-night?"

Placing her arms around his waist, she pulled him closer. "It's available."

When he moved his hand down to caress her butt, her sharp intake of air caused him to stop.

Jasmine glanced up into his eyes. "That's on the menu tonight too."

"I think I'll just take one of everything."

"That's a lot of stuff," she teased. "Are you sure your appetite can handle it all?"

Terrence nodded slowly. "Oh, without a doubt. When it comes to what you're serving, I'm a bottomless pit."

Jasmine laughed. "You know, my daddy used to have a saying. 'Don't let your mouth write a check your body can't cash.'"

"Trust me, sweetheart. You can take my words to the bank."

Terrence smothered her lips with his, wanting to taste every part of her mouth. As their tongues danced, he moaned in exquisite pleasure. "So, do you want to take my check to the bank and see if it gets cashed?"

Jasmine led him out of the dining room and up the stairs. It was the first time a man had seen this floor of her house since Brian. Stepping into the bedroom, she felt his arms go around her from the back. "I love the way you smell. I love the way you look—this outfit is so sexy on you. I love you."

They both froze when they realized what he said. She turned to face him with questions in her eyes. He traced his fingers softly down her cheek. "I realized it earlier today when I thought about the fact that I couldn't wait to see you, to hear your voice, to just be with you. You're wonderful, kind, and caring. I'm a happier, better person because of you and I can't imagine living my life without you in it. I love you, Jasmine."

Jasmine swallowed the lump in her throat to fight back the tears that threatened to fall from her eyes. What she had had with Brian could only be classified as puppy love. That relationship was full of expectations that each person would fulfill the other, make each a whole person. But what she felt for Terrence was grown-folks love. Having someone who was already complete added more to your life. When she planned her seduction for tonight, she had wrongly assumed that she had wanted to make a physical connection with him. When in reality, making love would bring full circle the emotional ties they had already begun to share. "I feel the same way."

Leading her to the bed, he sat on the edge and pulled her between his legs. Reaching up, he pushed the sweater up and over her head. The soft material fell to the floor without making a sound. Tracing the outline of her breasts, he then moved his hands down to her pants. Unzipping them, he slid them over her waist and down her legs, allowing her to step out of them. Gazing at her body, he whispered, "Perfect."

When he leaned back, he carried her with him and she covered her body with his. Returning the gesture, she placed kisses on his forehead, eyelids, nose, and finally his mouth. She had never known how much of a turn-on kissing could be, but his expert tongue caused her to moan in sheer pleasure. The clasp on her bra came undone, and then with one smooth motion he turned their bodies until he lay above her. With focused attention, he moved his assault of kisses down her neck until his lips caressed one breast while his hand stroked the other.

"Oh, Terrence," she whispered. Was there ever a time when a man had taken such care with her?

Slowly, his lips continued to move lower. When he traced the outline of her belly button, she thought she would go crazy from the sheer pleasure that ran through her body. But when his teeth pulled on her underwear, she knew insanity was too mild a word to describe what was happening to her. She rose up just a little, and her panties were discarded in a matter of seconds. The moment his lips touched her core, her hands grabbed the covers at her side. When his tongue began to work its magic, the scream that had threatened to escape her lips since they entered her bedroom couldn't be withheld any longer. "Yes, oh yes."

Her heart rate increased and she felt tremors start at her toes and work their way to the top of her head. The powerful sensation of pure satisfaction overtook her and her entire body exploded into a thousand wonderful pieces.

It took her a few minutes before her breathing returned to normal and her grip on the sheets loosened. There was no way she could ever talk about this experience, because there weren't any words in the English language that could describe what she felt.

Standing beside the bed, Terrence removed his clothes and retrieved the foil packet from his pocket. Rejoining her on the bed, he lay on top of her, his eyes filled with desire. He wanted to connect with her in a way that left no doubt of his commitment to her. He had come to the West Coast to create a fresh start for himself, and had found the love of his life.

The moment he entered her, Jasmine's mind became completely free of all doubts about him. He had proven himself to be strong, caring, loving, and all hers. Each stroke filled her with passion and contentment. This feeling was what she had been searching for all her life. This was it. The woo-woo. That one true thing. The everything. This was love.

Ten

Jasmine sighed in contentment and leaned her head back against the cushioned headrest, eyes closed. She had decided to take this Friday off and indulge herself with an herbal body wrap, followed by a hot stone massage. After the body wrap and massage, she was now pampering herself with a pedicure and manicure at the spa. It had been at least five years since she'd enjoyed a day-long beauty treatment at a spa and she had all but forgotten how relaxing the experience could be.

Years ago, booking a full day of services as a birthday present for her mom, she'd hoped the experience would be a time for them to enjoy each other's company. And while Jasmine had savored every moment of the day, her mother complained a few times about the cost—reminding her daughter that they could buy groceries for a week with the money spent on facials, massages, and manicures. Inhaling deeply, Jasmine decided that this would become a monthly ritual. If she could feel this way each time she came, it was definitely worth the money.

"This is the life."

The sound of Dawn's voice from the station beside her interrupted Jasmine's memories, but she was too relaxed to look in her direction. "You are so right. I could definitely get used to living like this, instead of waiting for a special occasion."

"Speaking of special occasions," Dawn said, "did he give you any hints about tonight?"

"Nothing," Jasmine said, still not raising her head or opening her eyes. "Just that he wanted to do something nice to celebrate our anniversary."

"Can you believe it?" Dawn said, practically moaning from the foot massage. "It's been six months. And you thought you guys wouldn't last one date."

Thinking back to her assessment of a relationship with Terrence, Jasmine was glad to have a persistent friend nudge her in his direction.

"Not to mention that he's taking you to meet the family for Thanksgiving—in just two short weeks."

Jasmine suddenly sat up and opened her eyes, panic evident in her expression. Turning to Dawn, she said anxiously, "I don't think I can do it."

Dawn turned to face her friend, surprised at Jasmine's sudden panic attack after they'd just spent the last two hours trying to get rid of life's stress. "Can't do what?"

"Meet his parents. And his sister. And his niece and nephew. What if they don't like me? What if his mother and I don't hit it off? What if—?"

"Whoa, slow down," Dawn said, hoping to calm her friend down. "There's no need to be nervous."

She heard the words; she just wasn't sure she believed them. "His family is so close. His parents, sister, aunts, uncles. They'll all be there."

"Don't worry," Dawn said confidently. "You'll be just fine. They'll love you, just like he does."

"But what if—"

"You're getting yourself worked up over nothing. Everything will be fine. You'll see."

Jasmine closed her eyes again and leaned back, feeling only slightly reassured by Dawn. Trying to get back to her state of bliss, she thought of the past six months of her life. And what a wonderful six months it had been.

She and Terrence hadn't gone more than a few days without seeing each other and they never went a day without talking to one another. He'd introduced her to sports by taking her to a few basketball and football games, and she'd taught him simple songs on the piano. There had been many times when she'd given a private concert, just for him.

Even his work hadn't been a hindrance to their relationship. She had attended a few functions with him, but he always told her that she had a choice. He wouldn't force her to go or compromise her principles. Her personal life could not have been better.

Professionally, things were busy as usual. Her caseload at work was still more than one person could bear, but she made concerted efforts every day to make a difference in the lives of the people she helped and tried not to let the pile of growing files on her desk get her down.

She also spent time with Monica, who still seemed to be struggling with managing the troubling situations that arose on an almost daily basis. They'd had several conversations and Jasmine was glad to mentor her since Monica worked so hard to give her clients all the help they needed.

"Are you ready for your facial?"

Jasmine and Dawn opened their eyes as the woman came to escort them to another part of the spa. Yes, life was definitely good.

Terrence sat in his office finishing up a conference call. Just after 2:00 P.M., he checked his calendar and realized he had one more meeting in about fifteen minutes. Planning to be finished by three, he knew that was plenty enough time to take care of his errands. He'd given his secretary explicit instructions: no appointments or meetings after three today. The jeweler closed at six and he needed to pick up her engagement ring before he headed out to Richmond.

Never in his wildest dreams had he thought his move to San Francisco would result in his finding the love of his life. But that's exactly what happened. And six months later, he was ready to make the ultimate commitment. Tonight was the night he would dust off his knee pads and kneel—all in preparation to pop the question.

Noticing the flashing light, he quickly checked his voice mail before heading to the conference room for his last meeting of the day.

"Terrence. Richard Montague. I need to talk with you about a pressing legal matter. Please give me a call at your earliest convenience. You can reach me on my cell."

Terrence didn't even replace the headset before dialing. When your biggest client had a pressing problem, you returned the call immediately.

"Richard? Terrence. I just got your message. What can I do for you?"

"I'd prefer not to discuss this over the phone," he said hurriedly. "I'm actually on the West Coast this week.

Can I come to your office today? I have a meeting with my sales force at three, but I could be there around five P.M."

Terrence thought of his plans with Jasmine. There was no way he could meet that late. It would throw everything off. "I'd really like to accommodate you, Richard, but I have plans this afternoon that are nonnegotiable."

Richard hesitated and Terrence held his breath. If Richard insisted, what was he going to do?

"I understand," he said finally. "I realize this is very short notice. I'll just stay the weekend. I have plenty of work here to keep me busy. How about I come to see you first thing Monday morning—eight o'clock?"

Terrence sighed in relief. "I'll be here."

"Thanks, Terrence. I'll see you Monday."

Terrence hung up the phone and stared at it for several seconds. That was the strangest phone call he'd ever received from Richard. He'd worked with him for the last five years, and their dealings in various situations had settled into a pattern. Typically, Richard would give Terrence a brief overview of the situation that needed attention. From that information, Terrence would recommend a plan of action. Rarely did he not share information with Terrence over the phone, and even less often did their dealings require a face-to-face meeting without any background information on the subject matter.

But Terrence could tell by the tone of his voice that this meeting was different. He sounded almost desperate, and somewhat secretive. Terrence hated putting Richard Montague off, but he did say that Monday morning would be fine.

"Terrence, they're waiting for you in conference room C."

The voice of his secretary over the intercom brought him back to reality. Grabbing his portfolio and suit jacket, he headed for the door. "I'm on my way."

Thirty minutes later, Terrence pulled out of his building's garage, trying to contain his excitement about his plans for the evening. Tonight would be one night Jasmine would never forget.

Jasmine sprayed the perfume on her pulse points before slipping on her panty hose. Terrence had been tight-lipped about his plans tonight, and had only told her to dress up. Taking his advice, she and Dawn went shopping and she settled on a red off-the-shoulder, long-sleeved satin top that hit just below the hips, and a pair of black chiffon flare pants. She accessorized this with a pair of diamond earrings and a pendant that belonged to her mother. As she finished dressing, she slid into her shoes just as the doorbell rang.

It'd been a long time since she'd seen a man in a tuxedo, and damn, did he look good! If she didn't think he'd put so much effort and time into planning this evening, she would have suggested they bag the whole thing and stay in.

"Get that look off your face," he warned, stepping into the entryway.

"What look?" she said innocently.

"The look that says we don't have to go anyplace to have a good time."

"Well, it sounds like a good idea to me," she said, turning her head toward the staircase.

"Forget it, Jas. We're going out tonight."

"Okay, I'll be on my best behavior," she said, pretending to pout. "Just let me get my wrap and I'll be ready to go."

Before she could turn to retrieve it, he reached out for her and pulled her close. Giving her a passionate kiss, he whispered, "You look absolutely spectacular, and for the record, I was thinking the same thing—to hell with my plans." Taking a step back, he smiled. "But since we're all dressed up, we might as well hit the road."

Jasmine stepped out onto the porch and stopped dead in her tracks. "You didn't."

"It's a big night for us—six months. We might as well do it up big."

"But a limousine?"

The driver opened the door, and they eased into the plush seats. Inside were six roses and a card. *To the woman I love. These have been the best six months of my life.*

"They're beautiful, Terrence. Thank you." She tried to keep the emotion out of her voice, but the night was already more than she ever could have expected.

"And now, this." He reached in his pocket and handed her a scarf.

"And what am I supposed to do with this?"

"Put it on."

She turned the piece of fabric around in her hands. "Put it where?"

"Over your eyes."

Jasmine waited for the punch line because she knew he couldn't be serious. But after several seconds, she understood that this was not a joke. "Are you telling me I need to be blindfolded?"

"The driver has been instructed not to move until he gets the signal from me . . . and I don't give the signal until that little piece of fabric is tied around your eyes."

"But that means I won't be able to see anything."

"I knew that master's degree of yours would come in handy. See how easily you figured that out?"

The delight in his eyes caused Jasmine to relax and go with the flow. Wrapping the scarf around her head, she suddenly felt vulnerable.

"Can you see anything?" he asked, waving his hand in front of her face. When she didn't react, he was satisfied that all she saw was darkness.

Tapping on the partition, he signaled for the driver to take off.

"This is silly, Terrence," Jasmine said as she felt them pulling away from the curb. She hated feeling out of control.

"Then humor me."

Jasmine sat back, trying to get into the spirit of her mystery night, while keeping her impatience at bay.

"We've been riding for at least thirty minutes. Are we going back into the city?"

"Be patient, sweetie," he said. "We'll get there when we arrive."

"Napa Valley!" she said suddenly. They'd been talking about taking a weekend trip for months.

"I'm not saying a word so you might as well stop trying to guess."

"How about . . ."

Terrence laughed and put his arm around her. "How about I find a way to keep you quiet?"

One second later, she felt his lips on hers and she leaned back into the plush seats as his tongue and hands did an intimate exploration that definitely kept her from saying anything else.

Twenty minutes later, the limo came to a stop and she heard the engine cut off.

When the door opened, Terrence took her hand and helped her out of the car.

"Step up," he instructed.

She did as she was told, but now that her lips were no longer occupied, she made full use of them, letting out a few complaints about the blindfold.

"Stop complaining and keep walking. I promise you, it'll be worth it."

After a few more seconds, he said, "Now step up three times."

She could tell by the change in weather that she was now inside a building, but she didn't hear anything. Would a restaurant be this quiet? Maybe it was a play or a concert. But she didn't hear anything.

After walking a few more steps, she heard the bell of an elevator. When she walked yet a few more steps, the door closed and they ascended. When the bell chimed and she heard the door open, they stepped off and walked about twenty feet. By this time, she had convinced herself that she was in a hotel. Maybe he rented a suite for the night. Coming to a stop, Terrence turned her toward him.

"Okay, Miss Impatient, you can take off the blindfold."

She ripped it off without regard for her hair or makeup, her curiosity getting the best of her. She couldn't take not knowing one second longer. She turned her head from side to side, finally making a full turn to confirm that her brain had actually registered what her eyes were seeing. Finally she rested her eyes on him. "You have got to be kidding me?"

Her response was a combination of surprise, shock, annoyance, and disbelief.

"Nope. No joke."

Looking around again, she couldn't believe that this was their grand destination for the evening. "Are you telling me that I went through a full day at the spa, a shopping spree, two hours at the hair salon, and a blindfold for you to take me to your loft?"

Without saying a word, he opened the door and stepped aside.

Not sure whether to be angry or amused, she walked in and stopped. Immediately her hands covered her mouth to prevent her from screaming in utter amazement. The tears welled up in the corner of her eyes and she could only guess what her makeup was going to look like now.

Words could not adequately describe the room she had just walked into. There had to be at least two hundred candles illuminating it with the scent of vanilla wafting through the air. Rose petals covered the floor and vases filled every possible space with more red roses. Silver and red balloons floated against the ceiling with colorful ribbons dangling from them. Soft music played in the background and she felt as if she'd stepped into the most romantic place on earth.

Following him into the living room, she saw it and this time she couldn't hold back her scream of joy. "Oh my God," she repeated several times.

"You like it?"

All the words she could possibly say at this moment lodged in her throat, and this time she didn't care what the tears did to her face. Taking a few tentative steps, she gently ran her hands across it. She turned to Terrence and tried to speak but no words would come out except "Oh my God."

"Do you want to try it out?"

Nodding slowly, she removed her wrap. She stepped

around it and took a seat on the bench of the Steinway grand piano. The minute she struck the first chord, the rich, powerful sound resonated around the room, ringing off the hardwood floors. She closed her eyes and let her fingers and the amazing sounds take over.

Her mother had enrolled her in piano lessons when she turned seven years old, sharing with Jasmine that she'd always wanted to learn but her family couldn't afford the lessons. To Jasmine's surprise, and her mother's delight, she fell in love with the instrument and looked forward to her weekly sessions with Mrs. Clandowsky, who taught her until she graduated from high school. The lessons and the used upright piano were the only luxuries her parents allowed. When it came to Jasmine and her music, the starving kids in Africa didn't seem to come into play.

Terrence watched and listened in awe as she played a classical piece he had never heard. If someone would have told him that he would not only be listening to this type of music, but actually enjoying it, he would have laughed in their face. But that was exactly what happened. She'd opened up a whole new genre to him and he enjoyed the relaxing feeling it invoked.

Playing the final note, she removed her hands from the keys just as Terrence began to applaud. "Each time I hear you play, I think it couldn't get any better. But you continue to pleasantly surprise and amaze me."

Slowly lowering the lid over the keys, she ran her fingers across the mahogany wood. Handcrafted, perfectly tuned, and expensive. That last thought caused her to push back off the bench and stand. Over the years, she'd occasionally toyed with the idea of investing in a baby grand, but each time the deep five-figure price tag deterred her. That's when it hit her, how much he loved her. A single tear fell down her cheek. "I don't know what to say, Terrence. Thank you."

He moved beside her and wrapped her in his arms. "I know how much you love to play—especially Dawn's piano. You once told me that you don't play on a schedule anymore—that you play when the mood strikes you. I just wanted to make sure that when you were here, if you ever got the urge to make some more of your beautiful music, you could."

All she could do was hug and kiss him.

"Besides," he continued, "I want to practice some of the songs you've been teaching me."

"Excuse me, sir, are you ready for dinner to be served?"

The voice startled her and Jasmine turned. Dressed in butler wear, the older gentleman entered the area and picked up her jacket. "I'll be glad to hang this for you, ma'am."

"Thank you," she said, trying to decipher what was going to happen next.

Introducing himself as Monte, he escorted them to the dining area, where he pulled back her chair and waited for her to take a seat.

"I hope you like what I've done with the place," Terrence said.

His light humor caused a smile. "It's beautiful, Terrence." The table was set in bone china and decorated with tiny red confetti in the shape of a heart.

The butler returned with a bottle of Cristal and offered it to Terrence. When he nodded his approval, Monte popped the cork and filled the crystal flutes.

Monte quietly disappeared as Terrence raised his glass. "I'd like to propose a toast."

Jasmine raised her glass.

"To the woman who showed me what true love is

really about. You've taken over my heart, my soul, and my spirit. You've become an intricate part of me and I can't imagine living my life without you."

Jasmine swallowed deliberately, refusing to shed one more tear. "And to the man of my life. I'm so glad you challenged my theory. You are everything I could ever want or need."

They clinked glasses and took a sip just as Monte returned with the first course.

Over an hour later, Jasmine set her fork aside and begged for mercy. Shrimp cocktail, lobster bisque, and Caesar salad were the first three courses. By the time the roasted duck, sweet potatoes, and green beans arrived, she didn't think she'd be able to eat another bite. But when the duck melted in her mouth, she couldn't let it go to waste.

Monte removed their plates, promising to return with coffee and dessert.

Jasmine watched his retreat to the kitchen and shook her head. "He can bring out whatever he wants, but I am finished. I am absolutely sure that I can't eat another bite."

"Oh, don't say that," Terrence said. "We haven't had dessert yet."

Patting her stomach, she thought the buttons on her pants would pop off if she ate one more morsel of food. "None for me."

"Oh, I don't think you want to pass on the dessert that I have planned for tonight." Terrence signaled to Monte to bring on the final course.

"I'm serious, Terrence, if I don't stop now, I might not be able to fit these clothes tomorrow."

Monte set two coffee cups down, filling them both. As soon as the aroma rose from her cup, she smelled it.

Hazelnut. Her favorite. Unable to refuse, she took a sip and savored the rich flavor.

When Monte returned again, he placed a full raspberry cheesecake in front of them, setting down a knife, two forks, and small dessert plates. "I'll be in the kitchen if you need anything."

"You really know how to torture a girl," Jasmine moaned, refusing to look at it, knowing full well she'd want a piece. "You know this is my favorite, but really, I just can't eat it."

She reached for the cake to push it away when she noticed the writing. Initially, she thought it was just raspberry icing, but she could see now that there were words on it. Blinking twice, she wanted to make sure her eyes weren't playing a trick on her. Reading the words again, she looked up at Terrence, her eyes widened in anticipation.

He reached into his pocket and pulled out the black velvet box. "I know the cake says it, but I want to say the words, too."

Standing, he walked around to her before getting down on his knee. "The limo, the flowers, the music, even the piano are but a small representation of how special you are to me. Jasmine Monique Larson, will you marry me?"

By this time, the tears were flowing freely and Jasmine did nothing to stop them. As she nodded, her answer came out in a raspy whisper. "Yes."

Opening the box, he presented her with a two-and-a-half-carat princess-cut diamond set in a platinum band.

She didn't realize how badly her hands were shaking until she held them out to him. Slipping the ring on her finger, she stood and he stood with her. "I love you, Terrence."

"I love you too, baby."

Sealing the deal with a kiss, Terrence took a step back and pulled out his cell phone.

"Now what are you doing?" Jasmine said. How many more surprises could he have in one night? Whom could he be calling?

After dialing the seven digits, he waited a few seconds until someone answered. "She said yes!"

"Terrence, who are you talking to?"

Ending the call, he motioned to Monte, who went to the door. When he opened it, a slew of people came swarming in.

"What's going on, Terrence?" Jasmine asked, as at least twenty people entered the loft.

Grabbing her hand, he kissed her on the cheek and whispered in her ear, "It's our engagement party."

Jasmine took a look at the people who were filing in. Eric, Dawn, Monica, Marjorie, and several people from Terrence's firm. Before she could fully comprehend what was happening, Monica and Dawn swooped her away from Terrence.

"Congratulations, girl," Monica said, giving her a big hug. "I'm so happy for you. No one deserves a man like that more than you."

"I told you he was the man for you. Another perfect match, compliments of me."

Giving Dawn a hug, Jasmine playfully punched her in the arm. "You knew about this, didn't you?"

"Well . . ." she said, trying to sound innocent.

"We spent practically the whole day together," Jasmine said, thinking of their shopping spree and time at the spa. "You never said one word. I've never known you to keep a secret—especially one as juicy as this."

"Are you kidding?" Dawn said, with a hint of fear in

her voice. "Terrence would have skinned me alive if I had ruined his special night. He's been planning this night for a while. He ordered the piano weeks ago."

"And what if I had said no?" Jasmine teased. "All of you would have been standing outside his door for nothing."

"Oh, girl, don't even say that!" Monica said, grabbing her heart. "We all would have gone into a full-fledged panic mode, not to mention that you would have broken that poor man's heart."

The rest of the evening flew by in a blur to Jasmine. Accepting well-wishes and congratulations from a slew of guests, she felt the night couldn't have been any more perfect.

At almost midnight when they said good night to the last guest, Jasmine felt as if she were floating on a cloud. "This evening was absolutely perfect."

Hugging her close, he kissed her neck, her ears, and finally her lips. "I'm glad you enjoyed yourself . . . and that you said yes."

Resting her head against his chest, she relished the comfort she felt whenever she was in his arms. "Did you have any doubt?"

He responded by continuing his assault of kisses down her shoulder. In one quick motion, he swooped her up in his arms and carried her up the short flight of stairs and into his bedroom. He gently laid her across the bed and lit the candles he'd strategically placed before the evening began. When he joined her on the bed, he had already shed his jacket, shirt, and shoes.

Turning her onto her stomach, he began to rub her neck and shoulders before unzipping her top. As he worked his magic fingers down her back, Jasmine moaned in exquisite pleasure. When the massage was complete, she returned the favor, leaving no part of his body untouched.

When neither could take the anticipation any longer, he protected them and lay on top of her but didn't enter. "I love you so much, Jasmine. I didn't realize how much I needed and wanted someone in my life."

"This night was perfect. Thank you for the flowers, the piano, and the ring. But more importantly, thank you for your love. It is the best gift of all."

They made love that night with a tenderness and sweetness that mirrored the feelings they had for each other. When she finally drifted off to sleep, she felt safe, protected, happy, and content.

Eleven

Terrence hummed an upbeat tune as he settled into work on Monday morning. He and Jasmine had spent the remainder of the weekend in bed, making plans for the rest of their lives. Promising Jasmine that she could have any type of wedding she wanted, he was surprised, and pleased, when she asked for a small ceremony—in New York.

He'd called his parents on Sunday morning and told them the news. To say they were ecstatic would be an understatement. He'd shared bits and pieces of his courtship with Jasmine over the months, but his mother told him that it wasn't how much he told her that she knew Jasmine meant the world to him, it was the joy she heard in his voice that gave it away.

Yvonne yelled in pure excitement when he told her the news. He'd begun to open up to Yvonne over the past couple of months about his growing feelings for Jasmine, and she encouraged and supported him. She'd even given him advice on the piano and the ring. Knowing how Jasmine felt about material possessions, he wasn't sure she would accept such an extravagant gift or such an expensive ring. But Yvonne convinced him that when she looked at both, she wouldn't see money, she would see his love for her, and that would make all the difference in the world. And he had to give credit where credit was due, his baby sister was absolutely right.

"Mr. McKinley?"

"Yes, Stacy," Terrence said, putting aside his day-dreaming.

"Richard Montague is here to see you."

"Great. Send him in." Terrence stood and buttoned his suit jacket.

With so much activity going on this weekend, he'd almost forgotten about Richard Montague's strange phone call last week. Hopefully, whatever he needed to discuss wasn't as bad as he made it sound over the phone.

When the door opened, Terrence shook hands with Richard, motioning for him to take a seat. Declining Terrence's offer of coffee or juice, he obviously had a lot on his mind. His normally good-natured personality was noticeably absent this morning. Terrence wondered what could have caused a usually self-assured business-man to look as if his world was falling apart.

Richard, by anyone's standards, was a hardworking, self-made millionaire. He had begun his career working at a small auto parts manufacturing plant in Detroit when he was fifteen. His initial job consisted of cleaning the floors and bathrooms. But he never lost sight of his ultimate goal—to own his own business.

When the owner of the manufacturing plant retired, Richard, at thirty, called in every favor he could and mortgaged everything he had. To this day he wondered how he was able to get credit from three different banks. But his gamble paid off. When he took over, the company provided parts to a handful of carmakers and repair shops in his immediate area. Now, more than three decades later, he was the number-one supplier of auto parts in the world. Moving his corporate offices to New York fifteen years ago, Richard enjoyed all the lavish perks that came with his status and wealth.

Terrence had joined him on his yacht in Florida, his private island in the Caribbean, and had been invited to many of the soirees he held at his home in New York and in the Hamptons. Famous for his lavish parties and exotic vacations, Richard didn't have a problem showing off the wealth that he worked so hard to achieve.

But now, the man who normally exuded power and authority looked worried and concerned.

"I need your help."

That phrase wasn't new to Terrence. He'd heard that from clients all the time. So that didn't bother him. What did concern him was the feeling he had in the pit of his stomach that told him that this request for help would be like no other he'd been asked before. "What can I do for you?"

Richard removed a handkerchief from his pocket to wipe his face, a nervous gesture not often seen with successful businessmen. They could bluff their way through anything. The sixty-something-year-old had spent enough time with Terrence for him to know when things were not going well. And today was one of those days. His thinning white hair, typically worn combed straight back, had several strands falling loosely to the side.

The clear blue eyes, normally bright with enthusiasm, somehow appeared dimmer. His appearance revealed not only the seriousness of Richard Montague's request, but that it also must be extremely personal. Richard Montague had never encountered a business problem that caused him to be this upset as long as Terrence could remember. Pulling out a notepad and pen, he prepared to take notes.

Placing the handkerchief back in his pocket, Richard replaced his glasses. "I'm not sure if you're aware, but I have a lovely three-year-old granddaughter."

Taken aback by the subject, Terrence set his pen aside. They rarely talked about their personal lives, so his statement made no sense to Terrence. Maybe talking about his family would help ease him into talking about the real issue. That was fine with Terrence. After Richard's phone call on Friday, he had shifted some appointments around to give him extra time in case he needed to take immediate action. He had the time to listen.

He'd recalled a few years ago Richard mentioning that his daughter was pregnant out of wedlock, but he hadn't heard anything since. "I remember you mentioning something a while back."

Reaching in his coat pocket, he pulled out a wallet-sized picture and leaned across the desk to hand it to Terrence.

"She's pretty," Terrence said, staring at the blond-haired, green-eyed child, placing the photo on the desk. "I'm sure you must be very proud."

Nodding in agreement, Richard unbuttoned his suit jacket and leaned back in his chair before continuing. "Her name is Hayley, born on New Year's Eve. She's smart, funny, and loves horses. I just bought a colt for her this past summer. He'll be there when she's old enough to ride."

Terrence listened intently, but didn't say anything. Nothing so far had sounded to him like a pressing legal matter, but he figured Richard would get around to it shortly. After all, Richard didn't stay on the West Coast for the weekend just to talk about his granddaughter and her horse.

Richard tried to continue, but when he opened his mouth nothing came out. Embarrassed, he briefly looked away, averting his eyes before turning his attention back to Terrence. "My daughter, Chelsea, Hayley's mother, has had a few challenges in her life."

Terrence nodded, mainly because he had no idea what else he was supposed to do. This conversation had him at a total loss. Was this going somewhere?

"Two years ago, my wife and I found out she had a ... um ... a ..." Richard struggled to get the words out. "Chelsea had a drug problem."

Terrence sat back in his chair. He finally understood what Richard wanted and why it had him so worked up. It was a personal matter. Terrence needed help for his daughter with a drug arrest. Not a criminal lawyer, he'd guessed that Richard was here to ask for a referral. "I know someone who can ..."

"We put her in rehab," Richard continued, oblivious to the fact that Terrence had tried to respond to what he anticipated was the next request. "Margaret and I kept Hayley while she completed her stay at a center upstate. When she came back home, everything appeared to be going well. She'd decided to go back to school and had enrolled in several business classes at a community college. Excited about getting her life back on track and making something of herself, I offered her a job at our corporate headquarters. She flat-out refused, determined to make it on her own. She even moved into her own apartment."

Terrence watched Richard walk over to the small bar

in the corner of the office and pour himself a cup of coffee. Stalling for time more than satisfying his thirst, Terrence sat quietly, waiting for the rest of the story.

"When Margaret died last year, things in Chelsea's life just seemed to fall apart. She began to miss days at school and sometimes would be late picking up Hayley from day care, or worse, not picking her up at all. On several occasions, I had to arrange to have Hayley taken to my house and I'd wait hours for Chelsea to show up."

As Richard wiped the sweat from his brow, Terrence could tell that sharing this information wasn't easy for him.

"Three months ago, Chelsea left Hayley alone in her apartment for almost twenty-four hours. The police broke down her front door after a neighbor called to report the crying she'd heard. They found the little girl sitting on the kitchen floor, half dressed and food scattered about. Because the police were called, social services got involved and took temporary custody of Hayley."

Terrence finally got the message. It wasn't a criminal lawyer he needed—it was a family law attorney.

"The hearing is supposed to be in three weeks and Chelsea is devastated. Even though she had began using again, the thought of permanently losing her daughter scared her senseless. She became more determined than ever to get her life back together. She checked back into rehab and was just released a month ago. This time she had a reason to succeed—keeping her daughter."

Walking back to the chair in front of Terrence's desk, he sat back down with a look of relief on his face. He had gotten through the toughest part of the story.

His next words were spoken with strong conviction. "I see the old Chelsea again, my baby girl before the drugs and the destruction. She finally agreed to take a job at our corporate headquarters as an administrative assistant and has shown up with a good attitude and ready to work—something I hadn't seen from her since before Margaret died."

At the thought of his late wife, Richard's eyes softened and he fought hard to keep any tears from falling. "Margaret had always been able to handle Chelsea, reach out to her when she was having problems. But I never had that relationship with her, and I wonder now if that was a mistake on my part."

Realizing he was starting to ramble, Richard cleared his throat. Rising, he buttoned his jacket and resumed the demeanor of the confident businessman Terrence usually dealt with. "I'd like you to represent Chelsea and help her get her daughter—my grandchild—back where she belongs—with us."

Terrence leaned back in his chair, contemplating Richard's request. "I understand the importance of Chelsea's upcoming court appearance, and I sympathize with your situation, but I have to tell you, I don't think I'm the best person for the job. We don't have a family law practice, but I can call—"

Richard watched him reach for his Rolodex and leaned forward, placing both hands on the desk. "I don't want a family law attorney. I want you."

"But—" Terrence started, hoping to explain to him that the only family law he'd practiced was during law school when he'd volunteered at Legal Aid.

"So far, we've managed to keep this situation low-key. While it's not directly related to my business, I don't think my stockholders would appreciate a story on the eleven o'clock news about the problems my family is having."

Terrence tried to think of the best way to get his point

across. This type of request was nothing new. Lawyers saw it all the time. Clients wanting them to help in an area that was outside their expertise. But Terrence preferred to direct his clients to someone who had the experience they needed. "I'm sure another attorney would be just as discreet. Let me—"

Richard didn't let him complete his sentence. "Last year, I paid you over one million dollars in legal fees, and even followed you when you changed firms. All I'm asking is that you do whatever is necessary to help resolve this issue in my favor."

Terrence stood, deciphering the hidden message in that last statement. The conclusion he came to didn't sit well with him at all. "Are you saying that you'll drop me as your corporate lawyer if I don't take on this case?"

"I'm saying I want my granddaughter back with her mother."

Both men stared at each other, neither needing to speak. The ultimatum had been put on the table and there was no room for negotiation. However, Terrence wanted Richard to spell out exactly what he was saying.

"If I don't agree to represent your daughter, you'll take your business elsewhere?"

Richard shrugged. "It's always good business practice to periodically reevaluate my legal ties."

The room went silent for several minutes. Finally, Terrence sat. "I'll review the file and let you know."

Reaching in his briefcase, Richard pulled out an accordion file. "All the information is right here."

Before he took the file, Terrence wanted to make his position perfectly clear. "This isn't a yes. It's a commitment to review the information."

Pointing to the front of the file, Richard said, "This is

the name and address of the foster family Hayley is staying with. I'm sure they haven't led perfect lives either."

"And what do you expect me to do with that information?"

"I'm not telling you what to do with it. I'm just letting you know I want this hearing to result in a favorable ruling for my family."

Terrence walked across the room and opened the door. "I'll call you."

Stopping just as he was about to walk through the door, Richard held out his hand, and after only a slight hesitation, Terrence shook it.

Terrence wanted to slam the door, but instead closed it quietly and uttered a slew of expletives. Getting involved in this situation didn't feel right. But neither did telling the partners he'd just lost a million dollars in revenue.

Glancing down at the file, he decided that the least he would do was what he'd agreed to do. Review the file and see if it contained information that would satisfy his conscience enough to take on this case.

Three hours later, Terrence buzzed Stacy. He'd read the file twice and had spent the past two hours contemplating his decision. "Can you get Mr. Montague on the line?"

Closing the file, he placed the documents to the side. While waiting for the call to come through, he weighed his options one last time.

"Terrence, Mr. Montague is on line three."

"Thanks, Stacy."

The conversation was brief and to the point. Terrence would represent his daughter and Richard would keep his company's legal business with Davidson & Warner.

* * *

"You did what!" Jasmine exclaimed, staring at him in complete shock.

Terrence and Jasmine had just ordered dinner when he relayed the story of his earlier meeting with Richard. This was the not the reaction he had expected. He actually thought she might offer some insight into the proceedings. The hearing was in New York, but the process was generally the same.

Jasmine sat stoically, silently fuming at Terrence's revelation. In the time that they had been together, how could he think she would react any other way after hearing something like this?

Driving to Richmond and taking her to dinner to discuss wedding details had been Terrence's original plan for the evening, but wedding plans had quickly become the last thing Jasmine wanted to discuss. "So you sold out."

Now it was Terrence's turn to go into shock. "What is that supposed to mean?"

"What part of that phrase don't you understand?"

Terrence reeled in some of his growing anger. "I take on a case for a client and you call me a sellout?"

"Correction, Terrence. You've take on a case from a *million-dollar* client. What would you call it?"

Realizing they were drawing attention from other customers, Terrence leaned forward and lowered his voice. "I call it providing legal service."

"Fine," Jasmine said. "Would you be providing this 'legal service' if he weren't a client, or if his billables only equaled a couple thousand dollars a year?"

That question hit Terrence in his gut. The thought crossed his mind, but hearing it out loud made it sound unethical. Yet he refused to believe it was as simple as she was making it out to be. "That isn't the point, Jasmine."

Placing her napkin on the table, she pushed her chair back. "And that statement doesn't answer my question."

"What is your problem?" he said, wondering how this could make her so angry. "Why does this bother you so much?"

Jasmine shook her head in amazement. Could the man she planned to marry actually sit across from her and ask her that question? Shouldn't he know the answer? "I'm ready to go home."

Terrence took a deep breath, feeling their discussion spiraling out of control. "I think we need to both calm down and talk about this rationally."

Waving for the waiter, she pulled out her wallet. "I don't."

The waiter stood at the table glancing from one to the other. "Did you need something?"

"Yes," Jasmine said without looking at Terrence. "We won't be having dinner after all. If it's too late to cancel the order, just bring me the bill."

Terrence couldn't believe the turn of events the night had taken. Reaching in his pocket, he pulled out his wallet and waited for the waiter to return. "I'll take care of the bill."

"That's not necessary," she spat out. "I'm more than capable of paying for my own food."

"Come on, Jas. You're being childish."

The waiter returned and before she could hand over the money, Terrence gave him his Black American Express card. The gesture and his comment infuriated her more.

"That's the answer to everything for you, isn't it?" she said, indicating his exclusive credit status.

Now Terrence had really lost the direction of this conversation.

"Money," she said, seeing the dumbfounded look on his face. She put her wallet back in her purse and pulled her jacket off the back of the chair. "You and your clients think it can solve everything."

Standing, she zipped up her jacket and put her purse on her shoulder. "No need to take me home, I'll grab a cab."

"The hell you will," he said, but his words fell on deaf ears. She was already halfway to the exit.

Hot on her heels, Terrence caught up with her just as she stepped outside.

"You left your credit card," she pointed out without turning around.

He reached out for her, but she still didn't look at him.

"You're just going to walk out?" he asked incredulously. "Just like that . . . you're leaving?"

The statement stopped Jasmine and she turned to face him. "What is that supposed to mean?"

"It means that we're engaged to be married," he said, taking a step toward her, only to watch her take a step back. "We have a disagreement and you just walk away. Is this how we're going to handle challenges in our relationship?"

Listening to him, Jasmine admitted to herself that he had a point. There was only one way to solve the problem. "I don't know if I can have a relationship with someone like you."

Terrence felt the stake pierce through his heart at her words. How could they go from being engaged to possibly not having a relationship at all in a matter of an hour? Then it hit him. *Someone like you.* Those words mirrored what she had said when she first met him. That she didn't date *someone like you.*

"Are we back to your dating theory? After all this time?"

"I guess so," she said slowly, as the reality of the situation started to sink in.

"So that's it. You don't even want to talk about it?" he asked, unable to fathom the thought that she was prepared to walk out of his life.

"Are you taking this case?" she asked, refusing to let any tears fall, even though they hovered in the corners of her eyes.

"I've already said yes," he answered.

"Then the answer to your question is no. I don't want to talk about it."

Walking to the valet, she asked the attendant if he could get her a cab.

Terrence followed and handed his ticket to the valet. "You may not want to speak to me, but you will not take a cab home."

The young teenager glanced from one to the other, not sure what to do. Get the car or call a cab.

"Fine," she said.

The young man nodded in understanding and ran to get the car.

Terrence had never experienced the silent treatment with anyone like he was experiencing at this moment. Since she said, "Fine," she had yet to say another word. And he was too worked up to try to get her to talk to him. What was her problem anyway? Why was this so hard for her to understand?

He pulled up to her house and before he could turn the car off, she'd already opened the door. Heading up the walkway, she didn't look back as she opened the door and shut it behind her.

Debating his next move, he got out of the car and knocked on the door. When she didn't respond, he knocked again. He pulled out his cell phone and dialed her number. Voice mail. Not sure what to do, he stood on the small porch for several seconds before knocking again. Finally, when she still didn't answer, he got back in his car and drove home, confused, frustrated, and alone.

Pulling back the curtains, Jasmine watched him drive off as a slow tear made its way down her cheek. How could something that she thought was so right not work? Holding out her hand, she stared at her ring and thought back to a few short nights ago when he got down on one knee and declared his love. When she said yes, it was not only because they loved each other. It was because of their shared values and principles. But she'd been wrong. They didn't share those things after all.

How could he have even considered taking on such a case? Didn't he have any idea how this would affect their relationship? Either he didn't know her or he didn't care. Whichever one it was—it meant the end of their relationship. As painful as it would be, she might have to do the one thing she never thought she would. Live without him.

Twelve

Jasmine sat in her office the next morning around nine-thirty putting drops of Visine in her eyes. It had been six hours since she'd last cried, but the remnants still remained. Hoping to get through the day without someone asking about her puffy, red eyes, she bought an extra bottle of Visine and decided to work with her door shut.

He'd called at least five times last night and twice this morning before she left for work. Not wanting to deal with him, she'd let the calls go straight to her voice mail.

Sitting back, she surveyed her desk. Files were everywhere. Each one represented a family that needed her help. So many cases, so few social workers. The increasing stack of files served as a constant reminder that the profession was in desperate need of help. For the caseload they had, the agency needed twice as many social workers. And in the end, the only ones to truly suffer were the children and families who needed to look to them for assistance and guidance. How could they get all they need when a social worker's time was so limited?

Jasmine had attended enough seminars, symposiums, and task force meetings to know the startling statistics. Abused and neglected children often had poor language skills and other developmental problems. They were at an increased risk for alcoholism, drug abuse, depression, and suicide. The reports of child abuse were in the multi-millions each year in this country, yet there just weren't enough resources to give each one the time and energy they deserved.

But through all the statistics and hopelessness that had been a part of her profession, she always maintained the hope and belief that she could make a difference. However, today, as she glanced at the many cases, for the first time in her career she was overwhelmed and tired. How could she possible help them all?

"Jasmine?"

Sitting up, she pulled herself together and tried to get her emotions under control. "Come in, Monica."

Monica stepped inside and shut the door; the pink message paper in her hand shook slightly.

Jasmine instinctively stood. The news couldn't have been good. "What happened, Monica?"

"It's Candice Worley," she said, barely above a whisper.

Jasmine didn't need a refresher to place the name. It was the first case she'd had where the judge ruled against Monica's recommendation. The judge sent Candice back to her mother, convinced that her drug addiction and unsteady employment had been addressed.

"We just got a call from the hospital."

Jasmine grabbed her purse. "I'll go with you."

* * *

The emergency room was filled with people of all ages. A child crying in his mother's arms, an older man holding a bloody cloth over his hand, and a very pregnant woman trying to complete her admittance paperwork. But all of that faded in the background as Monica and Jasmine checked in with the information desk before being escorted through the automatic double doors.

No matter how many times Jasmine made this walk, the apprehension and fear always showed up. Today was no different.

After they identified themselves to the doctor, he led them to a small room, motioning for them to sit. Jasmine remained standing.

"The child was brought in around six this morning. It appears that the mother brought her in, but left her in the waiting room. She had a broken arm and a slight concussion. She's going to be fine, but under the circumstances, we called social services."

Glancing at his notes, he turned his attention to Monica. "You're the caseworker that's been handling this case?"

"Yes," Monica said, trying desperately to maintain a professional demeanor, when actually she was mad as hell and wanted to scream and yell at someone—anyone.

"I understand she'd been returned to her mother about six months ago," Dr. Collins said.

Monica's back stiffened and she prepared for battle. She'd done everything she could to convince the judge not to return Candice to her mother. Even though she had been clean for a month, she was still only working a temporary job and had no transportation.

Monica had met with the mother several times, encouraging her to participate in parenting classes and some of the free computer classes that were available to her. That way, Monica could offer her assistance in finding her a job. If she did that, and stayed clean, Monica would recommend that Candice be returned.

But the mother insisted that she was ready to have her child back now, and the judge agreed. Monica refused to let this doctor make her feel guilty. "The judge made the decision to return Candice to her mother."

The doctor understood her tone, and quickly amended his comment. "I know you guys have it tough. All I'm saying is that if you need anything from me to keep the child safe, I'll be glad to provide whatever information is necessary."

Monica relaxed. "Thanks, I appreciate that."

The doctor stood and headed for the door. "Candice is probably a little groggy from the pain medication, but you can see her if you like."

"Yes," Monica said, "I'd like that."

"She'll be discharged in another day. Will you have found a family by then?"

"We'll have a home to place her in," Monica said, still fighting the tears.

Both women followed the doctor, saying a silent prayer for little Candice and her mother.

When Jasmine returned to the office and checked her voice mail, there were three messages from Terrence. After the morning she'd endured with Monica, she definitely wasn't in the mood to talk to him. But there was one phone call she did want to return.

"Dawn Westfield."

Dawn put down the file she was reading when she heard her friend's voice. "Are you okay?"

"I take it by your question you've talked to Terrence."

"Three times."

"I see."

"Each time he calls, I can hear the increased desperation in his voice," Dawn said, hoping to influence Jasmine enough for her to talk to him.

"Are you trying to make me feel sorry for him?" she asked, attempting to put on a brave front, when in reality she was falling apart.

"You don't have to feel sorry for him, but you should be feeling something. He said you cut him off just like that." Dawn snapped her finger to emphasize her point. "No explanation. No talking. Nothing."

"Look, Dawn, if you're calling me to plead his case, don't waste your breath." After the morning she'd had with Candice and Monica, she didn't think she was up to talking with Terrence even if she wanted to. Plus, she was annoyed with Dawn. "I can't believe you would take his side on this anyway."

"I'm not taking anybody's side, and I'm definitely not calling to plead his case," Dawn said. "To be honest, he didn't even tell me what the problem was. All he wants is a chance to talk to you. And I can't blame him for that."

Jasmine listened but wasn't sure she could agree. For the past six months, she and Terrence had shared everything with each other. Their past, their present, and even their dreams and aspirations for the future. How could he not know why she had a problem with him accepting this case?

When she didn't get any response, Dawn said, "You should at least see him face-to-face to return the ring."

Raising her left hand, Jasmine watched the diamond sparkle in the light. The right thing to do would be to give it back. And that's when it hit her. She was ending her relationship with Terrence. No more late night phone conversations. No more romantic dinners out. They would never take that trip to Napa Valley. She wouldn't be joining him on the trip to New York to meet his family over Thanksgiving. And suddenly, the impact of her abrupt decision weighed heavily on her heart. If he didn't understand why she was doing what she was doing, she at least owed him an explanation. Only then could she end it with a clean conscience.

"Okay, Dawn. I'll call him."

"You don't have to, he's right here," Dawn said quickly.

Before she could voice any objections, he came on the line.

"Jasmine?"

Just hearing his voice caused emotions to stir inside her. Images of their time together flashed through her mind. Flashbacks of the two of them eating pretzels at Fisherman's Wharf. The first time they kissed. The first time they made love, and the proposal and engagement party. Just hearing his voice almost made her forget whatever problems they were having. But all those wonderful memories didn't change their current situation.

"Hi, Terrence." Her voice was barely audible as she attempted to keep the emotions out of her tone. Feeling the lump in her throat grow, she realized she was not succeeding.

"Can we talk tonight?" he said, taking the fact that he finally got her on the phone as a positive sign. "I'll come to Richmond."

After the emotional day she'd had, she wasn't sure if she was up for talking to him so soon. Not to mention that her heart had a hard time agreeing with the decision she'd made in her head. Leaving him had been the hardest thing she'd ever had to do. Would she be able to uphold her choice if he walked into her house and she saw him, smelled him, held him? Could she handle it? But she realized that she couldn't avoid him forever. They had to see each other at least one last time—and it would be difficult no matter when it happened. "No. I'll come to you. I'll be there around seven."

Terrence started to object. He didn't mind being the one to make the drive. However, he knew if he said anything, it would just start another argument, so he reluctantly agreed. "I'll be waiting."

Terrence paused before continuing, not knowing how his next words would be received. "I love you, Jasmine."

"I love you too, Terrence." The words flowed out of her mouth with ease, because they were true. Regardless of their differences, she had never stopped loving him. But loving him and spending the rest of her life with him were two separate issues.

Jasmine got off the phone and laid her head on her desk. When had everything in her world become so overwhelming? Her job. Her personal life.

When she had started her career, she always prided herself on her ability to distance herself from the other social workers that thought there was never enough time to handle all the cases that came their way. They spent their time bashing the system, the resources, and the funding from the state and federal government. But Jasmine preferred to focus her energy on doing what she could with what she had.

She sometimes worked seven days a week to ensure that, to the best of her ability, every file that came across her desk got her attention. Of course, there were visits that weren't made as often as she would have liked. And it could take weeks to follow up on attendance at parenting classes, but she never felt like she was fighting a losing battle. Until now.

The only question she couldn't answer was, why now? Everything had been fine last week. But ever since she had had dinner with Terrence and he had talked about his latest case for Richard Montague, she couldn't shake the feeling that she was increasingly unsure about her ability to do her job.

If any of her staff were coming to her with the same question, she'd probably tell them that somewhere, deep inside, they'd had these feelings all along, and had kept them at bay by the sheer will to prove the naysayer wrong. The key was to hold on to that determination. But Terrence's case had exposed her to issues she preferred not to have to deal with. Would Richard Montague try to use his money and power to get a desirable ruling for his family? Could he have the resources to influence how this case would be decided? Would Terrence willingly participate if he did? Those questions stirred in her mind, but she wasn't able to come up with any answers.

Terrence hung his suit in the closet and got a pair of jeans and a T-shirt to put on. He'd gotten little done at work today and decided to call it quits around two o'clock. Rehashing their fight over dinner in his mind didn't help him understand what had made her so upset that she would consider ending their relationship. She knew nothing about the Montagues, yet she had decided that this case held so much importance that she would call off their wedding.

When she didn't return his calls, that's when he went to see Dawn. Her complete surprise showed in her face when he asked her to try to get Jasmine to talk to him, making it obvious that Jasmine hadn't told her they'd had an argument. Never one to share details of his personal relationships with outsiders, he only explained that they'd disagreed on an issue and that Jasmine wouldn't see or talk to him. Dawn—always the advocate for love—called Jasmine for him. Not wanting to take a chance on missing his opportunity to talk to his fiancée, he waited in Dawn's office until she returned the call.

Relief raced through his body when she agreed to see him, and he couldn't contain his happiness the moment she declared her love for him. It didn't repair whatever damage had been done to their relationship, but at least she acknowledged that her feelings about him hadn't changed.

Once he buzzed her in, he stood in the open doorway waiting for her to get off the elevator. She stepped into the hall and started toward him and it was only by sheer willpower that he didn't run to her and swoop her up in his arms. Dressed down in sweatpants and a sweatshirt, she looked as if her day had been just as rough as his. They'd just seen each other last night, but it seemed as if it had been years.

She entered the loft and he reached for her hand. Not sure if his kiss would be rejected, he held back and walked her into the living room.

Jasmine saw the piano and all the memories of that special night came gushing back. She inhaled deeply, but quietly, hoping to squelch the tears that threatened to make an appearance at any given moment.

"I'm glad you agreed to talk this out," he said, once

they settled on the sofa. "I've tried to figure out exactly what the problem is, but, Jasmine, baby, I really have no idea."

Jasmine couldn't believe what she was hearing. The fact that he could make that statement just proved that he really didn't know her at all. "After all I've shared with you about my career and philosophies, you can honestly sit here and tell me you have no idea why I reacted the way I did."

Taking a deep breath, Terrence tried to take it all in. He thought he knew her better than he knew himself, and he figured that her problem revolved around the fact that his client was considerably wealthy. But would that annoy her enough to make her throw away everything they'd built together? "You said that you thought I let money influence my decision to handle Richard's case—"

"And you're going to deny that?" Jasmine said, cutting him off in midsentence.

"I'm not going to deny that the fact that he's a big client didn't influence me," he admitted. "But it only influenced me to *look* at the case, not *take* it. I only agreed to represent his family after I reviewed the file."

Sitting forward, Jasmine stared him directly in the eyes. "Tell me, Terrence, what could you have possibly read in that file that would have made you turn the case down?"

Confused, Terrence didn't answer right away. The information he reviewed had a summary of what had happened the day the court took Hayley away, Chelsea's record of her drug rehabilitation, and notes from the social worker scheduling times to meet with and interview all the parties involved. "It was general information about the situation."

"Information that really didn't play a role in whether you were going to say yes to Richard."

"How can you say that?" Terrence asked, feeling like they were talking in circles. "I told you I didn't agree to take it until I had a chance to see exactly what was going on."

"Whether you want to admit it or not, your mind was made up before you took one look at that file."

He started to object, but she held her hand up to stop him.

"You weren't going to find anything in that file that would prevent you from taking the case, because you weren't looking for it. There was no way you were going to turn this down. That file could have said anything and it wouldn't have made one bit of difference in your decision. There was no way you were going to turn down a million-dollar client. The stakes were just too high."

Terrence exhaled and rested his head in his hands. For several minutes, neither said a word. He then realized he was fighting a losing battle. "That's such an unfair statement, Jasmine."

"Unfair is different from untrue," she pointed out.

Raising his head, he rephrased his words. "Then it's an untrue statement."

With her hands folded across her chest, she shrugged. "I don't believe you."

At that moment, his patience ran out and he snapped, "Do you ever get down off you soapbox?"

"What is that supposed to mean?" she said, raising her voice slightly.

He stood abruptly and began to pace. "You give these speeches—no, sermons—about how people *like me* only exist to serve the almighty dollar, making one business deal after another, with little regard for what's morally right. Yet people who, in your mind, serve the community, *like you,* are the only ones on God's green earth who have any moral backbone. People *like you* are the only ones who help those in need, put others before themselves, and give back to those less fortunate. Well, here's a news flash for you, Jasmine. Your thinking is wrong!" he said.

"Money and power do not automatically make people unwilling to do the right thing," he continued. "It does not always lead to manipulation and corruption. As a matter of fact, think about this. Those soup kitchens you work in a couple of times a year? How do you think they bought the soup? Those special day camps you try so hard to get your kids in every summer? How do you think the transportation, activities, and cabins are paid for? Those computer classes that teach the parents you work with the skills that will land them jobs in the workforce? How do you think the equipment manages to stay up to date? I'll tell you how. *Money.* From people *like me.*

"So do all us rich people a favor, baby, and get off your high horse. As a matter of fact, you should start saying thank you to people *like me.* 'Cause without people *like me,* people *like you* wouldn't have any soup to serve, camps to go to, or computers to use."

Terrence finished his speech and stopped pacing. His heart, racing at breakneck speed, felt as if it would burst right through his chest, and he wondered how long he'd been harboring these feelings but had not shared them. During their courtship, Jasmine would make little comments here and there, and he would push them aside. They'd be watching a news story about a CEO who flew his associates to a resort in the Caribbean and she would comment on the waste of money. Leaving the movie theater, she would mention how celebrities don't always do enough for the needy. He hadn't realized until this moment that her judgmental attitude had bothered him this much.

"Are you finished?" she said quietly.

Terrence sat back down, physically exhausted. "Yeah."

"Let me ask you something," she said, maintaining a calm demeanor. "You agreed to represent Ms. Chelsea Montague. Have you met her?"

"Of course not."

"Have you talked with her on the phone?"

"No, but—"

"Have you contacted the social worker on the case to get her perspective on the situation?"

Terrence heard the growing agitation in her voice with each question and each of his answers. "Not yet."

"Have you arranged to speak to the child to see for yourself if she was afraid of her mother, missed her mother, or never wanted to see her mother again?"

It was clear why Jasmine was asking these questions, but he gave the simple answer. "No."

She leaned forward, her eyes direct and hard. "Yet you could determine by reading a few notes in a file that this child would be safer and happier with her mother."

Terrence had nothing to say. He had done none of those things, and he knew how Jasmine would interpret his lack of action.

Rising, Jasmine removed her engagement ring and held it out to him. "You determined that Hayley should be returned to her mother because of the million dollars attached to that decision, not because it would be in the best interest of the child."

Terrence stood as well, but refused to take the ring. "Jasmine, we can—"

"No, Terrence," she said, interrupting his attempt to explain how they could work this out. "We can't."

For a brief moment, they just stared at each other, each waiting on the other to compromise, to offer the olive branch. But neither was forthcoming.

Jasmine picked up her jacket and her purse. "I'm leaving. I wouldn't want me, my soapbox, or my high horse to get in the way of your path to partnership."

He watched her place the ring on the coffee table and walk out. Terrence remained in the same spot, unable to move. Finally, he plopped onto the couch as the reality of the situation sank in. She had just walked out of his life and left him with a broken heart.

Jasmine's hand shook as she tried to get the key in the ignition. After several tries, she was finally on her way back to Richmond. Trying to be strong only lasted for a short while. The minute her car crossed the Bay Bridge, the tears began to fall and she felt her heart shatter into a thousand pieces.

Thirteen

Dragging herself into work the rest of the week took everything Jasmine had in her. The sleepless nights and bouts of tears had taken their toll on her. It was a wonder she could function at all. Managing to hold it together during the workday, she found the evenings an entirely different story. Avoiding his calls had only magnified her loneliness, but talking to him would only make letting him go harder.

Even her guaranteed stress reducer hadn't worked. The comfort, joy, and peace she usually found in her music were surprisingly absent. No matter what she played or when she played it, the final note left her feeling empty and alone.

Checking her watch, she couldn't believe it was close to five o'clock. Where had the day gone? She'd barely gotten through a couple of items on her to-do list. Instead of trying to force it, she decided to call it a day.

The overnight bag sat in the corner and she curved the corners of her lips into a slight smile when she thought of her conversation with Dawn the night before. Refusing to let her sulk all weekend, Dawn had told her that either she could join them for dinner that night and shop with her tomorrow, or she would not have a moment's peace.

Not really in the mood for either, Jasmine agreed only to avoid eating alone, watching television alone, and going to bed alone. After making Dawn swear on a stack of Bibles that she would not invite Terrence over or even mention his name, Jasmine promised to be there around seven. Dawn, an early holiday shopper, couldn't contain her excitement. She'd managed to kill two birds with one stone. She got Jasmine out of the house and she could start her holiday shopping before the rest of the world started the day after Thanksgiving.

Thanksgiving. The day set aside for family. The day she was supposed to be in New York. The day she should have been spending with Terrence and his family.

They had bought their tickets a month ago and were scheduled to leave late Sunday morning, spending the entire week. Having already requested the time off, she looked forward to matching the faces with those she'd seen in his photo album on their first date. Jasmine especially looked forward to meeting Yvonne.

Having spoken with each other several times over the past few months when Yvonne had called Terrence, they'd developed a friendly rapport Jasmine hoped would become a real friendship. Younger than Terrence by almost five years, Yvonne seemed to possess a level of maturity that Jasmine found endearing and refreshing. They'd spent countless hours talking and laughing about Terrence, and Yvonne loved to share childhood stories whose sole purpose was to embarrass her brother.

There was the time that Terrence had gone to see

Nightmare on Elm Street with an older cousin, defying his parents who had forbidden him to go because they knew it would probably frighten him. But Terrence jumped at the chance when his cousin offered to take him. It took him weeks to begin sleeping with the lights off again. As soon as his parents would say good night and shut the door, he'd run like a madman to the light switch to turn it back on. Yvonne even hid under his bed a few nights, scaring him half to death.

Then there was the time when Terrence had a crush on an older woman—he was twelve and she was fourteen. Hoping to impress her, he jumped off the diving board at the community pool, doing a flip and landing in twelve feet of water. Not a great swimmer, he figured he could just hold his breath and float to the top. Instead, he sank to the bottom and the lifeguard had to pull him to safety. His friends, and Yvonne, teased him the rest of the summer.

Focusing on her work now, she pushed thoughts of New York out of her mind. This Thanksgiving would be spent at home. Putting away several files, she began to clear her desk so that she could leave. She thought back to Terrence's words the last time they were together. *High horse. Soapbox.* Those words had been swirling around in her head for days. Aside from how she felt about the situation with Richard Montague, could there be some truth to his statements? Did she come across as a preachy know-it-all who self-righteously insisted that her way was the only way—the right way?

The knock on her door snapped her back to reality as she reclined in her chair. "Come in."

"Do you have a minute?"

Marjorie Davis entered her office and took a seat. When Jasmine had first started with the agency, Marjorie was her supervisor. Marjorie took Jasmine, inexperienced and fresh out of school, under her wing, much the same way Jasmine was now doing for Monica.

Now, with Jasmine a supervisor, Marjorie had become her manager. They worked well together over the years and Jasmine still considered Marjorie to be a great mentor and boss.

Now forty-one, Marjorie had joined the agency ten years ago. Prior to that, she counseled in a drug rehabilitation clinic, helping young men put their lives back together after succumbing to temptations. Today, she spent most of her days in meetings. She rarely went out in the field. But Marjorie never forgot what it was like, and for that, Jasmine was appreciative because she could always relate to what her staff was going through each time they went to court or made a home visit.

"I just wanted to stop by and see how things were going. We haven't really touched base all week."

Jasmine made a few clicks with her mouse and pulled up her status report. "I had meetings with two mothers this week, Sandy Jensen and Maria Sanchez. They've both been attending their parenting classes regularly and things seem to be going well with their jobs. Their cases come up next month, Sandy's is the week before Christmas and Maria's is a week later. I'm going to recommend that their children be returned to them. Hopefully, they'll be able to start the New Year as a family unit again."

Marjorie heard her read her notes, but she was more interested in the tone in which she spoke. The information she provided was accurate and complete, but the enthusiasm was missing. Whenever Jasmine had the opportunity to reunite a family, the joy shined through. Today, that joy was missing. "I didn't mean with your cases, I meant with you."

Jasmine paused. Office gossip could be brutal, even if you typically didn't open up about your private life. But the past few months, Jasmine had been more forthcoming about her relationship with Terrence, and everyone in the building had heard the story of the proposal. Now it was payback time. She'd been short with staff this week, unfocused on her work, and no longer wore the ring. There was no way that would go unnoticed by anyone, especially her boss. "I'm fine."

Marjorie didn't believe her. "I know this job can be tough. When you add in trying to balance it with a personal life, it can at times be overwhelming."

"Are you saying you have a problem with my performance?"

"Oh no," Marjorie stated emphatically. "Quite the contrary. While I think you've been a little preoccupied this week, you are definitely one of our stars. My goal is to keep it that way."

"I understand," Jasmine said.

"No, Jasmine, I don't think you do." Marjorie remembered a time many years ago when she felt as Jasmine did now. Loving the job was one thing, but being able to do it day in and day out sometimes became a struggle. Someone had helped Marjorie overcome the hurdle, and now she wanted to return the favor by helping Jasmine.

"One of our worst enemies in this profession is not the drugs, the alcohol, the abuse, the neglect, the poverty, or the judges. It's burnout. Sometimes, it just gets too hard to deal with the coldness and the reality of the situations that we encounter on an almost daily basis. And I don't want that to happen to you."

"It won't," Jasmine said, trying to sound convincing,

even though she'd been experiencing some of the burnout symptoms lately.

Marjorie heard the words, but the sincerity behind them wasn't there. "You're scheduled for a vacation next week, right?"

Jasmine thought of her planned days off. The seven days she was to spend with Terrence and his family. The seven days of vacation she no longer needed.

Getting no response, Marjorie continued. "I don't mean to pry, but I know your plans suddenly changed."

Jasmine looked away so she wouldn't see the pity in her eyes.

Trying to make an awkward situation comfortable, Marjorie explained, "Monica only gave me the details because she was concerned about you. You haven't quite been yourself this week."

There was no arguing that point.

"Knowing you, you're probably going to just come in to work, taking Thanksgiving Day off."

Jasmine didn't have to say anything. Marjorie could see the answer in her eyes. That's exactly what she had planned to do.

"When was the last time you took a vacation—a real one? One with plane tickets, hotels, good restaurants?" Marjorie asked. It had been more than five years. That, Marjorie could guarantee.

"I just took one . . ." Jasmine racked her brain trying to think of the last time she took any time off from work. She came up empty.

"I'm ordering you to take this week off *and* take a vacation. Go somewhere. Get away. You deserve it." Marjorie paused before she continued. "And I suspect that you need it."

Jasmine appreciated the caring gesture, but how

could taking a vacation improve her attitude about her job and help her get over Terrence? "That's not necessary. With so many people out of the office next week, it'll be good for me to be here just in case something comes up."

Marjorie stood and headed for the door. "If you don't take the time off, I'll consider it insubordination."

"How could you?" Jasmine asked, surprised at her stern tone.

"It's my opinion that you are well on your way to burning out." Marjorie's eyes quickly softened, along with her voice. "And I won't let that happen to my star. Take the time off and take pictures."

"Do I come across as someone on a soapbox?"

The question came out of the blue and Eric and Dawn glanced at each other over the dinner table. Neither spoke.

Jasmine had arrived at their home about a half hour ago and they had just sat down to eat when she decided to see if there was any truth to Terrence's assessment of her. Noting their reaction, she set down her fork and sighed. "I guess that's a yes."

"Why do you ask?" Dawn wondered, still not providing an answer.

Even though Eric and Dawn knew that she and Terrence were no longer together, Jasmine had yet to share the details of their breakup. Tonight, she decided to lay the situation out to them.

For the next half hour, Jasmine rehashed everything from the moment they sat down for dinner to discuss their wedding plans up until the message she received on her answering machine last night telling her good night and that he loved her. She missed their nightly phone conversations. Even though it was obvious that she wasn't going to talk to him, Terrence still called every night, leaving a message on her machine that wished her a good night's sleep and said that he loved her. Jasmine wondered if she would have been able to sleep at all if it wasn't for his voice on her machine every night.

Ending the recap, she followed it up by talking about the challenges at work and her boss's orders to take a vacation.

"So that's why I asked about the soapbox."

"I see," Dawn said slowly.

Now that she had shared the information with two seemingly objective people, Jasmine asked the question that was in the forefront of her mind. "Who do you think is right?"

Eric immediately looked down at his food and continued eating. He had no intention of getting in the middle of this. He probably would have left the table if he didn't think that would be too rude.

"I love you like a sister, Jasmine, but you can be a bit preachy and judgmental at times," Dawn said. "It's like having money is an automatic strike against someone with you. Every time a person with some level of wealth does something you don't agree with, you associate it with their money, status, or power."

"I guess that means you think Terrence is right?" Jasmine said, wondering why Dawn never said anything.

"But you were right too," Dawn continued. "Terrence all but admitted that he was influenced by the fact that he was about to lose a major client. I can understand why you took the position you did. Maybe he should have contacted Chelsea, talked to the social worker, or made arrangements to see the child. But instead of condemning him for it, maybe you should have helped him."

"Again," Jasmine said, slightly frustrated, "you've done a good job in telling me how wrong I am."

"I'm just saying that you can still work it out with him."

Shaking her head, Jasmine couldn't see that. "The bottom line hasn't changed. If this happened again with a different issue, different client, the results would still be the same. He'd still side with the money."

"But is that wrong?"

Jasmine didn't respond right away, but instead picked up her fork and took a bite of chicken.

Dawn watched her friend struggle with this situation. "What you need to do is talk to him."

Talking to him wouldn't solve or change anything. They were just too different to make a marriage between them work. "I have talked to him and the bottom line is that we just don't see things eye to eye."

"Then you're never going to have a successful relationship," Dawn said, hoping to talk sense into her. "Isn't that right, Eric?"

"Oh no. You're not going to drag me into this. I'm just an innocent bystander who wants to eat his dinner," Eric said, looking up for the first time since this conversation started. And he meant it. He was not interested in getting involved in other people's love lives the way his wife was. The only thing he could do was be there for Terrence.

He'd been a total wreck all week, and while he didn't share with Eric what the problem was, it was evident that the fact that they couldn't work it out was tearing him apart. Thank goodness he was busy with work because

Eric would bet that was the only thing that was keeping him sane right now.

"That's ridiculous," Jasmine said in response to her statement. "One failed relationship does not sentence me to a life of singleness."

"What about Brian?"

"What about him?" Jasmine asked, seeing no correlation between what had happened with Brian and what was happening now. "You can't blame that breakup on me. He left me, remember? He went to Chicago and never looked back."

Dawn could hear the crack in her voice and knew that even though she didn't have any feelings for Brian, the pain of what he had done still lingered so many years later. "What if he did call? Would you have been willing to try to make it work between you two?"

"I don't believe it," Jasmine started, her voice rising with emotion. "You're taking Brian's side on this? You were there every night while I waited for him to call. You stood right beside me and watched me open that stupid Christmas card. How many nights did I cry myself to sleep because of him?"

Dawn didn't want to upset her friend further, but she wanted to help her work through this so that she could give her relationship with Terrence the chance that it deserved. "If he had called and declared his undying love for you and asked you to join him in Chicago, would you have gone?"

Jasmine started to speak, but Dawn wouldn't let her.

"No, Jas. I want you to really think about your answer."

Jasmine thought back to that time in her life when she was so blissfully in love. She and Brian had planned their lives out until he decided to make amendments to their plans that didn't include her. But she was also finishing up her master's degree and wanted to begin her career—in California. "No, Dawn. I probably would not have gone. He would be asking me to give up too much."

Dawn relaxed her shoulders in relief. Jasmine had finally been honest with herself. That relationship would have ended whether he called her or not. "And what about Terrence? Is he asking you to give up too much?"

Again, she told Jasmine to think about her answer.

When Jasmine didn't respond, Dawn decided to do it for her. "I think he's been just the opposite. He's supported you, loved you, and hasn't asked you to change one thing."

"He's asking me to change what I believe in. My principles," Jasmine said, saddened by the reality of her situation.

"No, Jasmine, he's not," Dawn said, hoping to get her to see her point. "He's asking you to trust his judgment. The same way he believes in you, you need to believe in him."

Tired of discussing the situation with Terrence—especially since she was beginning to question her decision to break if off—she decided to change the subject. "I just need some time to think."

"Will you at least think about contacting him?"

Jasmine thought about it, but she couldn't commit. "He's leaving for New York on Sunday. I'm not going to do anything until he gets back. I need time to think."

Dawn started to say something but caught herself. An idea began to form in her mind. All Terrence and Jasmine needed was the opportunity to talk in an atmosphere that would encourage them to work things out. She needed a place free from interruptions from work, friends, and family, a place where they could concentrate on each other. The wheels started turning in her head and she pulled her plan together quickly, in a matter of seconds. If she could make this work, this would be her greatest matchmaking success of all.

"Are you going to take you boss's advice and get away during your time off? Go somewhere where you can relax?"

Jasmine sat back in her chair, pleased that the subject of Terrence McKinley had finally been dropped. If the truth were told, Dawn's assessment of the situation had started to make sense. Did she overreact? Should she reach out to him? Quickly, she decided against it. She didn't want to react out of emotion, she wanted to take the time to think her relationship with Terrence through. This week off would give her that time.

"Where would I go that wouldn't cost me a fortune at this late date?" Jasmine didn't need to be a travel agent to know that securing an airline ticket and hotel accommodations the week of Thanksgiving for seven days would cost her well into the four figures.

Casually, Dawn snapped her fingers. "I have an idea. I'm not sure if it can work out, but you might be interested."

"What is it?"

"Eric's mother called last week and said that they weren't using the house they have on the island of Antigua this year."

"They did what?" Eric said, jumping into the conversation for the first time.

"I told you," she said to him, before turning her attention back to Jasmine.

"I didn't know Eric's family owned property in the islands. How come you guys have never gone?" Jasmine said. This wasn't the type of news Dawn would keep a secret.

"They purchased the property earlier in the year and planned to spend time there over the holidays, but that was before Eric's sister Michelle got pregnant. She's due in two weeks and they didn't want to travel that far and miss the birth of their first grandchild."

Jasmine remembered that Eric had shared the news of his sister's pregnancy several months ago.

"They want to stay in D.C., just in case," Dawn continued. "Isn't that right, Eric?"

Dawn and Jasmine focused their attention on Eric, who took a bite of his food and slowly nodded in agreement.

"So why isn't someone else using it? I'm sure they could have made a ton of money renting it out for the week." Jasmine said. She could think of at least three people she knew off the top of her head that would jump at the chance to spend a relaxing week in the Caribbean.

Dawn shook her head no. "They still have that 'new owner' mentality—only wanted family to use it. And with Michelle's delivery so close, no one really wants to take them up on their offer."

Jasmine and Dawn talked about everything. How could she not have told her about this? "Why haven't you mentioned anything about it before?"

"They kept it hush-hush, planning to surprise us with the news just in time for the holidays. Besides, I knew you were going to be in New York."

The sting of her canceled trip pierced her heart. "If they only want family to use it, why would they give it to me?"

"Are you kidding?" Dawn said, hoping that Jasmine was warming up to the idea. "You're just like family. How could they say no? Plus, I'll promise them you won't have any wild parties on their property."

"I don't know, Dawn," Jasmine said thoughtfully. "This is really short notice. I'd be leaving on Sunday and I'm sure an airline ticket would cost a small fortune."

"I'm sure we could go online and find a halfway decent last minute deal."

"I'm still not sure I want to go anywhere."

"We're going to be in D.C. for the holidays, and since you don't want to talk to Terrence until you have time to think, what better place to do it?"

Dawn could see that Jasmine was still not completely convinced. "Picture it . . . beautiful beaches, ninety-degree weather, peace and quiet."

Jasmine hated to admit it, but the idea of a week in the islands started to appeal to her. "I guess you could check with Eric's folks and let me know what they say."

Dawn smiled in victory. "It's after eleven on the East Coast, but Eric will call them first thing in the morning. Right, honey?"

Again, he just nodded his head.

"You know," Jasmine said, starting to get excited about the idea of spending part of the holiday season in the Caribbean. What better way to take a break from her personal and professional challenges? "The more I think about this, the better it sounds. Let them know I'm willing to rent it from them."

Later that evening, Dawn crawled into bed, careful not to wake Eric. She and Jasmine had stayed up late enjoying hot fudge sundaes and planning out their day of shopping. It was almost 2:00 A.M.

"Don't try to be quiet, I'm not asleep," Eric said. Sitting up, he turned on the lamp beside the bed.

"I hope I didn't wake you," she answered sweetly.

He stared at his wife with scolding eyes, waiting for her to explain.

"What?" she asked innocently.

"Don't *what* me, Dawn," he said as if he were talking to a child. "You know what."

"It was just an itty-bitty, teeny-weeny white lie," she reasoned.

"My parents don't own a house in Antigua!"

"I know!" she said sweetly.

Eric didn't know whether to curse her criminal mind or celebrate it. "This could blow up in your face."

Snuggling close to him, she wrapped her arms around his waist. "Not if we think positively."

"What's this 'we' stuff? You and your matchmaking have nothing to do with me."

Kissing him on the lips, she assured him her plan would work.

"And how are you going to get him there?" he asked.

Patting him on the back, she just gave him one of her million-dollar smiles. "Don't worry, babe. I've got everything under control." And with that, she turned off the light and got busy with a little lovin' of her own.

Terrence lay in bed with the television on in the background. It had been a week since his blowup with Jasmine, and nothing. She wouldn't return his calls, open the door when he came by, or accept any of the gifts of flowers and candy he sent. How could she turn off what they had so quickly? It made a brother wonder if she ever loved him at all.

Quickly, he discarded that thought. No one was that good of an actress. Even if she could fool him into believing it with her words, the body doesn't lie. Her tender kisses, her sweet caresses, her moans when they made love. Those were authentic.

It was Saturday morning and he had the entire day ahead of him. He had originally planned to drive to Napa Valley with Jasmine to get wine to take to New York with them. But not only did it appear that his day trip was not going to happen, neither was their trip to New York.

Spending Thanksgiving without her had never crossed his mind, and now it had become his reality. He'd already purchased the tickets and knew his family would love to see him—with or without a fiancée. But he wasn't sure if he was up to it. There would be questions, looks of concern and pity, and maybe even a backlash against Jasmine.

Jumping out of bed, he thought about his options for the day. He could go to Napa as planned or he could just go to work. Anything had to be better than sitting here thinking of her.

Deciding to go to work, he headed for the shower just as the phone rang. Knowing it was a long shot, he checked the caller ID. She hadn't returned any of the messages he left, but he still held out hope. No such luck.

"Hi, Yvonne."

"Hey, big brother. I just wanted to check and see what time you guys are getting in on Sunday. Marcus and Delaney can't wait to see their Uncle T, and none of us can wait to meet the woman who has turned your world upside down."

Everyone had been looking forward to seeing him,

as he hadn't made a trip home since he moved. However, he just didn't think he could deal with his family right now. They would surely want to know why he was traveling alone after getting engaged a week ago. Maybe the solution was just to stay in town. "Listen, Yvonne, I was going to call you and Mom today."

Yvonne could tell by his voice that he had news she probably didn't want to hear. "Please don't tell me you're not coming."

Terrence heard the disappointment in her voice and chose to ignore it. "It's just that I've got this case heating up and if I don't spend some serious hours on it this week, I won't be ready for an upcoming hearing."

"But what about Jasmine, we were looking forward to meeting her."

"And she was looking forward to meeting all of you." Terrence didn't think it was exactly a lie. "But she understands."

"Can't you work from here?" Yvonne asked. "Between your laptop and the Internet, I'm sure it will be like you're right in your own office."

"Except for the lack of a law library, my secretary, and my paralegal," he said, trying to lighten the mood.

"But everyone's been looking forward to seeing you," she said, hoping to guilt-trip him into changing his mind.

"I'm sorry, Yvonne, but it can't be helped. I promise I'll be home for Christmas. It's just a month away."

Yvonne heard the word and wondered if he caught his slip. He said "I'll" be home instead of "we'll." That could only mean that something must be going on with Jasmine. "Are you sure everything's okay?"

Terrence and his sister had always been close, but he just wasn't ready to talk about it. Besides, he reasoned, he and Jasmine would work it out, so there was no need to involve his family in his situation. "Everything's fine. I'll call you next week."

Yvonne knew her brother well enough that if he wasn't ready to talk about something, there was nothing she could say or do to make him change his mind. She just hoped that whatever was going on between them could be worked out. The past six months had been the happiest she had seen her brother. She would hate to see what would happen to him if his relationship with Jasmine didn't work out. "Call me if you need me."

"I will."

Terrence hung up the phone and thought about his sister's last words. He'd tried to cover his reasons for not coming, but he wasn't quite sure she fell for it. Holidays were important to his family, and missing one would definitely raise eyebrows. Hopefully, the fact that he promised he would be home for Christmas would appease them.

After taking a shower and dressing, Terrence grabbed his keys to head for the office. Just as he opened his door, the phone rang. Contemplating answering it, he glanced at the caller ID. The Westfields.

"Hey, Terrence."

"Dawn?"

"Quick question for you."

"Shoot."

"Ever been to Antigua?"

Fourteen

The plane banked left over the water and Jasmine stared down at the clear, blue ocean. Having flown cross-country to Florida, her connection out of Miami left on time, so it was just a matter of minutes before she would touch down in a place travelers called paradise. At first, she'd been reluctant to accept the offer from Eric and his family. Traveling alone to an island? Was it safe? What would she do?

But the more she thought about it, the more she realized she needed to get away. Marjorie was right, she hadn't taken a real vacation in years and the thought of sitting in her house for the next week with no Dawn, no work, and no Terrence nearly drove her crazy. Once she'd finally made the decision to go, her excitement began to grow.

The house was in a small, private community, with security at the front gate, which eliminated her concerns about safety. She'd also spent Saturday night on the

Internet, researching the island and the many things to do. With an array of shops, historical sites, and water sports, she realized that seven days might not be long enough. Once she added in the six or seven books that were in her to-be-read pile, Jasmine found that she had more than enough to keep her busy for the week.

Hearing the announcement to prepare for landing, Jasmine tightened her seat belt and put her seat back into the upright position. With a full flight, she was glad to get a window seat. That ensured that she wouldn't have to get up to let someone out if she were sitting in the aisle or squeeze between two others by sitting in the middle seat. This way, she was able to look out the window and keep to herself.

Checking in at the ticket counter in Florida, she lost count of the number of couples snuggling and giggling, waiting for boarding to start. She didn't need to take a survey to realize she was the only person traveling alone. But she refused to let that fact play with her mind. She'd only been to an island once before—when she and Dawn went to the Bahamas for spring break during their sophomore year of college. So she wasn't going to let anything—especially couples in love—spoil the good time she planned to have.

Armed with her computer printouts, books, sunscreen, and swimsuits, she'd loosely mapped out how she'd spend her days. Between the sightseeing, the shopping, and the beach, her goal was to return to the house completely exhausted at the end of the day. That way, she'd have no choice but to sleep like a log during the night, keeping her from the sleepless nights she'd experienced the past week because of her thoughts of Terrence.

Just as Dawn promised, a driver was waiting for her at baggage claim and assisted her in loading up her luggage, ready to take her to her new home for the next week. Surprisingly, the ride was just a short fifteen minutes from the airport, in Long Bay. When the driver turned into the gated community, Jasmine couldn't believe her eyes. The grounds were breathtaking, with lush green grass, palm trees, and shrubbery throughout. When he put the car in park after turning into a driveway, Jasmine didn't move. Surely this wasn't the house Eric's parents owned—the one that she would be staying in for the week? When the driver popped the trunk and then opened her door, she got her answer.

Stepping out of the car, she felt the sun beaming down on her and the warmth completely engulfing her. Shielding her eyes from the sun with her hands, she stared at the beautiful structure. Changing clothes in Florida from casual pants and light sweater to shorts and a short-sleeved top proved to be a smart move, as it had to be about eighty degrees. And knowing how much she loved the water, she had made another good choice of having her hair cornrowed straight back. That way, she wouldn't have to be bothered with blow-dryers and curling irons.

"I have the key, ma'am. If you'll just follow me."

The accent was so heavy that she almost didn't understand what he said, but she got in step behind him, ready for the most relaxing week of her life.

The house, nestled on a small hill, sat slightly off the main road. When they reached the front door, he opened it and stepped aside, allowing her to enter first.

"You'll need to punch in the code," he said.

Almost forgetting the small piece of paper Dawn had given her at the airport, she quickly retrieved it and punched in the five numbers, and the beeping sound stopped.

"Would you like me to take your bags to the master suite?"

"Yes, thank you," she said, stepping fully into the entryway.

Watching him disappear down the hall, Jasmine took the opportunity to explore. The living room and dining room were combined in a large, charming space. The living area had two beige love seats with a couple of chairs surrounding a dark wood coffee table. A fireplace was nestled in the far wall. There was also a large television with DVD player attached. At the back of the room was a sliding glass door that led out to the wraparound deck. Beyond the deck was the pool. And beyond the pool was the ocean. The view was spectacular.

Making her way into the kitchen, she found it open and airy, and it impressed her that it contained all the modern equipment a gourmet chef would use. Checking the refrigerator, she saw that Dawn was right. There were a few items for her to eat tonight, but someone from the community association would come by tomorrow morning to pick up a grocery list and shop for her for the entire week.

Jasmine slowly shut the refrigerator door and stood still, surveying her living quarters one more time. Refusing to stay for free, she forced Dawn to charge her the going rate for the week. She gave Dawn a check yesterday, but now she began to wonder if Dawn was completely honest with her. Somehow, she had an inkling that the amount she gave Dawn would barely cover a couple of days in a place like this—and definitely not the entire week.

"Ma'am?"

Hearing the driver call her name, she went back to the living room.

"Is there anything else I can do for you?"

Reaching in her purse for a tip, she said, "No. Thank you."

Waving her gesture off, he started toward the door. "Not necessary. Everything, including a tip, has been taken care of. My number is on the refrigerator. Just call when you need transportation. I can take you anywhere on the island you'd like to go. Enjoy your stay."

As soon as the door shut behind her, complete silence prevailed. Almost immediately, she thought about Terrence. How much more fun would this be if he were sharing this with her. But he had landed in New York a few hours ago to spend the week with his family and she was here. For a moment, all the hurt and pain rose to the surface. *Don't even go there, girl!* Determined to start her vacation off right, she decided not to unpack right away, but to change into her swimsuit, grab a book, and enjoy the rest of her day by the pool.

After rubbing sunscreen in all the places she could reach, she settled onto a patio chair and opened up her book. By page ten, she was hooked. She'd read romance novels as a child, but had put them away as an adult. The fantasy world the characters inhabited didn't fit with the reality of life. But on a whim, she had picked up a couple of them at the airport in Florida, and to her surprise, the characters and the plots were intriguing and interesting.

When she was halfway through the book, the sun began to set and the air turned a little cool. Heading inside the house, she decided to fix a salad before enjoying a relaxing bath in the oversized tub in the master suite. Just as she sat down to eat, her cell phone rang.

"Wanted to call and make sure you made it and that everything was to your liking."

Jasmine looked out past the pool, listening to the waves crashing against the shore. "Are you kidding? This place is spectacular. I may never come home."

"I'm glad you're enjoying it," Dawn said. Phase one of her plan had been accomplished.

"There's just one thing?"

"What?" Dawn answered cautiously.

"Are you sure I gave you enough money for this?"

When she didn't get a response, Jasmine had the sneaking suspicion that she'd been right in assuming that she had been undercharged. But just to confirm it, she asked the question again.

"Dawn, are you still there?"

"Can you hear me?" Dawn asked, pretending they'd suddenly had a bad connection.

"Yes, Dawn, loud and clear," Jasmine said, not fooled by her tactics.

"I can't hear you," Dawn yelled, making a static sound with her mouth. "I think you're breaking up."

Jasmine doubted that there were problems with cellular service on the island and decided to let the subject drop. "We'll talk about it when I get back."

Amazingly, their connection became crystal clear. "Oh, that's better. I can hear you now."

"Very funny."

"Seriously, Jas. You were slightly undercharged, but just consider this an early Christmas present."

The tone in her voice caught Jasmine off guard.

"Take this week to really figure out what you want," Dawn continued.

"What's that supposed to mean?" Jasmine asked, noting that the light and joking tone she'd used a few seconds ago had become somber and serious.

"Just what I said . . . I hope this week will give you clarity."

"Dawn, what are—"

"Sorry, Jas. I gotta go," she said abruptly. "We have a dinner with one of Eric's clients tonight. I'll talk to you later."

Before she could respond, Dawn had hung up.

Strange.

Almost two o'clock in the morning, her body was still on California time—making it close to midnight there. Physically exhausted, she hoped that sleep would come easy tonight. To help it, she filled the tub with warm water and scented bath gel, before easing her body into it. Soft jazz was playing in the background. Leaning back on the bath pillow, she closed her eyes and replayed Dawn's cryptic words. *"I hope this week will give you clarity. Take this week to really figure out what you want."*

It wasn't difficult to decipher the hidden message. Dawn simply wanted Jasmine to realize how much Terrence meant to her and allow him back in her life.

Crawling into bed, exhausted and completely relaxed from her full day of travel and tonight's soaking, she closed her eyes and waited for sleep to take over. But thirty minutes later, she was still awake. Even though she hadn't talked to Terrence since their fight, he still called her every night to leave a message on her machine to say good night. This would be the first night since they met that she'd have to go to sleep without it.

On a whim, she reached for her cell phone and dialed her home voice mail. Terrence didn't know she'd taken this trip, so he would assume that she was home.

She waited for the prompts to enter her pass code and listen to her new messages. Just as she hoped, his voice was there.

"You haven't told me to stop calling, so I won't. I just wanted to tell you good night and sweet dreams."

The words and his voice comforted her, but they also confused her. Was Dawn right? Should she trust his judgment? Were her expectations beyond the reach of anyone? All the questions and Terrence's voice swirled in her head as she drifted off into a fitful sleep.

The knock at the door startled Jasmine out of her sleep. Just after 9:00 A.M., she hopped out of bed and grabbed her robe. She had no idea who it could be. No one knew she was here. Then she remembered the groceries she planned to order today.

In the bathroom, she did a five-second rinse with mouthwash, and stopped in the kitchen to grab the grocery list she had written out before she went to bed. According to the tentative schedule she'd made for herself before leaving home, she planned to spend the day checking out the shopping areas. Hopefully, by the time the person returned with her food, she'd be dressed and ready to start her day. "I'm coming."

Opening the wooden door, she reached out to unlock the screen door when her hand froze. Blinking twice, she wanted to make sure that her brain actually confirmed what her eyes were telling her. After several seconds, the truth sank in and her reaction was immediate. She slammed the door in his face.

* * *

Terrence stood on the other side of the door, shell-shocked. In his wildest dreams, he never thought she would be the one on the other side of the door. What was she doing here? How did she . . .? Then it hit him. Dawn, the queen of matchmaking, had struck again.

Jasmine leaned against the closed door, trying to stop her body from shaking. He knocked a second time, but she didn't move. A mixture of anger and excitement ran through her body. If she opened the door again, she couldn't be sure whether she would slap him or kiss him.

Taking a deep breath, Jasmine finally opened the door. Opting not to slap or kiss him, she instead just stood still.

"Oh my God," he said slowly, before breaking into a smile.

Jasmine felt her heart flutter at the sight of him. Dressed for the islands in black shorts and a white top, his muscular frame offered proof of his commitment to his physical well-being. It had only been a week since she'd seen him, but she swore he looked ten times better than she remembered.

Leading him into the living room, Jasmine began to pace, talking to no one in particular. "I should have known better. How could I have been so stupid? All the signs were there. Dawn worked overtime to make this trip happen. Wasn't it obvious she had something up her sleeve? How could *no one* in Eric's family have wanted to use this place over the holiday?"

She stopped her ranting, turning her thoughts from Dawn and focusing on Terrence. "And you. Do you get your kicks from setting me up? Was this your idea, and you got them to play along? How did you . . ."

Her next words died on her lips as Terrence's long strides led him directly in front of her. Before she could stop him, he pulled her body against his and kissed her fully on the mouth. Not hesitantly or tentatively, but with purpose and conviction. He didn't plan it. Hell, she wasn't even supposed to be here. But the minute he saw her, all the feelings of missing her, needing her, and loving her came rushing forth and the only way he could satisfy them was to taste her again—if just this one time.

The shock of the kiss caught Jasmine completely off guard and her initial reaction was to push him away, but when her hands moved up, she couldn't do it. Instead she wrapped them around his neck and pulled him closer. Rubbing her hands at the nape of his neck, she didn't realized how much she needed—craved him— wanted him until this very moment. Unable to control the pure passion raging through her, she leaned into his kiss, fitting her body in the contours of his.

Terrence's hands were everywhere, reacquainting himself with her body. The thin, silky material of her nightgown and robe did nothing to hide her curves. In seconds, her robe dropped to the floor. Terrence moaned in pleasure as he lowered the spaghetti straps on her gown down her shoulders.

That was when the reality of her actions hit Jasmine. Jumping out of his arms, she tried to speak, but couldn't. Breathless, happy, and angry all at once, she turned on her heels and headed for the master bedroom. Slamming the door, she sat on the bed trying to regain control.

Yanking the phone off the receiver, she dialed San Francisco. When the answering machine came on, she hung up and called her cell phone. When the call went straight to voice mail, she decided to leave a message. "You can't hide from me forever. You better hope the anger I'm feeling now subsides by the time I see you. Call me. And I mean today."

She ignored his knock at the door.

"Jasmine?"

No answer.

"Are you going to come out?"

When he only received the silent treatment, he tried again. "You can't spend your entire stay in that room."

It only took him a second to realize that they were both set up by Dawn, but judging from her words a few minutes ago, she obviously thought he was in on it. "I didn't know you were going to be here."

"Yeah, right," she yelled through the door. "And there really is a Santa Claus."

"I'm serious, Jas," he said. "But as long as we're here, don't you think we should talk? How can you just let what we have go? Don't you want to see if we can save our relationship? Don't you think we're worth the effort?"

When she didn't respond, his frustration mounted. "I love you, Jas, but I swear you're making it harder and harder."

After waiting several more seconds, he realized she wasn't coming out, which meant she wasn't interested in working things out with him. "Fine. Have it your way. I'm outta here."

She stared at the door hearing his footsteps grow lighter as he made his way down the hall toward the front door. Heading for the door, she was about to open it when she heard him return.

"The driver already left. Do you have a number to a cab service I can take back to the airport?"

Finally opening the door, she eyed him suspiciously. Did he really have no idea what Dawn was up to? Were the two of them both victims? "There's a list of numbers on the refrigerator."

Without saying another word, he headed for the kitchen. She followed and watched him pick up the phone. Suddenly, the thought of him leaving caused panic. Regardless of whether he had participated in Dawn's scheme or not, she didn't want him to leave. "Wait. Hang up the phone."

He replaced the receiver, but didn't speak. Following her back into the living room, he sat on the sofa with her, taking a spot just a few inches from her.

Refusing to let on how much his nearness affected her, she focused on their present situation. "Why are you here?"

Reaching out, he ran the back of his fingers down the side of her face and whispered, "I've missed you so much."

Closing her eyes, she relished his touch and remembered all the things she loved about him. And at this particular moment, she tried hard to justify the reason they weren't together.

"Haven't you missed me at all?"

More than you know. The words were on the tip of her tongue, she just couldn't speak them.

Leaning forward, he kissed her eyelids, then her nose, and then rested his forehead against hers. "God, I've missed you so much."

Unable to resist any longer, she admitted it. "I've missed you, too."

Sitting back from him, she tried to maintain her composure. "What are you doing here, Terrence?"

"It's simple," he said. "Dawn."

Thinking of the load of bull Dawn had fed her when

they had dinner on Saturday night, she wondered if she'd used the same story on Terrence. And Eric? Was he a willing participant in her devious plan?

"Eric forced me to stop by their house for dinner a few times last week since my evenings had suddenly become free."

She didn't have to guess what he meant by that statement.

"I mentioned that I'd decided not to go to New York for the holiday. I just wasn't up to seeing my family."

Jasmine tried to set aside the guilt she felt about his decision not to see his family—no doubt because of their breakup. She remembered how she didn't want to see anyone after Brian left. The questions, the advice, the sympathy. Friends and family could mean well, but it could be emotionally draining.

Knowing how close Terrence was to his family, she hated that she may have caused him to cancel his trip.

"Yesterday morning, I get a call from an excited Dawn. She gives me a story about an unused family house in the Caribbean. I told her thanks, but no, thanks. But that didn't deter Dawn," Terrence said.

Jasmine couldn't argue with him on that point. Once Dawn got an idea in her head, nothing could stop her.

"Knowing I already had scheduled the time off, she thought a vacation would do me some good. I told her I wasn't interested in going four thousand miles away, just in case you decided to return my call. But she told me that you were going to be joining Eric's family in D.C., trying to encourage you to join me. I couldn't stand the thought of going to New York without a fiancée and I definitely didn't want to spend the holiday alone in San Francisco, so I finally agreed."

The story sounded reasonable, but Jasmine still wondered if he had known she would be here. "Why did you knock?"

Terrence could still hear a little doubt in her voice. "I thought the person in this house was going to be my neighbor. Dawn told me to come here to get the key to the house I would actually be staying in."

The doubt finally disappeared in her expression. If it was one thing Terrence had never done, it was lie to her.

"I can't believe she would go through all this trouble. This could have completely blown up in her face," Jasmine said.

"I have to say, Dawn is definitely a piece of work. But I have to admit," he said, taking her hand in his, "I don't mind it this time. She got us together. She got us talking."

Jasmine thought of the week ahead. How could they possibly share this house when they were in the process of breaking up?

"So what do you want to do?" Terrence said, as if he read her mind. "I don't have to stay here. I can check into a hotel, I can even catch the next flight home. But I want you to know that my first choice would be to stay right here with you and try to work out whatever went wrong in our relationship because I still love you."

Jasmine decided to be completely honest with herself and admit that she didn't want him to leave. Not sure if the could work through their problems, she wanted the chance to find out. That chance was taken away from them when she refused to see or talk to him in the week since she broke it off. "There're two other bedrooms, you can pick whichever you want."

Terrence exhaled slowly and said a silent prayer of

thanks. The moment he got back to the States, he was going to treat Dawn to dinner. She'd lied, cheated, and manipulated both of them. But he didn't care. She'd managed to accomplish the one thing he couldn't—get Jasmine talking to him again.

Rising, Jasmine headed for her bedroom. "I'm going to get dressed. I'd planned to do some shopping today."

"Would you like some company?"

The relaxed smile, the sexy eyes, and the chance to spend time with him were too much for Jasmine to resist. And she didn't want to. "Sure."

A half hour later, they locked the front door and headed out into the late morning sun. As they settled in the back of the car, Jasmine secretly smiled. All the romance novels, relaxing baths, or dips in the pool couldn't compare to having him here. The only mystery was whether they could work out their differences.

Four hours later, Terrence and Jasmine sat in a quaint restaurant on Radcliffe Quay, one of the oldest parts of St. John's, Antigua. The breathtaking view of the harbor gave them a chance to watch the yachts and cruise ships come in and out. Ordering entrées with local flavor, they were both starving from their day of checking out the different shops around the island.

"Once again, the sellers at vendors' mall must have seen you coming." Jasmine laughed, taking note of the many plastic bags Terrence had filled with T-shirts, handmade crafts, and other souvenirs.

"I can't help myself. Who could resist three T-shirts for ten dollars!" Terrence said, glancing down at all his purchases. "My niece and nephew will love it."

At the mention of his family, Jasmine's good mood faltered a little. It was an innocent statement, but it reminded her of where they were supposed to be this week—in New York, celebrating their engagement with his family.

Terrence watched the change in her demeanor and figured out what she must be thinking. He knew this because he was thinking the same thing. "Don't worry about it, Jasmine. You'll get to meet my family another time."

The implication of his words wasn't lost on Jasmine. He was assuming that they would work things out and get back together.

Both caught up in their own thoughts, they waited for their food in silence.

When they returned to the house, the sun began to set and they sat on the patio, relaxing after their day of touring. Aside from the comments about the canceled trip to New York, the subject of the status of their relationship lingered in the background. Neither brought it up, but they both understood that if they were going to be able to patch things up completely and move forward, they would have to talk about it.

"We need to talk, Jas."

Jasmine had been avoiding it long enough. "I know, Terrence."

Standing, he walked toward the edge of the deck and looked out. "You want to take a walk on the beach?"

They left their shoes on the deck. It was less than a one-minute walk out the back of the property before their feet sank into the sand on the private beach. They weren't alone. Several couples were out for late night strolls. The waves, washing up to shore, served as great background music as they walked hand in hand.

"You were right, Jasmine," Terrence started. "I didn't want to lose an important client. I let the circumstances of my business relationship with Richard influence my response to his request. I promise you, I won't let that happen again."

Somehow, she didn't take pleasure in his confession. "You were right, too, Terrence. Soapbox. High horse. I've climbed up on both of them. I had no right to judge you like I did."

"I know you feel strongly about your beliefs and principles, and I respect that," he said. "I would never ask you to compromise or change for me. I trust you to do what's right for you."

Jasmine remembered her conversation with Dawn when they had talked about trust. When she made choices about any of her cases, there were always others that didn't agree with them. The parents, the judge, and sometimes the child. But she would always tell them the same thing. To trust her. To know that she was making the best decision with the information she had.

That's what Terrence was trying to do. But her stubbornness hadn't allowed him to do the very things she expected others to do for her. She was so used to fighting everyone's battles that she hadn't been able to allow people in her life to make their own choices and decisions. She paraded around as if she had all the right answers, and as a result she alienated the man she loved.

"I need you to do the same for me," Terrence continued. "I want to be able to share my life with you. All of my life. That includes my work. If I'm to do that, I have to know that you won't be ready to pounce or judge me for any decision I make, or any client I decide to represent."

Jasmine let the words sink in, knowing it would be a challenge for her to change.

"You are great at what you do. You were born for it," Terrence continued. "I would never try to tell you what decision to make about a case or what recommendation to make to a judge. All I'm asking is for the same from you."

Stopping, he turned her toward him and placed his arms around her waist. "I want to make this work between us. I can't imagine that two people who love each other this much should be apart."

"Me either," she whispered.

"So where do we go from here?"

"I want to give you what you want, Terrence. I just don't know if I can change overnight. But I'm willing to try."

He kissed her sweetly on the lips. "There's something else."

"What?"

"Can we agree that when we have problems, we have to stay and work them out?" Terrence said. "No running away?"

Jasmine nodded in agreement.

"My parents have been married thirty-five years and I'm sure they've had some major issues where they were on opposing sides, but they always talked it out and eventually worked it out. I think we should take a lesson from them."

"I love you, Terrence. And I know that I can be stubborn at times."

He raised his brow.

"Okay." She laughed. "I can be stubborn a lot of times. But I'm willing to work on that. I know you are a wonderful person and a fantastic lawyer. I won't second-guess your professional decisions."

He leaned his face down and gave her several short kisses on the lips before taking them fully and slipping his tongue inside.

The passionate kisses and declarations of love had worn her down, and she didn't want to spend one more night apart from him. "Let's head back."

The sultry sound of her voice aroused Terrence, and without hesitating he led her back to the house.

Entering the bedroom, they could barely get out of their clothes between the kisses. Leading him to the bed, Jasmine reached for him, when he suddenly stopped.

"What's wrong, Terrence?"

Rubbing his hand across his chin in frustration, he picked up her shirt and threw it to her. "I didn't exactly think I'd be making love this week when I got on that plane."

Jasmine's confusion shown on her face. Then it hit her. "It's after eleven, do you think any stores are still open?"

Putting his shorts back on, he shook his head in disappointment, before breaking into a smile.

"You think this is funny?" she asked.

"Oh, believe me, sweetheart, the only reason I'm laughing is to keep from crying."

"We're going to fix this problem tomorrow, right?"

"Without a doubt, but for now we'll have to settle for holding each other."

And that's just what they did. They talked well into the wee hours of the morning, developing a closeness at a much deeper level.

Fifteen

When Jasmine awoke, she was alone in the bed, but she could smell the coffee. Hazelnut. Her favorite. The groceries must have been delivered that morning. Stretching, she had never felt so satisfied . . . so complete in her life. Her boss and Dawn were right. This vacation was exactly what she needed to assess what she wanted in life. And now, the answer was so clear. She wanted Terrence.

With them reaching an understanding about their issues, there was nothing to stop them from being together. Terrence had decided not to represent Richard and she had agreed to refrain from being judgmental. Now they could focus on repairing the broken pieces of their relationship.

"I thought you might enjoy breakfast in bed."

Jasmine sat up when Terrence entered the bedroom carrying a tray filled with coffee, a croissant, and eggs. "Did you cook this?" she asked skeptically. She recalled the many other attempts he'd made at cooking for her.

A few times, it was pretty good, but most times they ended up ordering out.

"I only had to scramble the eggs," he said, pretending to be offended by her questions.

She narrowed her eyes and stared at him, waiting for him to tell the whole truth.

"Okay," he confessed, "it took me three tries, but I tasted them and they're quite edible."

Jasmine laughed as she made room for him on the bed. With the fork, she picked up a bite of eggs and smelled them.

"Very funny," he said.

After putting them in her mouth, she had to admit they weren't that bad. "My compliments to the chef."

"Thank you very much," he said, bowing.

Breaking off a piece of her croissant, he fed it to her. "So what's on your agenda today—other than finding a drugstore?"

The inside joke wasn't lost on Jasmine and she quickly agreed that condoms had become a top priority.

"We don't have to stick to my plans," she said truthfully. "I made those when I thought I'd be here alone."

"I know we don't have to, but I want to." Terrence had only thrown some clothes and toiletries in a bag when he decided to take this trip. He'd hoped to spend this time figuring out how he could bring Jasmine back into his life. But thanks to Dawn, the problem had been solved. "I want you to enjoy all the things you planned, and hopefully, with me joining you, it will make our time here that much better."

"Okay," Jasmine said, reaching toward the nightstand for her list of activities. "Let's see. Today I planned to swim with stingrays."

Terrence waited for her to crack a smile, to let him know she was joking, but it didn't happen. "You're going to do what?"

The apprehension in his voice amused Jasmine. She thought twice about doing it, but decided to go ahead and be a little adventurous. But hearing the tinge of fear in his voice let her know Terrence wasn't exactly comfortable with the idea either. "Oh, come on, T. Don't tell me you're afraid of a little fish."

Terrence's ego wouldn't let him cave in to her teasing. "Me? Afraid? Of course not."

"Yeah, right," she said, not believing one word.

"I'm serious," he said, gaining some confidence in his voice. "Those 'little fish' as you like to call them can be dangerous. Are you sure you're up for it?"

When she'd made the reservation, she double-checked their cancellation policy, just in case she chickened out at the last minute. But there was no chance of that happening now. Nothing would stop Jasmine from taking this island adventure. "I'm sure. We leave in one hour."

With that, she popped the last of her croissant in her mouth and headed for the bathroom. "Let me know if you want to cancel. I'm sure we could find some kiddie tours, maybe something where you could swim with goldfish."

"Ha, ha," Terrence said. "Just don't look to cling to me the first time one of the 'little fishies' comes racing toward you."

Two hours later, Terrence stood on the edge of a small cliff looking down into the calm, crystal-clear waters. He'd been stalling for the last twenty minutes, asking their tour guide questions about the island and the reefs, adjusting his swim trunks, and making sure he had enough sunscreen on. But he had run out of ways to delay the inevitable. Others in the tour group had been in the water for almost fifteen minutes, including Jasmine.

"Come on, honey, the water feels great," Jasmine said, loud enough so the other people in the group could hear her, making it quite obvious that he was the last one to get into the water.

Thanks, Jas. Now everyone's looking at me. "Let me just take off my watch," he said, pointing to the timepiece he knew was waterproof.

Taking his time, he walked over to their beach bag, taking extra care to close the bag and snap it shut. A few minutes later, he stood in the same spot he'd just left—right on the edge of the water.

Jasmine swam over to him with a quirky grin on her face. Talking to him as if he were a baby, she tried to encourage him to get in. "Come on, Terrence, baby. It's okay. The little fishies won't bite you. You can do it. I'll be right here with you."

That was the last straw. It was now or never. Hearing her laugh, he had no choice. He sat down and eased into the water, preferring not to jump right in as the others had done. Moving stiffly at first, he tried to avoid the attention of the stingrays, but after a couple of minutes, his body began to relax and he began to enjoy the warm sun, the water, and even the swimming stingrays.

"See, I told you it wasn't that bad," Jasmine said, swimming up beside him.

Terrence thought of the stories Jasmine would tell about this day. The teasing would be endless. Eric, Dawn, Yvonne . . . no one would let him live this one down. Every family gathering, every office party, every time someone came to visit, Jasmine would tell this story. "Just promise you won't tell anyone about this—my rep will be ruined."

Jasmine's eyes sparkled and the corners of her mouth curved up. "Oh, I don't know, Terrence. That's asking an awful lot of me. I was intending for this to be my lead story each time someone asked me if I had a good time on my vacation."

Terrence playfully splashed water at her. "Very funny. I know you wouldn't do that to the man you love."

"I do love you," Jasmine admitted. "But this just might be too good to keep quiet. If you want me to keep a secret like that, I'll have to get something in return . . . something big."

"Are you bribing me?"

"You bet," she said. "This is good stuff."

Terrence put his hand over his heart, pretending to be hurt. "I don't believe you would resort to blackmail."

"I know . . . but it would be so hard not to tell Eric, Dawn, Yvonne . . ."

"Okay, okay," Terrence said, deciding to give in to her demands. As he thought of what he could offer in exchange for her silence, it suddenly came to him. Swimming next to her, he reached for her hands. "I got it."

"I'm all ears," she said. "And it better be good."

"How about this?" he asked, raising her hands to his lips and kissing them. "You keep my secret and I'll give you a two-and-a-half-carat diamond ring set in a platinum band."

All signs of joking left her face as his offer hung in the air. When they had agreed to get back together, she hadn't considered whether they would get reengaged. She thought he might want to take things one step at a time.

"Do we have a deal?" Terrence said, anxiously waiting for her response, holding his breath in anticipation of her answer.

"Yes!" she said, wrapping her arms around him. "We have a deal."

Dawn joined her husband in the study that night with a look of victory on her face.

"What's got you in such a good mood . . . did you win another case today?"

"It's not a case, but I believe it's a win nonetheless," she answered, kissing him on the cheek. "Have you heard from Terrence?"

Eric set down his book. "No. And I'm not sure if that's a good thing or a bad thing. I can't believe I let you talk me into taking part in your devious scheme."

"Yeah, yeah, yeah," she said teasingly. "But you have to admit, it was a brilliant plan."

"Brilliant or psychotic depending on how you look at it."

Dawn did a little dance around his desk, humming. "However you want to classify it—it worked. Jasmine was pretty pissed when she left a message on my voice mail, but since then I haven't heard from her. That means they are too busy enjoying their reconciliation on the island of paradise."

Eric watched her celebration and decided to burst her little scheming bubble. "Why doesn't it mean that they haven't reconciled and are so angry with you that they haven't called because they can't stand the thought of talking to you?"

Dawn stopped her dance to consider his take on the situation. "No," she stated confidently. But the more she thought about it, the more her confidence wavered. "How could they not get back together? They're on an island in the Caribbean. Beautiful sunrises. Warm weather. The lure of the ocean. You can't help but fall in love when you're there."

"If you say so," he said, turning his attention back to his book.

"You think I should call her?" Dawn asked, plopping into a chair, all the enthusiasm she had felt moments before evaporating.

"You think?" he said sarcastically, putting his book back on the shelf. He could tell by the direction of this conversation that he wouldn't get any more reading done this evening.

Checking her watch, she saw it was almost eight o'clock, which meant almost eleven in the islands. Worried that she may have made things worse instead of better, she decided to call her friend back tomorrow.

"I'm curious," Eric started. "How in the world did you get that house on such short notice? The Caribbean is usually sold out this time of year."

"I didn't," she confessed. "I was working with a client last week who unexpectedly had a death in the family. He usually takes his wife and kids to the house during this week, but decided to stay in town for the funeral. I caught him just in time. He was about to call a colleague to see if his family wanted to use the house."

Eric didn't see anything wrong with that story, so he asked her why she lied to Jasmine about it belonging to his parents.

"Are you kidding me?" Dawn asked in surprise. "You know Jasmine. The minute I said, 'I have this client who, according to his tax return, made 2.3 million dollars last year, who has this house in the Caribbean—one of five houses he has around the world—and he's not using it this year. How about it . . . you want to go?' "

"I see your point," Eric said truthfully. "I just hope this plan of yours works. Otherwise, you've probably damaged your friendship with Jasmine beyond repair."

"Don't worry, Eric," she said, regaining some of her earlier confidence. "Don't you have faith in the power of love?"

Eric laughed at his wife's dreamy look. Nothing gave her greater joy than seeing other people happy. It was one of the things that attracted him to her. "Come here," he said, in a low, seductive voice.

She walked over to his chair and straddled him. "Yes, Mr. Westfield?"

"Let me show you how much I believe in the power of love—our love." He began unbuttoning her blouse, kissing each open space created.

"Uumm," she moaned. "I like the way you use your power!"

The flickering flames of the fireplace illuminated the living room in a romantic glow as Jasmine and Terrence listened to jazz and drank from a bottle of wine. They had returned from their stingray adventure and decided to celebrate their reengagement eating their dinner on the floor, in front of the fireplace. Now, hours after the food was gone, they remained on the floor, talking.

"Do you want to go to New York for Christmas?"

This was a subject that Jasmine had been trying to avoid. What must his family think of her? One minute she was accepting his marriage proposal, and then next minute calling it off, only to once again accept his proposal. Would the warm telephone relationship still be there, or would his family be distant, expecting her to prove herself? "I'm not sure your family would be interested in meeting the person who has wreaked havoc in your life."

Refilling her glass, he said, "I don't think you'll have to worry about that."

Jasmine knew he was probably trying to make her feel better, put her at ease about meeting his family, but she couldn't be fooled so easily. "That's easy for you to say. You aren't the one they'll consider wishy-washy."

Terrence pulled her between his legs and held her close. "They won't feel any different about you, because I didn't tell them about our temporary separation."

Her body stiffened. "Why not?"

"Because I just didn't want to believe that we were over—that the power of our love and commitment wasn't strong enough to work out our problems."

Jasmine tried to make sense of what he was saying. "But I gave you the ring back. We weren't speaking."

"It didn't matter. I held out hope that we would work it out. That way, when we got back together, my family wouldn't know anything had happened."

Jasmine kissed him as a way of saying thank you. "I'm glad we talked things through. I recognize that I need to curtail being so judgmental about people. Sometimes you forget there's more than one way to help. Thank you for reminding me."

He kissed her forehead. "And you made me admit what I knew all along. In my profession, we do make compromises. But those compromises must be examined carefully to make sure that we can live with the decisions we make."

Tonight, they didn't bother to go back into the bedroom. Instead, he laid her back and gently caressed every part of her body. They made love well into the wee hours of the morning, making promises of love and commitment that would last a lifetime.

As the week went by, they continued to explore all the island had to offer. On Wednesday, they toured the wilder side of Antigua, experiencing mangrove swamps, exotic birds, and coral reef snorkeling. Avoiding most of the tourists, they were able to enjoy the beauty of these areas that were off the beaten track.

Thursday, they remained at the house for a Thanksgiving feast of island food, prepared by a local restaurant. They enjoyed the flavorful chicken, rice and peas, and a medley of island vegetables. As they sat down to eat, they both took a moment to share what they were thankful for, including each other.

Friday, they spent the day on a catamaran cruise to the other side of the island. Besides great snorkeling, they were able to indulge in some deep-sea fishing. The entire group, along with the crew, cheered when Terrence caught a snapper—the biggest catch of the day.

On Saturday, they decided to spend their last day hanging out by the pool. Grilling hamburgers, they sat on the patio basking in the afternoon sun.

Having finished their lunch, Terrence motioned toward the pool. With a wicked grin, he stood and removed his tank top. "Ever been skinny-dipping?"

Jasmine quickly looked around as if others would be watching. "Are you crazy?"

When he reached for his waistband, Jasmine stood. "Someone might see."

Terrence turned completely around three times. "Who? There's no one here but us."

Not waiting for a response, he stepped out of his shorts and underwear and ran down the few steps and jumped into the water. "Oh, come on in. The water feels great."

Jasmine walked down to the pool, still not convinced.

Swimming to the edge, he grabbed her ankles.

Trying to step back, she almost fell in. "Boy, are you insane!"

With playful eyes, he said, "In the next few seconds, you're coming into the water. The only thing you need to decide is whether you want to ruin that nice pair of linen shorts you're wearing."

While she thought about it, he gave her ankles a slight tug.

She let out a short scream, but couldn't stop laughing. "Okay, okay."

She crossed her hands and began to pull the bottom of her shirt over her head.

When she heard Terrence humming stripping music, she decided to have a little fun. With her top off, she twirled it around her head before tossing it to the side.

That caused Terrence to whistle and clap his hands, encouraging her to continue with the show. Shaking her hips from side to side, she turned around and slowly eased her shorts past her hips, stepping out of them and kicking them over by her top. For the grand finale, she shed her bra and panties in two quick moves and did a quick shimmy in the buff before jumping in.

For the next couple of hours, they frolicked and laughed like a couple of teenagers. They worked each other into such a sexual frenzy that by the time they got out of the water, they couldn't even make it inside the house. They made love on the patio. It was the only time that week both of them got a sunburn—all over.

The next morning, as they waited to start the boarding process, Jasmine looked around at the people returning from their stay on the island. Couples hugging, kissing, and laughing. Newlyweds carrying souvenirs of their honeymoon. And Jasmine, resting in the arms of her man.

"You all right?" Terrence asked, noticing the far-off look in her eyes.

What a difference a week could make. She had flown down feeling melancholy as she watched other couples embrace affectionately. Now she was a part of that group. Part of a couple. "Perfect," she answered.

Sixteen

Placing the luggage just inside the door, Terrence threw his keys on the table and followed Jasmine into the living room. It had taken a little maneuvering to get them on the same return flight, and Jasmine didn't even balk when he upgraded them both to first class.

Plopping down on the couch, exhausted from a full day of travel, Jasmine kicked off her shoes and leaned her head back with her eyes closed. Even though they gained three hours, she was going to use every second of that time to catch up on some much needed sleep.

Sitting beside her, he rested his arm behind her. "I love vacations, but it's nothing like coming home and sleeping in our own bed."

"Our bed," she said, "I like the sound of that."

"Hey, *mi casa est su casa.*"

Resting in his arms, she opened her eyes. "That's so sweet. And *mi casa—*"

Before she could finish, her eyes caught the glare off the table. Her ring.

Terrence followed her eyes until they rested on the shiny object. "Somebody left that here about a week ago. It's been sitting in the same spot, waiting for the owner to claim it."

When she had walked out on him, he sat on this couch for hours, staring at the ring, wondering how things had gotten so out of control. But he refused to move it. It belonged to her and if anybody was going to move it, it was going to be her.

Picking it up, she fought the tears in her eyes.

"Allow me," he said softly.

He placed it on her ring finger, right where it belonged. "Don't move."

Terrence stood and walked over to the bookshelf. He held out another shiny object to her. "This kinda goes with the 'my house is your house' theme we have going here tonight."

Jasmine handed him her key ring and watched him slide it through the hook. "You know, this means I can come and raid your refrigerator at any time."

"It also means you can stock it any time, too," he joked.

"Touché," she responded, playfully punching him in the arm.

Interrupted by the ringing of her cell phone, she pulled the device off her hip and recognized the number immediately. She turned the phone outward so that he could read the name. "Do you think I've punished her enough?"

Raising his hands, he sidestepped the question. "That's between you and her. I told you to call her four days ago—if for no other reason than to thank her."

Pushing the talk button, she decided to put her friend out of her misery. "Hello?"

"Why haven't you called me back? I've been worried sick," Dawn said, relieved that she'd finally got her on the line.

"I'm sorry, who is this?" Jasmine said politely.

"Don't even try it, girlfriend. I've left three messages at the house and four on your cell phone. You haven't returned one of my calls."

"Oh," Jasmine said, not quite ready to let her off the hook. "This must be the woman who tricked me into taking a vacation. Or maybe it's the woman who lied to me so that she could play more of her matchmaking games. Perhaps it's the woman who pretended to be my friend, to have my best interest at heart, only to stab me in the back."

Dawn couldn't tell whether Jasmine was serious or not and she started to question whether her island getaway had been a good idea. But the thought of setting her friends up on a romantic vacation was just too good to pass up. If what she had done had actually made things worse, she'd have to do something quick to make things right with her friend. "Look, Jas, I just thought that if the two of you could talk you would work it out. You were miserable without Terrence and he was lost without you. The two of you belong together. I was just trying to help things along. I know it was a little extreme, but you know me—I'm kind of an extreme person."

Hearing the panic in her words, Jasmine couldn't let her game continue. "You're lucky your stinky little plan worked."

"What?" Dawn said, catching her breath.

"I said your stupid setup was a success," Jasmine repeated, giving up her attempt at sounding irritated. "Terrence and I are back together."

Dawn did her victory dance as all the doubts she had

harbored a few seconds ago vanished. "I knew it. Eric said it would never work, that you two would kill each other, before coming after me. But once again, Dawn, the matchmaker, has suceeded again."

"Yeah, yeah, yeah," Jasmine answered, rolling her eyes to the ceiling. "One minute ago, you thought your plan turned into a complete disaster."

It was too late. Her confidence had already been restored. "I should open up a business. Do this full-time."

Jasmine became serious. "I hope you realize this could have turned out very bad. What were you going to do if Terrence didn't want to come?"

"I wasn't worried about that," Dawn replied. "If I couldn't get him to fall for the same story you did, I was just going to tell him you were there. As bad as he wanted to talk to you, he would have gotten on that plane without a second thought."

Jasmine nodded in agreement. Thank God for persistent friends. Otherwise, she wouldn't be back with the man she loved. "There's one more thing you should know, Dawn."

"What?" she said, a slight concern in her voice.

"I'm engaged!"

"Hallelujah!"

Jasmine spent the next few minutes giving her a brief synopsis of their trip. When she finished, she had one question. "Tell me. Whose house was that anyway? 'Cause I know it doesn't belong to Eric's family."

Dawn hesitated. Things were going so well, she didn't want to ruin them by letting Jasmine know she had spent her vacation at the home of a Fortune 100 CEO.

"Dawn?"

"It actually belongs to a client of mine. He happened

to mention that his family wasn't using it this year, so when I formulated this plan, I called him to see if it was still available."

Dawn waited for the backlash about rich people and how they spent their money, but to her surprise it never came.

"Cool. Tell him I said thanks." Jasmine probably shocked her friend by forgoing her normal speech about the wastefulness of money she'd give Dawn each time she would tell her something like this. But Jasmine's thinking was starting to change. People had the right to do with their money whatever they pleased.

"That's all you have to say?" Dawn asked, dumbfounded by her response.

"That's it," Jasmine said, trying to conceal a yawn. "Besides, I'm beat. I'll call you tomorrow."

"Okay."

"And, Dawn?"

"Yeah?"

"Don't you ever pull something like this again."

Jasmine's tone told Dawn that she meant it. But that was fine with Dawn. She had been in a constant state of panic the entire time they were in the Caribbean since she hadn't heard from either of them. She never wanted to experience that feeling again. Her days as a matchmaker for Jasmine were over. But of course, that was an easy decision to make, since Jasmine had already found the love of her life. "Don't worry, Jasmine. I won't do this again."

The next morning, the alarm sounded way too soon. Reaching across Terrence, who had yet to stir from the noise, she tried to find the snooze button. As soon as she tapped it, he grabbed her and spun her around until he lay on top of her.

"Where do you think you're going at six o'clock in the morning?"

"I've got to get back to Richmond, change clothes, and be at work by eight-thirty. If I don't leave now, I won't have enough time to make it."

"You wouldn't have to leave this early if your stuff were here."

They both just stared at each other as his words hung in the air.

"What are you saying?" she asked, not wanting to misinterpret.

Terrence couldn't believe he let those words come out of his mouth. Even when he was with Felicia, they maintained separate living spaces. But he liked waking up to Jasmine every morning. After spending every night with her the past seven days, he didn't want to go back to sleeping alone. "Move in with me."

The words seemed like the next logical step, but Jasmine didn't know how to respond. Except for college, she'd always lived in the house she grew up in. With its tree-lined street, small backyard, and friendly neighbors, she never imagined living anywhere else. Even when she had accepted his proposal, she hadn't given any thought to where they would live.

He saw the doubt in her face. "What is it?"

"That house has been a part of me my entire life."

Having come this far, he wasn't going to let a little thing like housing come between them. "No problem. People commute from Richmond into the city every day. I just want to be with you."

Jasmine took note of how easily he changed for her. Then she thought about his and Dawn's assessment of her stubborn ways. Maybe it was time for her to give a little. "No need to rush to any decisions. How about we talk about it over dinner tonight? I'll come over after work. I'll bring clothes."

Terrence nuzzled her neck and slid his hand under her nightgown. "Are you sure you don't have twenty minutes?"

Jasmine arrived at work thirty minutes late. Terrence's request for twenty minutes had turned into forty and she was now trying to make a low-key entrance past the receptionist and into her office. Less than five minutes later, Monica came by.

"Wow. Look at you!"

Jasmine looked down at herself. "What about me?"

"First of all, that suit," Monica said, noting the gray double-breasted outfit with the skirt stopping a couple of inches above the knee. "No offense, but I haven't seen you looking this sharp in . . . well, never."

"You like it?" she asked, doing a quick turn and striking a model's pose. "It was a gift from Dawn two years ago. I guess I just never wore it."

"And that tan," Monica continued. "I can tell you've been lying in the sun. And I'm not even going to mention the hair, Miss Conservative-bob-cut Queen. Cornrows! What has gotten into you?"

Jasmine sat down at her desk and pushed the button to boot up her computer. "I'm sure the office gossip has told you that Marjorie demanded that I go on vacation."

"Yeah, but we were hoping you would go to New York

with your man." Monica tried to hide her disappointment that that obviously wasn't the case. "There's no
sun like the one in New York in November."

"I'll give you credit for half your statement. I didn't
go to New York, but . . ." She let her words trail off as
she flashed her ring.

"Praise the Lord!" Monica shouted.

"Ssshhh!" Jasmine warned, jumping up to shut the
door. "You'll have the whole office in here."

Lowering her voice, Monica gave her a big hug before
Jasmine took a seat. "I'm so happy for you, Jasmine. No
one deserves happiness more than you."

"I was already—"

"I know, I know . . ." Monica interrupted. "I've heard
your 'I'm happy all by myself' speech before. But you
have to admit, you may have been happy, but now you're
happier."

"Okay, I'll give you that much," Jasmine admitted.
What she felt when she was with Terrence wasn't like
any feeling she'd had before. When she awoke, he was
in her thoughts, and when she closed her eyes she
thought of him. During the week that they were apart,
the last emotion Jasmine would use to describe her state
was happy. "But enough talk about me. How was your
holiday?"

Monica took a seat and pulled a letter out of her
pocket. "It was good. I spent time with my family and
had time to think about the direction my life is going."

The seriousness with which she spoke grabbed Jasmine's attention. She stood.

Placing the letter on her desk, Monica sat back and
waited.

Jasmine continued to stare at Monica. "I don't have

to look down and read the words to know that it's a letter of resignation."

"I'm sorry, Jasmine," Monica started. And she was. Working for Jasmine had been a wonderful learning experience. It was the job she couldn't take anymore. "I just can't do this."

"Do what? Monica, talk to me."

"The abuse, the neglect, the pain, the suffering, the babies who need so much, the parents who try so hard. Even when I experienced success, there was another stack of possible failures waiting in folders on my desk."

Handing her the box of Kleenex, Jasmine walked around her desk and sat beside her. "I'm not saying this job is not without its difficult moments, but what we do is important. We protect children, we strengthen and preserve families, and we support the women and men who open up their homes and hearts to care for foster children."

"I know that's what the brochure says, but it's so hard to actually carry out that mission. It seems like there's never a break, never a moment when you can sit back and take a breath. There's always another situation on the horizon."

Monica didn't have to explain what she meant. Jasmine understood every word. "That's because you're looking at the big picture."

"I don't understand."

Jasmine tried to explain the way she viewed her job. "In the business world, they always teach you to look at the big picture, to see what the end product will be. You can't do that here, because until the cycle of abuse and neglect no longer exist, we have no end product," she said.

"In this job, you have to look at one piece of the picture at a time. One child. One placement. One mother off drugs. One father who stops hitting. One restored family unit. One successful adoption. One day at a time. One victory at a time."

"I just don't think I'm strong enough," said Monica, feeling like a failure. "I know I let you down."

Jasmine gave her a hug and offered her words of encouragement. "Oh, that's where you're wrong, Monica. You haven't let me down. I'm extremely proud of you. You have more strength than you know."

"You think so?"

"I know so," she answered with conviction. "I also know your heart. You have a heart to serve. Whatever you decide to do, wherever you go, you'll be helping someone."

"Thanks, Jasmine. And you're right. I will be helping others. I've taken a job at Young Girls, Incorporated. A nonprofit group in Los Angeles."

"Wow," Jasmine said. "Relocating?"

"It's a wonderful opportunity. I'll be managing a program for girls ages fourteen to eighteen. Preparing them for life, whether they want to go to college, get a job, or start their own business. It's an exciting organization that was started four years ago with a donation by Stanley Kensington, the owner of a software development agency. He funds the program with a million-dollar grant each year."

The small smile that touched Jasmine's lips was not only in response to Monica finding a job that would make her happy, it also reminded her of Terrence's comments when they had broken up. *"Someone needs to buy the soup, pay for the camp, upgrade the computers."* Thank you, Stanley Kensington.

"So when's the big day?" Jasmine asked.

"I've already started turning my cases over to Brenda to handle while you search for a replacement. My last day will be in two weeks. I'll spend the holidays moving to L.A., and then I'll start the first of the year."

"I'm gonna miss you, girl," Jasmine said, not stopping the lone tear from falling down her cheek.

"Ditto. You've been a great mentor and role model for me."

"And you've helped me, too," Jasmine confessed.

Monica leaned back in surprise. "Me? How?"

"Before I left for vacation, I felt overwhelmed with this job. I, too, was starting to feel like I was fighting a losing battle. You are absolutely right, the minute you finish with one case, two more are waiting to take its place. But what I just shared with you about what we do was spoken from my heart, not a brochure. I truly believe in those words, and telling them to you today reminded of why I do what I do."

"Then we've both given each other something to cherish," Monica stated.

Standing, Jasmine cleared her throat to keep her swelling emotions at bay. "Have you told Marjorie yet?"

"No, I wanted to let you know first."

"If you don't mind, I can let her know. I have a meeting with her in a hour to get a status report on what happened during my time off."

"Sure, just let her know. I'll stop by later to talk with her."

Marjorie set aside her paperwork when Jasmine walked into her office. Jasmine didn't have to say one word for Marjorie to know that her time away from the office had been good for her. She had a glow that not even that golden tan could create. Her light was shining from the inside, and in their line of work that light needed to stay bright. "I heard you were back in the office. Rejuvenated, refreshed, tan, and engaged."

"Doesn't take long does it?" Jasmine said, referring to the rumor mill.

"Not when it's good news." Motioning for her to take a seat, Marjorie took note of the stylish suit, another indication that she was feeling much better.

"First, let me thank you for making me take that time off. I didn't realize how badly I needed it until today." Jasmine opened her portfolio and started to write. "But now that I'm back, I'm ready to work."

They spent the next hour reviewing caseloads and discussing staffing and a new program designed to give special attention to young adults leaving their foster families and moving out on their own for the first time. It was during the discussion of the last topic that Jasmine told Marjorie of Monica's decision.

"And what did you say to her to help her change her mind?" Marjorie asked.

"Nothing."

Marjorie removed her glasses. "That's not like you."

"What do you mean?"

"Every time a social worker wants to leave, you give your speech about fighting for the little person, helping those in need, not letting the underdog down."

Her boss was right. Jasmine said those words so many times to so many people that it could be classified as the Jasmine Larson guilt-you-into-staying speech. But she realized making others feel guilty wasn't the answer. "I'm through giving that speech."

Leaning back in her chair, Marjorie waited for an explanation.

"I've probably given that speech to ten social workers over the years, and all of them changed their minds and stayed. But where are they now? Gone." She remembered Ola, Colette, Spencer, Larry, and all the others who'd turned in their notice, ready to move on, only to have Jasmine convince them to stay. However, it was only a matter a time before those same people were, once again, preparing to quit. They moved on anyway. "I've come to realize that this job isn't for everyone, and if anyone chooses to go, it's not because they are giving up, selling out, or have stopped caring. It's simply because this wasn't the job for them."

Marjorie hesitated with her next words, and hoped Jasmine would accept them. "I don't know how to say this without it sounding condescending, so I'll hope you hear my heart in this."

Jasmine waited.

"I'm very proud of you."

Jasmine nodded her head in understanding. She was proud of herself, too.

Eric stopped reading when he heard the knock on his door.

"You need to learn how to control your wife," Terrence said, trying to sound mad and irritated.

"Hey, man," Eric said, holding his hands up in defeat. "Don't you know that's the secret to a successful marriage—let the woman do whatever she wants?"

Terrence leaned against the door and crossed his arms at his chest. "I have to be honest with you, man. The moment that door opened and I saw Jasmine on the other side, I didn't know whether I wanted to wring your wife's neck or buy her dinner."

"Well, from what I've heard, you should be leaning toward the dinner," Eric said.

Terrence stepped into the office and sat. Having no meetings with clients scheduled for the day, he was dressed down in slacks and a button-down dress shirt. "Remind me to get your wife an amazing Christmas gift."

Eric set his files aside, glad to see his friend happy again. "It's great that you and Jasmine were able to work things out. I've known both of you quite a while and you are both happier together than you've ever been apart."

"Then I guess there won't be a problem for you to stand beside me as my best man."

Eric rose out of his chair and gave his friend a quick hug. "Congratulations, man. It's great that the wedding's back on."

"We had a long talk in Antigua, and we finally reached an understanding, and we've learned to respect each other's opinions."

"And Richard? How did he take the news that you weren't taking his daughter's case? Did he follow through on his threat to pull his business?" Eric hated asking the question, because Terrence would have a lot of explaining to do if this client suddenly went away.

Terrence shifted uncomfortably. "I'm still looking into it."

"Are you saying you may still take it on?" Eric said, unable to hide his surprise. "Isn't Jasmine under the impression that you turned down this case?"

"I never told her that. I told her that I wouldn't let money make me make bad choices."

Eric thought of his conversation with Dawn last night. It was clear that Jasmine thought that Terrence had decided not to take this case. "What are you saying?"

Terrence thought back to that walk on the beach and realized that she may very well have assumed that he would not be representing Chelsea in this matter. "I'm saying I'm still looking into it. I'm waiting on some more information before I make a final decision."

"And what if that information tells you not to take it? What are you going to do?"

"Tell me something, Eric," Terrence said thoughtfully. "What would you do?"

Eric had hoped to avoid having to answer that question, but he understood why Terrence would ask. Situations like this were common in their field of work, and every day people in their positions made decisions, based not on what was black or white but rather gray.

Eric's partnership vote was coming up and he couldn't imagine not doing everything he could to hold on to a major client. The ramifications to someone's career over something like this could be brutal if it weren't handled correctly. "Everyone deserves legal representation. If that's what Richard is asking for, then, as a lawyer, you have the right to give that to him."

Terrence read right through his convoluted answer. "You're saying you'd take the case."

Deciding to give the straight answer, he said, "I'd take the case."

Walking to the door, Terrence thought about his next move. "Thanks, Eric. I'll catch up with you later."

Seventeen

Wednesday, Jasmine used her key and entered Terrence's loft around six o'clock. He was working late, so she decided to treat him to a special dinner. Unpacking the ingredients from her bag of groceries, she combined herbs and spices to create a tasty marinating sauce and poured it over the chicken. Placing the covered pan in the refrigerator, she headed for the bedroom to change clothes.

Stepping into the closet, she hung up the suit that she'd worn that day, along with some clothes she'd brought from home for the rest of the week. Setting her shoes on the floor beside his, she put on a pair of stretch pants and a jersey top. It felt like home.

An hour later, Terrence opened his door and froze. He'd never been greeted by the smell of food before—or loud music. "Jas?"

Stepping into the kitchen, he leaned against the doorjamb and watched her cooking something on the stove, with her back to him.

"I'm every woman, it's all in me . . . anything you want done, baby, I'll do it naturally. Whoa, whoa, whoa . . ."

With her feet moving and her hips swaying from side to side, Terrence enjoyed the free show for a few minutes before breaking into applause.

Startled, Jasmine jumped. When she saw him, her face turned a deep red as she turned down the music. "I didn't hear you come in."

"Don't stop on my account," he said, imitating her dance moves. "A piano player and singer! I didn't know I was marrying a woman with so many talents."

"Very funny . . . you're also marrying a woman who spent the last hour and a half in this kitchen. So I hope you're hungry."

Moving toward her, he placed a kiss on her lips and squeezed her backside. "Definitely hungry, just not necessarily for food."

Slapping him away, she turned to stir her green beans. "Food first . . . dessert later."

Removing his jacket and tie, Terrence headed to the bedroom. Walking into his closet, he hung his suit jacket up beside her clothes. They had decided to put off moving in with each other until after the wedding, but he was glad she opted to bring some items to his place.

As they sat enjoying their candlelight dinner, Terrence cleared his throat. He'd looked at the situation carefully, reviewed the information, and finally come to a decision about the Montagues. "There's something I need to talk to you about."

Jasmine didn't like his tone and put her fork down, giving him her full attention. The sinking feeling in her stomach prompted her to stand, but she forced herself to remain in her seat.

"I spoke with Richard Montague today."

If Richard decided to pull his business because he passed on his daughter's case, Jasmine wanted to be as supportive as possible.

He paused several seconds before speaking. "I wanted to talk to you about his daughter's case."

The hesitation could only mean one thing, but she remained silent. Let him say the words to her face.

"I'll be flying to New York tomorrow night for the hearing on Friday. I'll be coming back that night."

Jasmine pushed her plate away from her, suddenly losing her appetite. Silently, she counted to ten. A second ago, she had no doubt that this was what he was going to tell her, but she still let the words linger in the air, just in case this was a joke.

Terrence had braced himself for this conversation. He'd rehearsed his words over and over again, hoping to say them in a way that wouldn't lead to an argument. Judging from her initial reaction, he didn't succeed. In Antigua, they had agreed to respect each other's professional choices. If there was ever a time that promise would be tested, this was it.

Pushing back her chair, she stood. "I'm waiting for the punch line."

When he failed to speak, Jasmine headed for the living room without say another word.

He followed her, watching her pick up her coat and keys. "Where are you going?"

"Home."

"Jas, I thought we agreed to talk our disagreements out."

"And I thought you said you weren't taking that case."

Terrence remembered his words in Antigua. "What I

said was that you were right in saying that I let the money influence my initial decision."

"Is this some kind of joke?" she yelled. "That's the best you can do? What happened to your 'no games' rule? You're just playing with words. You knew exactly what you led me to believe by telling me that."

"I never said I wasn't going to take this case." Taking a deep breath, Terrence continued. "I didn't want to say anything to you until I knew for sure. When we were on the island, I didn't know."

"And what changed between last week and this week?"

"I did what you recommended, Jas," he said, reaching out for her. "You gave me some things to think about and I took your advice."

Jasmine raised her brow in curiosity.

"Richard made arrangements for Chelsea to fly out here so that we could talk. She told me about her problems and how she was going to beat them this time. The rehabilitation program she participated in had been a success and she's gotten great feedback from her supervisor. Already enrolled in college classes, she showed me her acceptance letter and her registration receipt."

Jasmine had to admit, she was impressed with the lengths he went to, but that didn't change the fact that he had led her to believe one thing when he ultimately did another.

"She seems to have pulled it all together," Terrence said.

"And what about the social worker?"

Terrence blew out a heavy breath. That had been his wild card, the information he'd been waiting on before he made a final decision. He'd gotten a call from her today.

"Terrence?"

"Laura Kemp is the social worker and I've spoken to her twice."

She could tell he was stalling for time, which only meant one thing. "What did Ms. Kemp say?"

"She's going to recommend that Hayley stay in foster care and that they have another hearing in three months, to make sure Chelsea stays on track with her recovery."

Picking up her keys and purse, she headed for the door.

Before she could open it, he caught up with her and blocked her exit.

She tried to move him out the way. "What the hell do you think you're doing?"

"You're not running away again," he said. "We made an agreement. No more running out at the first sign of trouble."

"I'm not *running* away," she pointed out angrily. "I'm *walking* away—from a liar."

"I can't win with you, can I?" Terrence said, throwing his hands up in frustration. "First you ream me because I accept this case without checking into the facts. Now that I've checked into the facts, you accuse me of lying."

"You didn't tell me the whole story in Antigua."

"Because I didn't know the whole story," he said. "I didn't talk to the social worker until today. I didn't want to tell you anything either way until I definitely knew what my decision would be."

"A lot of good that did," Jasmine said sarcastically. "You're fighting against what the social worker is recommending."

Taking a moment to gather his thoughts, Terrence wanted to calm down. The last thing he wanted this to turn into was a shouting match. "I understand her concern, Jas, but I talked to Chelsea. She's changed. She's ready to be a responsible adult. She'll be staying with Richard, so Hayley will have her grandfather and his staff around to help take care of her."

"That's just great," she huffed. "Richard and his millions of dollars will make everything all right."

Her sarcasm grated on his nerves and that's when it hit him. "You wouldn't want me to take this case regardless of what the social worker thought."

Jasmine refused to acknowledge his statement or look him in the eye, and that was when Terrence knew he was on to something.

"That's what this is about," he said, finally opening his eyes to the entire picture. "It's about your personal hang-ups when people with money and power get what they want, regardless of the issue. God Himself could speak right now to give that baby back to her mother and you would still be against it."

"That's asinine," she answered, a little too quickly. "The social worker recommends—"

"Are you telling me a social worker is never wrong? That they never make a bad call?"

Jasmine didn't answer right away, because the answer wouldn't have helped her position at all.

"Laura told me that she had met with Chelsea twice. That's only one more time than me. Now, I'm not telling her how to do her job, I'm just saying that in this situation I believe that Chelsea is able to take care of her child and keep her safe."

Jasmine's emotions were running at an all-time high. Over the years, she thought of the hundreds of recommendations that she'd made. The times she thought the parent needed more time and the judge sent the child back to the home, and they went on to become a successful family unit. That was just one example.

Terrence watched her body relax and a glimmer of hope passed through him that she was finally considering all that he had said. He reached out for her. "Are you going to respect my professional choice?"

On Monday morning Jasmine waited anxiously by the phone. Terrence had returned from New York late Friday night, saying the hearing went well and that the judge would give his decision that Monday. He explained to Jasmine that he told the judge that Chelsea appeared to have put her life back on the right track. With a full-time job, almost four months clean and counting, and a promise from her father that she could live in his house, where other supervision for the child would be provided, he thought the judge appeared to be receptive to the idea of giving the young mother another chance.

While Jasmine agreed to respect his professional choice, it hadn't been easy. She struggled to reconcile her personal feelings with his professional actions. Logically, what he said made sense. Chelsea deserved to have her side of the story told and he just happened to be the one to do it. The money, power, influence, and lifestyle that Richard Montague had didn't matter. As she came to understand and accept this, their relationship ultimately reached a deeper level. Finally, she was able to live up to her end of the agreement they had made in Antigua.

When her phone rang, she took a deep breath. "Jasmine Larson."

"Jasmine, it's Linda. I have great news."

Jasmine relaxed. It wasn't Terrence with news about Chelsea, it was her real estate agent.

After much consideration, she'd decided to put her house on the market. Setting their wedding for Valentine's Day, she had a little less than two months to find a buyer.

"I have an offer for your house."

Jasmine couldn't have heard her correctly. "How is that possible? I just put it on the market three days ago."

"That wasn't the response I was expecting," said Linda. Her clients were typically bubbling over with joy when she made a sale that fast, but Jasmine seemed a tad disappointed. "With the outrageous prices of homes in the city, Richmond is fast becoming a prime location for people looking for a nice house without the city price tag. And," she continued, barely able to contain her excitement, "they're offering asking price. Because your house is paid off, I don't need to tell you how much cash that's going to put in your pocket . . . and mine!"

Things seemed to be moving too fast for Jasmine. In a matter of a month she'd gotten engaged, broken it off, had doubts about her career, gone on vacation, gotten reengaged, and recommitted herself to her work; and now, in less than three days, she had an offer for a house that had been a part of her life for thirty years. She needed a moment to catch her breath.

"Jasmine, is everything okay?" Now Linda was concerned. Was Jasmine contemplating pulling her house off the market? "I thought this would be great news."

Jasmine must have sounded like a complete moron. What sane person wouldn't be ecstatic that her house was selling right away, especially that it also sold for the asking price? "It is great news." Still not sounding over-joyed, she seemed better than a few seconds ago.

"I'm sending over the contracts to the buyer tomorrow. I'll be in touch to let you know when the financing is finalized."

"Don't forget my stipulation," Jasmine reminded her.

"I know," Linda said, "you don't want to close until February."

Jasmine thanked Linda and hung up the phone. Her stomach swirled with fear and excitement. It was really happening. She was on her way to becoming Mrs. Jasmine McKinley.

About twenty minutes later, the receptionist buzzed, letting her know she had a visitor. As she approached the lobby area, she heard a commotion. Going to investigate, she found Monica, Marjorie, and several other women in her office gathered around someone—a very handsome someone.

"Hey, Jasmine. You told us your man was good-looking, but your description didn't do him justice," someone said. Turning her attention back to him, she continued. "I asked Jasmine to find out if he had a brother," Monica chimed in.

"I'm sorry to say I don't. But I'm sure if I did," he added, flashing a sexy smile, "he wouldn't have any problems taking out a lovely looking lady like you."

"Oh, handsome and charming," Marjorie added. "He's definitely a keeper."

With Terrence dressed for the corporate world in his dark blue double-breasted suit and power tie, Jasmine had to admit she did have one devilishly cute guy. "Okay, ladies, break it up."

Terrence entered her office and took note of the

rows of pictures lining the wall—babies, toddlers, teenagers, and adults. They were all ages, races, and nationalities. "Are all of these yours?"

"Every last one of them," she said, pride evident in her response.

"All success stories?"

She perused the hundreds of pictures on the wall that had accumulated over the five years she'd been with the agency. Memories of tears, joy, success, and failure passed through her mind as she scanned the faces. It was funny, she could call almost all of them by name—even the ones from five years ago. "Most."

He took his time looking at the pictures and Jasmine had a feeling he wasn't just scanning the faces, he actually saw each person for the individual that he or she was. "What brings you to this part of town on a workday?"

"I met with a client in Oakland and I thought about the fact that I've never seen where you work. I hope this isn't a bad time. If it is, I can come back another time."

Jasmine heard the sincerity in his words and it touched her that he wanted to share this part of her life on an intimate level, not just through their conversations at home. "No, this a perfect time."

Taking a seat, Terrence said, "Tell me about what you do."

For the next hour, Jasmine shared the process and procedures under which they operated. With the questions he asked, she knew that he was listening and had a genuine interest in what she was saying.

When she told him about the phone call from Linda, he practically jumped for joy. He offered to celebrate by taking her to lunch. As they were about to leave, his cell phone rang.

She couldn't get much from his side of the conversation, but she knew it was about Chelsea and Hayley.

When he ended the call, she waited for him to deliver the news.

"They sent Hayley home with her mother."

"I see," she said quietly.

"The judge said that Chelsea is much further along than the last time she left rehab. With the recommendation letter from her supervisor and the fact that she had already enrolled in school, the judge thought that she had shown strength and maturity in getting her life back on track and thought she should begin this holiday season with her daughter at home."

Jasmine grabbed her purse. "I'm glad for them. I really hope things work out."

Terrence listened for any hint of sarcasm or anger in her voice. There was none. "You're really okay with this?"

"Not only am I okay with it, I say this is also a cause for celebration—and lunch is on me."

The rest of the week passed quickly and all too soon they were cutting the sheet cake at Monica's going-away party. Everyone had chipped in and gotten her an electronic organizer as well as a pen set for her new desk.

"I want to thank all of you for making my time here special," Monica said. "I've learned so much that I know will only make me better at my next job. Thank you all for the gifts and I hope this isn't good-bye—but more like 'see you soon.' "

The group applauded her speech as Jasmine made her way to the front. Once she stood in front of the crowd, she gave Monica a quick hug. "You have been such a joy to work with and we will never forget you, and I hope you never forget us."

Reaching behind the table, she pulled out a framed collage of pictures of the children and parents she'd helped in the nine months that she'd been with the agency. There were close to fifty. "Always remember, Monica—you made a difference in their lives. You protected them, strengthened them, and supported them."

After the presentation, there wasn't a dry eye in the house, including Monica's.

Later that afternoon, Jasmine helped Monica take her personal items to her car. Jasmine pointed to her electronic organizer. "You better mark February fourteenth on your calendar."

"You don't have to worry about that," Monica joked. "I'm going to take my seat in the front row."

"The front row is nice, but I was actually hoping you would not sit at all," Jasmine answered. "I'd rather have you standing beside me."

"Are you serious?" Monica said, realizing what she was asking.

"Yes, I want you to be a bridesmaid."

"I would be honored."

For the third time that day, they gave each other a hug, hoping they wouldn't cry—again.

Eighteen

If the handkerchief she was holding were made of paper, it would have been shredded into pieces by now. It was one of the visible signs that Jasmine was extremely nervous.

The plane had landed an hour ago and now they rode in the back of a black town car, making their way to Long Island. Terrence had slept most of the five-hour flight, but Jasmine had found it difficult to keep her eyes closed for more than a few minutes. Smoothing out her slacks, she stared out the window.

"Why are you so nervous?" Terrence asked, trying to reassure her. "I told you, you have nothing to worry about."

"Haven't all your girlfriends been nervous when they met your family?" Jasmine asked, refusing to believe she was the only one that acted this way.

That was an easy one to answer for Terrence. "Only one of my girlfriends has met my family. But you're not a girlfriend, you're my soon-to-be wife." Kissing her hand, he hoped to put her at ease. "Don't worry, they're going to love you."

The car pulled into the driveway of a white colonial single-family home with several cars parked in the driveway and on the street. Terrence took note of the number of vehicles and tried to figure out a way to break the news to Jasmine. If she was nervous at the idea of meeting his parents, this situation might send her into cardiac arrest.

"Promise me you'll stay calm," he said, stroking her hand. "It appears there are a few more people here besides my parents."

Jasmine had already counted the cars. Even if only one person came in each car, it was more than she thought she could handle.

"You don't say," she said, trying to make light of the situation.

"Just ten or fifteen—but definitely no more than twenty."

Inhaling deeply, she didn't think she could get any more worked up than she already was. Opening her compact, she checked her hair and makeup one last time. The deep burgundy color of her lipstick matched the fitted sweater. Her black wool pants with black boots were a perfect complement, and fit the cold Northeast weather. Snapping the case shut, she smiled. "I'm ready."

Before all of their bags could be unloaded from the trunk, the front door opened and a young woman came running out, arms wide open. Jasmine didn't need an introduction. Yvonne.

"Terry," she yelled as she ran up to him.

"Terry?" Jasmine mouthed to him with a smile.

Giving him a bear hug, it was obvious she really missed her big brother. Standing back from him, she patted his stomach. "You look bigger. Somebody must be feeding you good. And I bet I know who that is."

Yvonne turned to Jasmine and gave her a smile so genuine it reached her eyes.

Terrence made the introductions. "Yvonne, I'd like you to meet—"

"Oh, please, Terry, we don't need all that," Yvonne said, before focusing her attention on Jasmine. "It's good to finally meet you, Jasmine."

Yvonne hugged her and, giving her an extra squeeze, whispered in her ear, "Don't worry. You'll be fine."

And just like that, most of Jasmine's nervousness disappeared.

"Now, let me see that rock," Yvonne said, glancing down at her left hand.

Holding her hand up, Yvonne turned it from side to side. "Not bad, big brother, not bad at all."

Reaching down for one of the bags, she started up the steps. "Come on in. Everyone is waiting."

The crowd was thick when all three of them entered the house and Jasmine felt like the main object on display. But her feelings of discomfort disappeared when the warmth of his family enveloped her. An older woman approached them first.

"It's nice to meet you, Aunt Gracie," Jasmine said before anyone else said a word.

Terrence and the woman stared at her.

"The photo album," she explained to them. "I remembered your picture from Terrence's album."

Impressed, Aunt Gracie embraced her. "It's nice to meet you, Jasmine. Terrence has told us a lot about you."

Taking a step back, Jasmine turned full circle. "Well . . .?"

Confused, Aunt Gracie looked at her nephew. "Well what?"

"What do you think? Rumor has it that you like to say exactly what's on your mind. So give it to me straight. What's your first impression?"

Aunt Gracie and Terrence laughed at the reference to her infamous brutal honesty.

Aunt Gracie put her hand under her chin as if in deep thought, taking a moment to concentrate. "Turn around again."

Jasmine obeyed but began to wonder if she'd bitten off more than she could chew. Could she handle Aunt Gracie's response?

"You're a little thin around the hips. How you gonna carry babies? And you should cut your hair. Short is sassy. Live it up a little. You're still young."

Jasmine took her advice with a smile as Aunt Gracie turned to walk away. But she quickly turned back to face Jasmine. "One more thing, I hope you ain't giving it up to my boy without a marriage license."

"Uh, that's enough honesty for today, Auntie," Terrence chimed in.

She gave Jasmine one quick wink of approval before she headed back to the kitchen to help prepare dinner.

Moving through the living room, they came upon an older man sipping on a beer.

"So this is the woman that got us all over here on this cold December day," he said, giving Terrence a pat on the back.

Terrence placed her hand on the small of her back. "Jasmine, I'd like you to meet—"

"Uncle Raymond," Jasmine said without missing a beat. "The sculpture you sent Terrence looks perfect in his home. I've even had my friend inquire about the artist. She may want to commission a piece from you."

Terrence thought he actually saw his uncle blush.

"That's so nice of you, Jasmine. Tell your friend I'll give her a good price just for knowing you."

They made their way to the back of the house and Jasmine spotted them before Terrence did—his parents. Swallowing hard, she tried not to fidget.

"Terrence!"

His mother came over first, giving her only son a hug from the heart. She looked just like her picture. She was about five feet four, and her petite frame and designer jeans and top made her look much younger than someone in their sixties.

When she stepped away from Terrence and held out her arms, Jasmine stepped right into them. It had been so long since she'd felt the hug of a mother and her emotions threatened to overtake her. They held each other for a long moment before Jasmine felt composed enough to step back. The drops of water formed in her eyes, but they didn't fall.

Squeezing her hands, Mrs. McKinley nodded in approval. "Welcome to the family."

Terrence's father joined them and gave her a sincere hug as well. And while he wasn't as talkative as everyone else, he made Jasmine feel a part of the family just the same.

Throughout the evening, Jasmine met so many relatives, including Terrence's niece and nephew, who thanked their uncle a hundred times for the T-shirts and key chains. There were also a few cousins, another aunt, and two more uncles.

"You hanging in there?"

Jasmine turned to the voice and smiled. "I'm doing okay."

"Let's take a breather."

Jasmine agreed and followed Yvonne upstairs. They entered the bedroom and Jasmine knew it must have been hers before she went to college. It still had a teenager's feel with posters of hip-hop groups and singers, cheer-leading certificates, and pom-poms hanging on the wall and pictures of football games, car washes, and proms.

They both sat on the bed and Jasmine relished the moment of peace.

"Terrence is a very special guy," Yvonne said.

Something in her voice told Jasmine that she wasn't just making friendly conversation. "Yes, he's wonderful."

"He's honest, loyal, and would never intentionally hurt anyone."

Deciding to cut to the chase, Jasmine went on the offensive. "It's obvious you didn't bring me up here to catch my breath, so why don't you just say whatever is on your mind?"

Yvonne smiled at her direct approach. "I don't know what happened between you two over Thanksgiving, and Terrence isn't talking. However, I do know that for that period of time my brother was miserable. He missed coming home to see his family, and even though he tried to cover it up, he sounded like he'd lost his best friend. And if you two were having problems, and that was what happened, then he lost his best friend."

Jasmine didn't know whether to be offended or touched that she was sticking her nose in her relationship.

"I just want you to know that I've never known my brother to be as happy in life as he has been since you came into it. Relationships aren't easy. I'm younger, but

I've been married six years and I can tell you, it takes work."

"Amen to that," Jasmine said, knowing the work she and Terrence had already put in before even saying "I do."

"And it's worth it, Jasmine. It really is. When you love someone—the hard work, the compromises, the give and the take, it's all worth it."

They rejoined the group downstairs and Jasmine spotted Terrence in the corner showing Marcus how to operate a remote-controlled car. As she watched him, Yvonne's words came back to her, and Jasmine knew she was right. He was definitely worth the work.

Later that evening, Jasmine helped Mrs. McKinley clean the kitchen.

"I hope you weren't too overwhelmed by meeting everyone. But they've waited a long time for Terrence to find someone to love," Mrs. McKinley said. "They weren't going to be able to hold out until Christmas Day."

"I will admit," Jasmine confessed. "I was extremely nervous, but you have a wonderful family. You've all made me feel very welcome."

When the last dish had been put away, Mrs. McKinley escorted Jasmine upstairs. "I know you must be tired, so instead of waiting for Terrence to get back from taking Gracie home, I can go ahead and take you to your room."

Walking down the hall, they stopped at the second door on the right. "You can sleep in Terrence's room. Terrence will be sleeping in the basement."

Jasmine couldn't help but smile at the arrangement.

Mrs. McKinley leaned in closer and gently touched her arm. "You two can do what you want on the West Coast, but on the East Coast—no marriage, no sharing."

Jasmine could only nod, hoping her embarrassment at having this conversation didn't show on her face. "Don't worry. The arrangements you made are fine."

"Good," she said, giving her a kiss on the cheek. "I'll see you in the morning."

Fifteen minutes later, Terrence knocked on her door. "This is a joke, right?"

You would have thought she had just asked Terrence for one of his kidneys the way he reacted to the news that they would not be sharing a bed.

"But we're going to be here a week," he said, trying to keep his voice low, so as not to wake his parents.

"I know," Jasmine said, seemingly unfazed by their sleeping situation.

"Seven whole days," he said, wondering if she fully comprehended what that meant.

"I think that's what a week is," she said, trying to hold in her laugh.

"You think this is funny, don't you?" he said, trying to work his way into the room.

"No," she said, pushing him out of her room. "I think it's sweet."

Terrence checked the hall before rubbing his body against hers. "Maybe we can get away tomorrow for a little afternoon delight."

"Oh, you are one naughty boy," she said, pushing him back off of her. The last thing she wanted was for his parents to catch them in a compromising position.

"Only if you let me be."

"Oh, I'll definitely let you," she teased. "In seven days."

"You sure do know how to torture a brother."

"Good night, Terrence." Giving him a kiss on the cheek, she stepped into the bedroom and shut the door.

* * *

As the week progressed, Jasmine experienced Christmas like she never had before. Just as she had played tour guide for Terrence, he was returning the favor. When she mentioned all of the places she wanted to visit, he laughed, just as she had done to him. Everything on her list was considered a tourist trap. But she didn't care, just as he hadn't.

They started with visiting Rockefeller Center and the giant Christmas tree. She even convinced him to go ice-skating in the rink just below it. As neither one of them had ever been on ice skates, to say it was an adventure was an understatement. Their bodies hit the ice so much, little kids began to take pity on them, showing them how to stand, stop, and make a simple turn. When they got home, every part of their bodies ached. But a hot bath and two cups of his mom's homemade hot chocolate helped them get ready for day two.

Terrence hadn't done any of his shopping, so they spent the day going from store to store in Manhattan. Starting at Macy's, they walked up Fifth Avenue to Lord & Taylor and on to Saks. Jasmine couldn't get over the elaborate decorations. It would take her at least fifteen minutes just to enter a store because she was too busy gazing at the window displays. It was unlike anything she'd ever seen before. With themes such as "Santaland" and "Muppets take Manhattan," she could understand why these streets remained crowded during the holiday season.

They also had a chance to view the Statue of Liberty, Radio City Music Hall, the Apollo Theater, and Ground Zero, where the World Trade towers once stood. And even though the temperatures hovered around freezing, Jasmine didn't mind at all. She even bought a few T-shirts and key chains of her own to take back to some of her children.

On Christmas Eve, Jasmine spent the day with Yvonne and her mom, preparing food for Christmas dinner. Jasmine thought of the many years she'd done this same thing with her mother. Stuffing a turkey, rolling dough for the crust of her mouthwatering sweet potato pie, and peeling potatoes to cut up for potato salad. Because her relatives were distant, both geographically and emotionally, it was usually just the three of them. This was the first time she'd celebrated a holiday with so many people, and she loved every minute of it.

Once Terrence's parents had retired for the evening, Jasmine sat in the living room drinking a cup of tea and watching the lights dance on the Christmas tree. The last-minute person that he was, Terrence had been upstairs wrapping gifts.

After a while, Terrence came rushing in and grabbed Jasmine by the arm, nearly causing her to spill her drink. "Come with me."

"What . . . the . . ."

He led her through the kitchen and out the back door.

"Oh my God," Jasmine exclaimed.

"Isn't it beautiful, peaceful?"

A steady flow of snowflakes floated from the sky.

"It's 12:07, which means it is officially Christmas Day," Terrence said, reaching into his pocket to reveal a long, wrapped box. Handing it to her, he asked her to open it.

"Shouldn't we wait until tomorrow?"

"It's already tomorrow, remember?"

Jasmine saw the excitement in his eyes and started to

tear at the gold wrapping paper. Holding a velvet box, she lifted the lid and gasped. The gold charm bracelet was exquisite. With a piano, music note, heart, and gavel hanging from it, he'd included all the things that were a part of her life. "I love it, Terrence. And I love you."

At four o'clock sharp the entire McKinley clan sat down to Christmas dinner. Delaney and Marcus, Terrence's niece and nephew, talked nonstop about what Santa Claus bought them, while the men talked football. They had exchanged gifts earlier in the day and Jasmine thanked Mrs. McKinley for the lovely silk scarf and Yvonne for the wedding planning memory book.

Jasmine was pleased that her gifts went over well. Both Yvonne and Mrs. McKinley couldn't wait to use their gift certificates for a day at the spa. Terrence and Jasmine had shopped together for Delaney and Marcus, giving them each a set of clothes, two books, and two toys.

After dinner, everyone gathered in the living room enjoying Troy's special eggnog. Yvonne warned everyone that her husband's concoction wasn't for the faint of heart. And when Jasmine reasoned that if she could smell the liquor before he handed her a cup, she knew Yvonne was right.

"How's that arthritis, Gracie?" Uncle Raymond asked. "Are you going to be able to play that piano so we can sing Christmas carols?"

Gracie stretched her fingers. "Sorry, Ray. Not this year."

Jasmine turned to Terrence to plead with him not to, but it was too late. His mouth was already moving.

"No need to fear—my Jasmine is here. She can play

better than anyone I know," he said, before he glanced at his aunt. "Present company excluded."

With a little prodding, Jasmine sat at the keys and waited for the first selection.

"How about 'The First Noel'?"

Jasmine played a few notes and soon everyone was singing. They went through "Jingle Bells," "Joy to the World," and at least four other songs before they decided to break for dessert.

As she enjoyed her pineapple upside-down cake, Jasmine couldn't help but feel she finally had a family again.

Nineteen

Recovering from the late night with the McKinleys and Troy's special eggnog, Jasmine wasn't surprised when she rolled over and it was almost eleven o'clock. Most of the family was probably already up and would have eaten breakfast, which suited her just fine. The amount of calories she'd consumed this week had to equal at least ten pounds.

Getting out of bed, she gathered up her toiletries and headed for the bathroom.

Just as she was going down the hall, Terrence's hurried steps rushed toward her. "I'm glad you're up."

Something in his tone told her something wasn't right. Walking back into the bedroom, he shut the door behind them. "You might want to sit down."

All the warning bells went off in her head. "I'll stand."

"I just got a call from Richard. Hayley's been taken to the emergency room. She took a bad fall and they're trying to determine how bad it is. She's been in and out of consciousness since the paramedics picked her up.

The attending physician, of course, called social services. Richard knew I was in town visiting family and he's asked me to come to the hospital. Will you come with me?"

Jasmine tried to hold her anger in check as the blood rushed to her head. Flashes of the children who'd been sent back to a home too soon came vividly to her mind. Especially Candice. "No, it will take me a while to get ready, why don't you go ahead?"

The judgmental tone in her voice left little room for interpretation. Terrence didn't need to guess how she felt or whom she was blaming. "Richard was too shaken up to talk, so I didn't get the details of what happened. Let's not jump to any conclusions."

It wasn't a far jump to make. She could only pray that the child wouldn't be the one to ultimately suffer for the mistakes of adults. "I'll see you when you get back."

"Jasmine . . ." he started. She had already pegged him and his client as the bad guys. How could she do that without having all the facts?

"Go," she said, opening the door for him. "They're waiting on their *lawyer*."

She tried to keep her tone even, but knew she was failing miserably.

He ignored her sarcasm but agreed with her statement. He needed to get there as quickly as possible. Giving her a quick kiss, he tried to ignore the fact that she didn't kiss him back. "I'll be back soon. We can talk then."

Watching him leave, Jasmine fell on the bed, exhausted. What could they possibly have to talk about that would make this situation right?

As she was packing the last of her items in preparation for their trip back to California, almost an hour since

Terrence had left, Jasmine found the social worker's assessment running through her mind. Why didn't Terrence just listen to her—follow her recommendation? She knew why: *one million dollars.*

Chelsea hadn't had violence in her past, but if she was using again, there was no telling what she could have done to that little girl.

Deep in her thoughts, she was startled by the knock at the door. "Come in."

Yvonne came in, taking a seat on the bed. "Packing up, huh?"

Not really in the mood to talk, Jasmine still couldn't be rude to someone who had been so nice to her this past week. "Yep. It's time to head home."

"I hear Terrence had to run out on business this morning," she hedged. Obviously knowing that something was very wrong, Yvonne hoped Jasmine would open up to her. Maybe she could help.

"A little girl lying in a hospital bed is not business." The words spat out before Jasmine could stop them. "Yvonne, I'm sorry. But this really isn't a good time."

"You don't have to tell me what's going on, but it looks like whatever it is is tearing you and your relationship apart."

She was right on that one, but Jasmine didn't say anything else. Sharing details about her relationships had never been her strong suit.

Standing, Yvonne headed for the door. "Our family loves you, Jasmine. Not because we know you so well, but because our brother does. If you need to talk, I'll be around."

The sincerity in her words didn't change the situation. Terrence may have assisted in sending that child back into an environment where she wasn't safe. All in the name of keeping a client. How could she work this out with him? How could she forgive him?

Placing her last bag by the door, she went to search out Mrs. McKinley, but ran into Yvonne in the kitchen.

"I wanted to say good-bye to your mother. Is she around?"

"She took Aunt Gracie to the mall. She's always the first one in line for the after-Christmas sale. That's why she didn't hand out gifts yesterday—she hadn't bought them yet."

Her attempt at humor was appreciated, but failed miserably. "Could you tell her thank you for her wonderful hospitality this week? I really enjoyed myself."

The words didn't sound like they were from someone leaving tomorrow. They were from someone leaving today. "I thought you guys weren't leaving until tomorrow?"

"I was able to change my flight to one leaving today—in two hours. I've already called a car service." Keeping her tone even, she didn't want an emotional scene.

"So, that's it? You're just going to walk on my brother?" Yvonne's voice elevated a notch and she tried to hold her anger in check.

"You don't understand what's going on, Yvonne," she said, hoping to avoid a harsh discussion.

"I don't need to understand," she said through gritted teeth. "All I know is that something is going on that has my brother at a hospital on behalf of an injured girl and you're walking out on him."

"Like I said, you don't understand," Jasmine answered, fighting the guilt.

Yvonne wasn't going to let her off the hook that easy.

"Then make me understand, because you're leaving me to be the one to tell everyone that you're gone."

"I'm not the bad person here."

"And neither is Terrence."

Just then, they heard the front door open. A few moments later, Terrence walked in, obviously seeing the bags by the door.

The tension in the room was thick and he looked from his sister to Jasmine and knew that he had walked into the middle of something. "Could you excuse us, Yvonne?"

Yvonne left the room, leaving the two of them to sort through their problems.

"Going somewhere?" he asked, even though he had guessed the answer. His bags weren't beside hers at the door.

"Yes, back to California," she said, stepping around him to avoid prolonging this conversation.

"Without me?"

"You're needed here," she pointed out.

"So, that's it? After everything we've been through?"

"Terrence, don't do this. You knew what you were getting into when you took this case. So if you want to blame anyone, blame yourself."

"It is not my fault that that little girl is in the hospital."

They heard a knock at the door and Jasmine turned to leave. "That's the car service to take me to the airport. Give my best to the Montagues."

Over the next two weeks Jasmine committed herself fully to her work. She hadn't heard from Terrence and she tried to convince herself that it was for the best.

For the first week, Dawn had been relentless in trying to get her to talk to Terrence, but Jasmine was tired of the merry-go-round her emotions were on when it came to her relationship. A clean break was for the best and she warned Dawn that if she tried any of her matchmaking tricks, that would be the end of the friendship. The seriousness with which she told her must have registered, because Dawn hadn't said one word about Terrence since.

Now she sat in her office, working long hours to make sure what happened to Hayley wouldn't happen to anyone else.

Terrence arrived home from work, exhausted. In the last two weeks, he had probably billed more hours than anyone, working ten- and twelve-hour days right through the rest of the holiday season. More times than he could count, he reached for the phone to call her, but he just couldn't bring himself to do it. He'd given it everything he had and then some. And it just wasn't good enough.

His parents had tried not to pry, but his sister was another story. After several phone calls to check on him, he finally opened up to Yvonne sharing what happened between them. After hearing the story, she still couldn't believe that they couldn't work it out.

Seeing them together over the holidays, Yvonne had thought they were in love. It was evident in the way they smiled at each other, kissed each other, and touched one another. Yvonne refused to believe that they couldn't work things out. Coaxing him to contact her proved fruitless and he warned Yvonne to let it go. He had done the chasing each time there was a problem and his heart just wasn't ready to take another disappointment.

He had decided to come to a new city for a change. To build something different and better than what he had had in New York. And up until last month, no one could have told him that he didn't get exactly that. A job that challenged him and a woman who loved him. But his love obviously wasn't enough for her. Missing her and loving her hadn't diminished over the past few weeks, but he had given all he could.

When he had seen Richard before he left New York, there was no hiding how distraught and preoccupied he was. Noticing the enormous change in Terrence, Richard questioned what the problem was. Terrence, consumed with the situation, shared with Richard why he was no longer engaged to be married.

After realizing his part in his breakup, Richard offered to contact Jasmine and let her know that she couldn't blame Terrence. But Terrence didn't need or want anyone's interference. If she was going to come back to him, she had to do it on her own. Otherwise, it would only take another issue or problem to arise and she would be gone—again.

Tossing his suit jacket across the chair, he headed for the kitchen to fix himself a quick dinner. As he waited for the microwave minutes to count down, he listened to his messages.

Richard's voice was the first one he heard and his words caused Terrence to smile in relief. He reached for the phone to call Jasmine, but after punching in the first two numbers, he hung up. He doubted that this bit of information would fix their problem. Their issues ran much deeper than Hayley Montague.

* * *

Jasmine finished her status report and prepared to e-mail it to Marjorie when the receptionist buzzed her line.

"Yes?"

"Jasmine, Richard Montague is here. He doesn't have an appointment but would like to talk with you if you have a moment."

She had no idea why he would come to see her. She'd never met the man, but her curiosity got the best of her. "Send him in."

Taking a few moments to clear her desk, she stood when he entered.

Dressed for work in a dark gray business suit, he shut the door behind him. "Thank you for seeing me on such short notice."

"No problem. Please, have a seat," she said, motioning him to a chair.

Richard declined her offer of refreshments, preferring to cut straight to the chase. Somehow he thought she would appreciate that. "I understand that my family has caused quite a stir for you."

Jasmine didn't know how to answer that. Had Terrence shared their situation with him? And if so, what exactly did he say?

"Don't blame Terrence for telling me about his personal life. He was so devastated when he prepared to leave New York that I basically forced it out of him."

Sitting stiffly in her chair, she wondered where this conversation was going. "Why are you here, Mr. Montague?"

"Richard," he offered with a friendly smile.

"Why are you here, Richard?" she repeated. The use of his first name didn't make her tone any more inviting.

Leaning forward, he removed his glasses. "To hopefully make right what is obviously very wrong."

"Which is?"

"You and Terrence apart."

Jasmine sat back in her chair. "I'm not sure I want to discuss my personal life with you, regardless of what you may already know."

"That's fair," he said, undeterred. "We don't have to discuss it, but I would like you to listen."

Jasmine nodded and he continued.

"I will admit that when I first asked Terrence to help me with the matter concerning my daughter and granddaughter, I did so because I wanted him to use whatever means were necessary to ensure that my granddaughter came home."

Jasmine wanted to say something, but chose to hear him out.

"If that meant bribing the social worker, then so be it. If that meant smearing the foster parents, I had no problem with that. If it meant making a personal contribution to the judge's bank account, that would have been fine with me. The only thing I was focused on was Hayley. That's why I came to Terrence. With a million dollars on the line, there was no way he could walk away from my request."

Jasmine's expression remained unchanged as he just admitted to being the scumbag she had thought he was the first time Terrence mentioned taking this case.

"And I was right. The minute I mentioned pulling my business, I could see the color drain from his face and his fear of telling the partners he'd lost one of his biggest clients. So when he told me that he would help me out and represent Chelsea, I wasn't surprised."

Richard paused and thought about his next statement and hoped she would finally see the truth. "What did surprise me was the call I got a few days later. He wanted to meet Chelsea, talk to the social worker, and find out for himself what was best for Hayley. I have to tell you, Ms. Larson, that was not a pretty conversation. Words were flying between us that would make a sailor blush. I told him in no uncertain terms that I didn't give a hoot about what the social worker thought, and he shouldn't care either. The only thing he should focus on was the hundred thousand dollars my company sent to his firm on a monthly basis."

Jasmine allowed a slight smile to escape her lips. While she was busy being mad at Terrence, he had been working hard to follow her advice.

"But he wouldn't let it go. He insisted that if he was going to take this case, he had to do it his way. Finally, I consented. When he walked into that hearing and spoke to the judge on behalf of Chelsea, it wasn't because of my threats to move my business. It was because of his belief that Hayley belonged with her mother."

Jasmine listened to everything he said and realized what a fool she had been. With all her talk of professional respect, she realized now that she had never gotten off her high horse. She was still riding high and fast—as if she had all the right answers. And in doing so, it had cost her Terrence.

"Thank you for coming by, Richard. I appreciate your honesty."

Richard had hoped for something a little more. "I know that you haven't spoken to Terrence since you left New York. Do you think that will change?"

"I'm not sure," she answered honestly.

Rising, he prepared to leave. "Just to let you know, Terrence doesn't know I'm here. I came here for selfish reasons. I didn't want his unhappiness on my hands."

Walking him to the door, Jasmine again thanked him for coming. "I appreciate you sharing your story with me."

As he turned to leave, he stopped. "One last thing, the injury to Hayley? She fell from the top of a jungle gym by accident. There were at least four witnesses—people I don't know—who saw it happen at a local park. She was returned to Chelsea yesterday. I left a message for Terrence."

Hours after he left, Jasmine sat at her desk figuring out how she could make things right again with Terrence. As many times as she had walked out when the going got tough, she wouldn't blame him if he never wanted to see her again.

When he needed her the most, she deserted him, and for that, she wasn't sure if he could forgive her. But the conversation with Richard had confirmed what she had been thinking the past few days. She was an idiot. But now that she knew that, she had to figure out a way to fix it. How was she going to prove to him that she wanted to commit to him and he would never have to worry about her leaving him again?

Twenty

Terrence only half looked up when Eric came to his office door on Friday afternoon. He'd taken on several cases the last couple of weeks and he planned to work late tonight, as well as all weekend, to stay on top of things.

"I have some good news," Eric said, taking note of the number of files scattered across Terrence's desk.

"Great, 'cause I could use some good news right about now," he answered, barely looking up from his computer screen.

"It won't be official until the first of the month, but you're looking at the newest associate to be made partner."

Terrence stopped typing completely and turned his full attention to his friend, expressing sincere happiness for the first time in weeks. "That's great, man. Congratulations. You deserve it."

"And that's not the best part," Eric said, watching him turn his attention back to his monitor. "Rumor has it, you're next in line."

Terrence's fingers froze as his words registered. That was what every lawyer wanted when he joined a firm. A year ago, he would have shouted from the rooftops at the good news. Now it rang a little hollow. Not because he didn't want the position, but because Jasmine wasn't there to share in his joy.

Eric watched the slew of emotions that crossed his face in a matter of seconds and could practically read his mind. "You can always call her."

Terrence snapped out of his daze and shook his head no.

"Fine," Eric said, heading for the door. "Why don't you join me and Dawn tonight for dinner? She's fixing her world-famous lasagna."

"Thanks for the invite, but I'll have to pass." Pointing to the papers on his desk, he figured there was no need for further explanation.

"She won't be there," Eric promised. "My wife has given up her matchmaking for good this time."

Terrence half laughed, only because he was half disappointed. How would they act if they were thrown together?

"I take it you're going to spend your evening in front of that computer?" Eric asked.

"Hey, I can't slack off now, I'm next in line for partner, remember?"

"You know what they say about all work and no play . . ." Eric reminded him.

"I'll remember that," Terrence said, already turning his attention back to his work.

"I want you out of here by six."

His commanding voice made Terrence pause. "You've got to be kidding?"

"I'm serious, man. You've been putting in some crazy

hours lately and I don't want you to burn out. You can work all you want starting tomorrow, but tonight go home. Relax. Watch the game. Do anything other than work."

"I'll see what I can do," he said, having no intention of leaving any time soon.

Eric didn't move, deciding whether to say his next words. "You can't work her out of your system."

Terrence stopped everything. There it was. The reason he had been pushing himself so much these past weeks. He'd hoped that the harder he worked, the easier it would be to live without her. It didn't work. It was just as hard today as the day he flew back from New York—alone.

Eric was right. He couldn't go on like this. He needed a break. "Okay, you got it. I'm outta here by six."

A short while later, Eric pulled out of the parking garage and dialed his cell phone. "Everything's a go. He'll be home by six-thirty." After a short pause, he smiled. "You're welcome."

Terrence pulled into his garage and cut the engine. Not able to stomach pizza or Chinese food one more night, he decided to skip dinner altogether. Facing another night alone, he thought about Eric's words. No matter how hard he tried, no matter how hard he worked—there was no getting her out of his system. He still loved her. Could he really let it end without giving it one more try?

He dialed her number without getting out of the car. If he left now, he could be there in less than an hour. Taking a deep breath, he felt his heart sinking when her answering machine came on.

"Jasmine, it's Terrence. Listen, I know things are really messed up with us now, but if you want to talk, please call me. I still love you."

He pushed the end button but didn't move. Contemplating going to her house, he wondered if she would let him in. But his ego wouldn't let him. What if she slammed the door in his face? What if another man was there?

Getting out of the car, he headed inside. He'd made the first move. Now the ball was in her court.

The first thing he heard when he opened the door to his loft was music. Not just any music—the piano. And not just any song, the song she had played the night they met. As he walked into the living room, the music grew louder and louder. He stopped short when he saw her playing, smiling up at him.

There were candles everywhere and the scent of vanilla filled his nostrils. The rose petals scattered across the floor paved a path from him to her. The other flowers, placed in vases around the room, added the perfect romantic touch.

The music stopped and she stood, dressed in the same attire she'd worn the night he gave her the piano. Before he could say anything, Monte appeared.

"If you'll follow me, sir, dinner is served."

Seated at the table, neither had yet to say a word. Terrence was the first to open his mouth, but Jasmine stopped him.

"Let me talk first."

Taking a deep breath, she thought of the words that would communicate how truly stupid she'd been. "Somehow, just calling you up and saying I'm sorry didn't seem adequate for how wrong I've been and how badly I've treated you. You have given me your love, your trust and respect, and I haven't given those things in return. Instead, I was selfish, stubborn, bullheaded, full of anger . . . You can stop me anytime."

Terrence laughed and reached across the table for her hand, but let her continue.

"I've seen so much in my line of work that I developed tunnel vision, becoming skeptical of everyone and everything. I never should have walked out on you in New York. You needed me, and I was too caught up in my own drama to be there for you."

Hearing her voice crack, he said, "Jasmine—"

"No, let me finish. Every time the going got a little rough, I bailed on you. I know that my track record isn't the best. But if you still love me like I love you, I'd like another chance."

"Can I talk now?"

Wiping her tears, she nodded yes.

"There has never been a day since the first day we met that you haven't been in my mind and in my heart. No couple is without their ups and downs, and as long as we can agree to work through them together, we'll be just fine."

Jasmine heard the words he'd said several times during their relationship. Could he really forgive her just like that? Put his faith back in her? "There's no way to prove what I'm saying is true until we have our next challenge."

He stared directly into her brown eyes and saw truth and love reflected back at him. "I trust you."

Jasmine signaled to Monte. "I thought we could start with dessert."

He laid the raspberry cheesecake on the table, this time with the words facing Terrence.

Jasmine reached in her pocket and pulled out her ring. "If your answer is yes, I'd be honored to put this back on."

He nodded yes and slipped the ring back on her finger.

Just then, she pulled out her cell phone and dialed. "He said yes!"

Before he knew what was happening, the front door opened and Dawn and Eric entered.

"Let me guess," he said, getting up to greet them, "an engagement party."

Walking up to Eric, he smiled. "That's what that little talk about working late was about. You manipulated me to make sure I would be home."

"Hey, I said my wife had retired from matchmaking. I said nothing about me."

Twenty-one

New York, Valentine's Day

The weather was crisp and clear and the room was full of activity. The cars were arriving in less than fifteen minutes and Jasmine was busy finishing up with her hair. She'd cut it last week into layers and the sassy look, just as Aunt Gracie had predicted, made her appear younger, vibrant, and lively.

With the stylist placing the veil on her head, she was ready to step into her dress. It had taken her only one day to find the gown that she would be married in. She and Dawn had gone to a boutique in the city and the strapless beaded dress seemed to be made for her. With the A-line floor-length skirt and three-foot train, it was perfect.

"Jasmine, the cars are here." Yvonne entered the room looking gorgeous in the bridesmaid dress. Similar to the bride's, it was strapless as well, but hung just below the knee. The shade of purple she wore made her look like royalty.

"Thanks, I'm just about to put on my dress."

The stylist turned to leave and Yvonne started to follow.

"Wait, Yvonne. Can you help me?"

Yvonne returned to the room and shut the door.

Jasmine stepped into the dress and turned around so that Yvonne could button the twenty-five buttons that lined her back.

"I wanted to apologize to you for the way I left the last time I was here. I know I was pretty rude. I shouldn't have treated you, or your family, that way after all you went through to make me feel welcome."

Yvonne finished the last button and stepped in front of Jasmine to take a final look. "Terrence told me the whole story after you left. You broke his heart that day and it tore me up to see him like that."

Hearing a hint of anger in her voice, Jasmine cast her eyes downward. She didn't need a reminder of how terrible she had been to him. She already knew.

"But you probably wouldn't be as good as you are at what you do if you didn't care so much about the children," Yvonne said, her anger dissipating.

"I do care," Jasmine said. "But I love Terrence with all my heart and that's what comes first in my life, for now and always."

The two women hugged just as the knock on the door came. "Jasmine," Mrs. McKinley said. "It's time."

The small church in Long Island was filled with family and friends who stood when the bride made her entrance. Escorted by Mr. McKinley, she radiated beauty as she stepped on the rose petals that Delaney had dropped on the floor a few minutes earlier. Monica and

Yvonne had already started to shed a tear, but Dawn was standing strong in her role as matron of honor. Terrence, in his black tails, looked as if he'd stepped straight out of *GQ*. She couldn't wait to stand by his side.

Terrence's breath caught the minute she walked through the double doors. He had heard that every bride was beautiful on her special day, but she was breathtaking. When he first took his place at the altar, his palms were sweaty and he was slightly short of breath. However, the moment his eyes locked with hers, a sense of calmness settled within him like never before.

Taking her hand, he helped her up the three stairs and they took their place before the minister, ready to commit everything to each other. When it came time for the vows, Jasmine spoke first.

"I did not know *what* love was until I met you. I did not know *how* to love until I met you. You have taught me the *true* meaning of patience, kindness, protection, trust, hope, and perseverance. That is what our love is filled with—now and forever."

"Jasmine, in a world so focused on outward things, you have taught me how to look inside myself and be true to myself. You are the music that makes my heart sing and the light that has brightened my world. I give you my heart, my body, and my soul—now and forever."

Instructed to exchange rings, they then lit the unity candle to signify two becoming one.

"You may kiss the bride."

He pulled her into his arms, and their kiss was filled with the passion and excitement of beginning their lives together.

"Ladies and gentlemen, I present to you Mr. and Mrs. Terrence McKinley."

ABOUT THE AUTHOR

Doreen Rainey graduated from Spelman College in Atlanta, Georgia, and currently resides in the suburbs of Washington, D.C., with her husband of ten years. She works for a CPA firm as their human resources manager. Her other works include *Foundation for Love, Just for You, Can't Deny Love,* and *The Perfect Date* (in the Valentine anthology *A Thousand Kisses*).

Doreen was named Best Multi-Cultural New Romance Author of the Year by *Shades of Romance* magazine and received the EMMA Award for Favorite New Author at Romance Slam Jam 2003.

Please visit *www.doreenrainey.com* or e-mail *doreenrainey @prodigy.net.*

More Sizzling Romance From
Francine Craft